Joyce Su
Madeira (

CW00541582

About the Author

Born in the Nibelungen city of Worms, Joyce Summer has been fascinated by stories and legends since childhood. What could be more natural than to devote herself entirely to writing at some point? After years of working as a manager in various banks and large corporations, she knows enough about politics and intrigue: so it was not difficult for Joyce to leave this life behind and go on a murder hunt with paper and pen. Her love for the island of eternal spring, Madeira, brought her to write her first crime novel in 2015. The proximity to water did it to her. Be it in their books, which always have scenes on the water, or in real life, kayaking.

JOYCE SUMMER

MADEIRA GRAVE

Avila Mystery #1

By Joyce Summer
www.joycesummer.com
Copyright German © Joyce Summer, 2017
Copyright English © Joyce Summer, 2023
Cover design by ©Joyce Summer, 2023

Content Editor
Georgia Rae Croeser of Georgia Rae Writing

Madeira Grave was first published in 2017 by Joyce Summer as
Madeiragrab– Comissário Avila ermittelt

Directory of Persons

Brigada de homicídios:

Comissário Fernando Avila–heads the "Brigada de homicídios" department and otherwise struggles with his new role of father-to-be.

Subcomissário Ernesto Vasconcellos–his right-hand man with a weakness for womankind, nicknamed "Belmiro".

Aspirante a Oficial Filipe Baroso–youngest member of the team.

André Lobo–Diretor de Departemento, head of Avila and his team, is also called "the wolf".

Doutora Katia Souza–coroner in charge.

Other persons:

Leticia Avila–wife of Avila, proud Catalan and expectant mother.

Inês Lobo–wife of Avila's boss and Leticia's best friend.

Francisco "Chico" Guerra–lawyer and best friend of Vasconcellos.

Teresa Ferro–ambitious gallery owner with changing gentlemen acquaintances.

Hugo Duarte–co-owner of the gallery.

Romario Palmeiro–leader of the new wing of the ruling party and owner of "Palmer's Winery".

Vitor Marsh–owner of a long-established Madeira Wine Lodge.

William Stuart Jr–aspiring politician and heir to an Aguardente factory.

Kate Stuart–his sister and current girlfriend of Vasconcellos.

William Stuart senior–father of William and Kate, owner of a large Aguardente factory.

Cecil Franco–rich old Madeiran.

Otavio Jesus–waiter at the golf club.

Aurelia Gomes–young Madeiran, helps with planning at the golf club.

Ignacio Coelho–President of the Golf Club.

Tadeu Parry–Head of Retail Banking at Banco Central do Funchal and golf partner of Diretor André.

Jorge Rocha–old Madeiran.

Luana Alves–old Madeiran.

*At one side of the palette there is white,
at the other black; and neither is ever used
neat.*

Winston Churchill

Prologue

Between the scent of earth and fresh grass, a tinge of metal now tickled his nose. Wet smacking from many mouths punctuated everything. He turned away and looked towards the Laurazeen forest.

Why had she done that? It had been so perfect. She had finally made him happy again. She had blown through his life like a summer breeze and had dispelled the heaviness that had settled on his marriage. Shortly after the wedding it had started: he no longer felt any joy in touching Milly. It was all about producing an heir for the old man's factory. But no matter how often they tried, Milly did not get pregnant. Every time at a certain stage of the month, he felt like one of those studs mounting a mare. Yes, that's what she was to him, nothing more than a mare. There was no longer this tingling feeling that they were doing something forbidden. On the contrary. In the big *quinta*, the walls had ears. As they made love, he imagined his father-in-law listening, hoping that now, at last, the longed-for heir to the throne would come. He felt old and used up, even though he was not yet thirty. During the day he slaved in the factory, in the evening he had to stand his ground at home.

Everything changed when *she* came into his life: Órla. The name alone was a promise. She was the granddaughter of Irish immigrants and her name meant "Golden Princess". And that is exactly what she was. Contrary to women's fashion, she wore her strawberry blonde hair loose. It fell in long curls over her shoulders. It was the first thing he had noticed about her. The long hair, bathed in a shimmering reddish light from the warm autumn sun. He had seen her for the first time in the harbour in Câmara de Lobos. Alone and unaccompanied, she was buying dried *bacalhau* from one of the fishermen, who had it dried there in large quantities on wooden poles. Yellowish-white pieces of fish hung down in dry, frayed trapezes. And between them stood Órla in her golden glory. Unmissable. Irresistible.

He did not hesitate and went straight towards her. Green eyes looked back at him, reflecting his happiness, which carried him away for the next few months as if in a dream. Órla bathed everything around him in a soft light that also filled the cracks in his marriage. Did Milly suspect something? Even if she did, she let it happen. She, too, noticed that the light-heartedness from their early days together had returned.

Until that damned day came. Órla had asked him to come to her little house near Madalena do Mar, which served as their love nest, one more time in the evening before the ball. When he arrived, he immediately noticed that something was different about her. Her long hair had disappeared. Short, red waves framed her face.

"Do you like it?"

He was stunned.

"Why did you do that?"

"My life will change fundamentally. Our lives. We need to talk."

10

There was an angry roar in his ears as he stormed out of the hut.

Three days later he returned and did what had to be done.

Carefully he opened the gate and pushed the remnants apart with the toe of his shoe. The throaty smacking, coupled with the soft grunting, was interrupted. Heads lifted briefly, then they bent down again, and it continued. They weren't finished yet, but the rest would disappear in the next few hours.

Quietly, he closed the gate behind him and let them finish their work.

Garajau,
01.08.2013–6:46

Avila tugged at Urso's leash. The dog had discovered something interesting under a car and didn't want to let himself be torn away.

Instead of obeying his master, the golden retriever tried to get under the car. Avila pressed the button on the leash pulley to give Urso a little more space. This was a mistake. Urso started barking and pulling with all his strength. Avila's forearm bounced along the spoiler of the car. Bloody hell! A painful click across half his arm. A black cat shot out from under the car then, leaping in one bound onto the man-sized wall of the next property. Immediately an angry barking sounded from several dog's throats. There were watchdogs on this property too. Meanwhile, Urso had come out from under the car again, not without wrapping the leash once around the tyre. Now he stood in front of the wall and barked at the cat. Avila noticed his stress level rising. He hated taking Urso out in their neighbourhood. There were dogs and cats everywhere. And most dog owners didn't walk their animal on a leash like him and Leticia. No, every now and then a gate was opened and the dogs ran out into the street.

There was a female dog in the neighbourhood who constantly roamed the streets and was extremely aggressive. Every time they came within her radius, Avila would start sweating. This morning too, he found himself constantly turning around and looking for that damn bitch. Once again, he wondered how his wife, who was much more petite and smaller than he, managed to command respect from this beast. At least she told him, when he complained about the other dogs again after another walk with Urso, that she had no problems with any of them.

Leticia. Avila's stomach cramped. Leticia, his wife, was not well. She was now seven months pregnant, and the doctor had prescribed as little exertion as possible for fear of a miscarriage. Long walks with the dog, along the steep ups and downs of Garajau and the surrounding area, were thus dead and gone.

So, Avila now had to watch out for and take care of how he satisfied Urso's urge to move. Fortunately, the presidency was quiet at the moment. His Subcomissário Vasconcellos and himself had no cases worth mentioning to work on. But Avila didn't want to take a holiday now either, he was saving it up so he could be there for his little family after the birth. At lunchtime, he usually raced from Funchal along the motorway to Garajau to check on Leticia. Afterwards, he treated Urso to a lunch run down to the big statue of Christ, the *Christo Rei*. The only positive thing about this was that he was no longer quite so out of breath when he went up the stairs at the police headquarters. The walks up the steep paths here in Garajau could really be called sport, that much was certain. Unfortunately, no positive result had yet shown up on the scales for this. The waistband of his trousers was as tight as ever.

Avila stopped briefly to enjoy the view down to the Atlantic. Fortunately, it wasn't so hot this morning, but the midday round would be quite an ordeal again.

Maybe he could skip the walk at noon today? Furtively, he looked over at his golden retriever. No, he really couldn't do that to the dog. Urso was sniffing at a high garage door behind which there were at least two dogs. They were trying to get a look at their counterpart on the other side by jumping as high as possible at the gate. Every now and then a brown head would appear, accompanied by heavy barking. Avila looked at the gate to see if it was really locked. But thankfully Urso seemed to have lost interest, he wanted to continue up the road. On the left side of the street, an old retriever could now be seen on top of the roof garden, limping and barking darkly as he paced up and down. He did not take his eyes off Urso. Next to him, a small mongrel ran excitedly back and forth, letting out its sharp yelp. Leticia had told Avila a few days ago that she always knew exactly where he was on the walk, depending on where the barking of the other dogs was coming from. *In a few weeks I'll probably be able to recognise the other dogs blindfolded by their barking*, Avila thought to himself, as a tabby cat appeared in front of him. He immediately pulled Urso closer to him by the leash. Let's not risk another scratch. But the retriever hadn't even noticed the cat, because at that moment he was sniffing at something left behind by another dog. Yuck. Avila quickly pulled the dog away before he got any more unappetizing ideas.

At last, they had arrived at the bottom of the statue of Christ. Avila took the small trail that led him and Urso close to the cliff. Down there was the small beach of Garajau. A long road wound and surpentined down. The beach consisted of grey rounded lava stones; one should not walk on it without bathing shoes. How long had it been since he had bathed there with Leticia? The last few times they had used the little cable car because Avila was worried that the climb up afterwards would be too strenuous for her pregnancy. Maybe he should take a little swim in the Atlantic tonight? Although, who was he kidding? The two walks a day with Urso were exercise enough for him. Tonight, he would sit nicely on the veranda with a glass or two of *Verdejo* and enjoy the view of their lush garden. Avila waved to the old lady who was feeding the pigeons again. As he walked around the statue, he startled a young couple who had clearly spent the night there. Should he caution them and make it clear that this was not allowed? But hadn't he also liked to spend the night outdoors with Leticia when they were students in Lisbon? He just nodded to the two and made his way back. Now came the part of the route he could well do without. He took a deep breath. The road wound up in a steep curve back to Garajau.

Mercilessly Urso pulled on the leash, he had apparently not registered his master's hesitation and was looking forward to the next part of the morning's adventure.

Avila sighed and began the ascent. Again and again, he had to stop and catch his breath. And the same again at noon today? He would miss the extensive lunch in the Rua de Santa Maria, the old quarter in Funchal. Disgruntled, Avila trudged up the hill with heavy steps. It felt like there was no end to it. He had to be at the top in a minute. The road bent at a house covered with flaming red bougainvillea. Another short steep climb, then he had finally reached the roundabout in front of the small main street of Garajau with all its shops. Panting, he paused. Urso pulled on the leash, determinedly dragging him up the street. There wasn't much going on here so early in the morning. The two small supermarkets were just getting their daily deliveries, the first residents were finding themselves in the two bakeries. Across the street, in the large hotel that took up almost a quarter of the right side of the road, it was still quiet. Only a few tourists were standing at the bus stop where the bus to Funchal halted. What were they doing there at seven in the morning? The smell of fresh *cornettos* and *natas* hit Avila's nose. He rummaged in his trouser pocket. On his way out, he had quickly pocketed some change. Leticia would certainly be happy to have breakfast together. He climbed the step to the bakery and made his way past the tables and chairs that were huddled close together under the canopy.

The first guests had already taken their seats with a *bica* and a *cornetto* and were reading today's *Diário de Noticias*, the Madeiran daily newspaper. A large article about the upcoming exhibition caught his eye. Leticia had told him about it. It had something to do with the golf club. But he had already forgotten what it was all about. Maybe he would make the time to find out more about it at lunchtime today. Otherwise, Leticia would end up accusing him of never listening to her again.

He tied up Urso's leash and entered the shop.

Barely five minutes later he came out again, loaded with several boxes of sweet pastries and a big paper bag full of still warm *cornettos*. Hadn't Leticia said this morning that she didn't want to eat so much sweet stuff? Guiltily, he looked at his purchases. Then he shrugged his shoulders. If need be, he would take the leftovers with him to the office to pass the time until lunch.

Urso stood up expectantly and wagged his tail. Avila absent-mindedly patted him on the head.

"Do you think there might be something left for you? The sweet stuff is not for you, my dear." Avila untied Urso and walked with him towards the hotel's passageway that opened onto their street. Avila's mobile phone started ringing. He fumbled in his trouser pocket and stopped paying attention for a moment. Urso took the opportunity to make a spirited leap towards the gate behind which two dogs were curiously watching their arrival. One of the boxes fell onto the road and the contents tumbled onto the asphalt. Immediately, Urso's interest in the barking dogs disappeared. He lunged for the *natas*, which had not survived the fall in one piece. Shaking his head, Avila looked at his dog. This critter was even more greedy than he was. The phone continued to ring persistently in his pocket. Finally, with the second box tucked under his arm, paper bag and leash in one hand, he managed to take the call.

Stress and anger resonated in his voice.

"*Tou*? Avila here."

On the other side, he heard the calm voice of his Subcomissário.

"*Hola*. It's me, Vasconcellos."

"Can't it wait? I'll be at the presidium in an hour at the latest."

"Unfortunately, no, boss. You should come to the presidium as soon as possible. Diretor André has called a team meeting for 8 o'clock. It's about the *Rali Vinho da Madeira*. He wants to talk to us about the security concept."

Avila cursed.

"*Caramba*! Okay, I'll be as quick as I can. I'll be glad when this stupid rally is over. The Diretor is driving me crazy. As if we have nothing better to do."

He hung up. Unfortunately, they had nothing better to do. At the moment, apart from a few small pickpockets, it was very quiet in Madeira. Good for tourism, certainly, but for Avila and his team it meant that they were also being called on to do tasks that normally fell outside their remit. And the director had even entrusted Avila and his team with the main responsibility of securing the Funchal section of this year's *Rali Vinho da Madeira*.

Avila pulled on Urso's leash. In the meantime, the golden retriever had removed any trace of *natas* from the road. With the rest of his shopping and a satisfied looking dog, Avila walked the few metres to his garden gate. The extensive breakfast with Leticia would not happen now. He had just twenty minutes left to be in Funchal at the presidium.

Funchal,
01.08.2013–08:11

Avila entered the small meeting room in the presidium. It was typical that Director André used this room again, with its cold, modern furniture. Functional and just the thing for a decent meeting, as he always liked to emphasise. He stood in front of a white multifunctional wall, or whatever the whole thing was called, and had a large map of Funchal's city centre pinned to it.

Avila preferred to hold his meetings in his office, which was the only one in the building with old furniture. Old, thrown together, but comfortable. He had so far successfully resisted any attempt at modernisation. It also had one of the most important utensils of all: a functioning automatic espresso machine with which he could conjure up a *bica* or even a *galão* at any time. *Now a nice strong espresso would do.* He was annoyed that he hadn't made a quick detour to his office. He was late anyway, so five more minutes wouldn't have mattered.

His two co-workers, sitting with their backs to the door, turned to look at him. Vasconcellos looked relaxed as always with his typical, slightly crooked grin, which, when applied at the right time, made one or two women's hearts beat faster at the station. But that didn't mean that the Subcomissário couldn't be tough as nails and not at all amiable at the appropriate times. His interrogation techniques were famous throughout the precinct, and he had already brought down many a suspect with them.

The young Baroso, who had meanwhile risen to *Aspirante a Oficial*, on the other hand, looked rather startled. His eyes were wide open and, as so often, he gave the impression of an astonished child rather than a policeman. Add to that his slightly tousled mop of hair, which always looked as if he had just gotten up or got too close to an electrical socket. But Avila also knew not to be fooled by this impression. When it came to investigations, Baroso was extremely efficient. Especially on assignments that required lengthy investigations, he could shine. More than once, he had contributed important clues to their cases with his tenacity and thoroughness. Looking ahead, Avila could guess the reason for Baroso's startled expression. The *Diretor de Departamento*, André Lobo, was standing there with his mouth agape, frowning at him angrily.

Avila nodded briefly to the group, sat down on one of the uncomfortable plastic chairs and waited out the storm.

"How can it be, *Comissário*, that you never show up on time for my meetings? Is this your way of showing me what you think of my tasks? I already realise that as *Comissário* of the *brigada de homicídios* you think that safeguarding our famous *Rali Vinho da Madeira* is beneath you! But that is not the case, my friend. The Rali attracts many tourists every year. And what do the tourists bring us? Revenue. And what do you think you get paid with in the end? We can't always hope to get cash injections for our police apparatus from the mainland. So, pull yourself together, Avila!"

Avila calmly took the lecture in his stride. The director was generally known for his quick temper. And just as quickly as he got upset, he calmed down again. On the whole, Avila was satisfied with his boss, who had his back. Especially when it came to dealing with the press or possibly even with the *Presidente da Câmara*, the mayor, in delicate cases, André Lobo was always on hand and on his side.

"So, where was I? Oh yes, we have a few well-known personalities from the mainland as guests of honour this year. In Funchal, we have to be especially careful because the crowds are very big here. The *Presidente da Câmara* wants us to be on high alert to prevent possible terrorist attacks."

"Terrorist attacks? Where does he get that idea? We're here on Madeira. At most there are a few pickpockets here." Avila couldn't help himself. What an unnecessary scare tactic.

"Times are changing, Avila. Terrorism is everywhere. Imagine if something happened. How would we feel then?"

"What exactly is your plan, *o Diretor* André?"

"My plan? You and your men make the plan! By tonight at the latest, I want to have a worked-out security concept that we can present to the mayor. Don't look at me like that, Avila. You've known what's coming for weeks. If you haven't prepared anything by now, then I can't help you either."

"*O Diretor* André, of course the Comissário started with us weeks ago, his team, helping to draw up a plan to secure the situation. We will present it to you in a moment", Vasconcellos now intervened in a calm voice.

"How? Really? I'm glad to hear that." Lobo looked at Avila in amazement.

The latter was just as surprised as the director. Vasconcellos winked at him. Avila took a deep breath. He could always rely on his Subcomissário. Especially when it came to issues that Avila put off purely out of protest,

Vasconcellos had already saved his head a few times. He would certainly make a much better Comissário than Avila later on. If he could curb the issue with his women a bit. That was his great weakness.

"Yes, and our Aspirante a Oficial Baroso will now explain the key points to you." Vasconcellos looked encouragingly at the youngest member of their team. With a flushed face, the latter gathered a few sheets of paper and stood up.

With a trembling voice he began to talk.

"Um, yes. We would very much like to present our concept to you, *o Diretor André*. We have identified the following points as possible targets for an attack: at the intersection of Avenida Arriaga and Avenida Zarco, and further on in Rua do Aljube. There, the cathedral in particular could be at risk…" The rest of Baroso's explanation was a mere babble for Avila. His thoughts were on Leticia and the upcoming changes in his life.

"Don't you think so, Comissário?" Lobo's deep voice interrupted his thoughts.

Guilty as a schoolboy caught copying, Avila looked up.

Diretor André raised his bushy eyebrows reproachfully. Apparently, however, his energy for another outburst of rage had already been used up for today, because he continued calmly:

"I wanted to know if you possibly also consider the shopping centre at the end of Avenida Arriaga to be at risk?"

Avila looked over at Vasconcellos, who nodded slightly.

"Yes, that is a possible point. We will have increased patrols there as well." He felt completely stupid, but if the higher-ups wanted to stick to this hysteria, they could be his guest.

"Very good. I like your attitude, gentlemen. I'm sure Funchal is in good hands." Lobo looked around with satisfaction, then nodded briefly and left the room.

Avila looked at his two co-workers. Vasconcellos was now grinning openly from ear to ear; Baroso's face still showed signs of nervous excitement. But at least there was now a slight hint of pride too.

"I'm really grateful to you. I'm sorry I've been neglecting things here for the last few weeks."

"But boss, we know there are more important things in your life now than work. And the wolf doesn't mean it, believe me." André Lobo was nicknamed "the wolf" by his co-workers because of his last name. When he was in a bad mood, he could remind Avila of one more often than not.

"Yes, but it must not get to the point where I forget my job over it. Even if I do indeed feel tasks such as these are not fitting for a *brigada de homicídios*." Avila looked chagrined.

Vasconcellos stepped forward and patted him on the shoulder.

"Believe me, Fernando, you are a good boss. And a good husband for Leticia. Even though I have no experience in such things, I'm convinced you'll be just as great a father." Baroso looked on a little uneasily, he wouldn't dare in his life call the Comissário by his first name.

Avila noticed that his cheeks had begun to tingle and he blushed slightly. To cover his embarrassment, he tapped the table in an awkward gesture.

"So, enough of that. I'd say the *espetada* is on me for lunch today. And I think a glass or two of Madeira wine should be mixed in there too. I saw a very nice new place on Rua de Santa Maria the other day, we really must try it. Or we could go to my favourite place above Caniço. You should definitely check out Nelson's barbecue skills."

Vasconcellos looked at his boss with amusement. It was clear to him that he was about to take the opportunity to eat one of his favourite dishes, beef kebabs grilled over an open wood fire.

Funchal, Golf Club, 01.08.2013–11:14

Leticia didn't have an eye for the blue of the Atlantic today, which could be seen over the green hill of the spacious golf course. Normally she liked to sit in the club president's office with a glass of Madeira wine and enjoy the exclusive atmosphere.

The fact that she didn't feel like it at all today was less due to the fact that pregnancy forbade her from enjoying her beloved Madeira wine than because of today's company. Next to the grey-haired club president, sitting in an armchair, was a very young, very blonde woman who was now craning her neck and wiping away imaginary tears from under her eyes with her index fingers. As she did so, she made light sniffling noises that did not fail to have an effect on Ignacio Coelho. Seeking her help but also serving a little reproach, the club president looked over at Leticia.

Then he turned back to the little blonde and patted her knee.

"But, but my dear. There's no reason to be sad. I'm sure we'll find a solution. What must Leticia do to make you feel better?"

Leticia looked at him in amazement. Could it be that this little bitch was getting away with this? At his age, he should be able to see through something like that, shouldn't he?

The little girl sighed audibly once more and then straightened bolt upright in her chair. Her voice suddenly sounded surprisingly clear and composed.

"Leticia puts me under so much pressure, she always wants something from me. I just can't take it anymore."

The club president turned to Leticia with a serious expression on his face.

"You must understand, Leticia. Aurelia needs some air. She's really not doing so well right now, after all it's the first time that she has had such a responsibility. So, show a little compassion."

Leticia looked down at herself. She saw her belly clearly bulging above the waistband of her trousers. And heard her doctor's voice asking her to take it easy. Had he guessed what was in store for her today? What kind of problems did Aurelia have? Had she only just made it to the bathroom this morning, half asleep, because the child was pressing on her bladder again? Had she then discovered that the waistband of her favourite trousers was now finally too tight and had to switch to the unbecoming but comfortable black pair with the elastic waistband? Leticia remembered with horror the saleswoman in Funchal who had stretched that very elastic with a meaningful grin. She had said, "You will be very grateful for these trousers, Dona Leticia." Right now, she wasn't grateful at all, looking at the tight powder pink skirt paired with Aurelia's ivory slim top. She felt like a fat black whale next to her.

The president shifted uneasily in his chair. He was probably worried that he was about to be the centre of a catfight.

Leticia drew in her breath. She did not want to take part in this theatre. With raised eyebrows, she looked at the smooth, chubby face of her counterpart, which was contorted into a tearful grimace. She would read this little bitch the riot act. That was when she felt something move in her stomach. Her little roommate must have sensed his mother's anger. *No,* thought Leticia. *This isn't worth all this. I'm really past that age. Let the younger one make her mark.* Leticia knew how exhausting the preparations for such a big event were. After all, she had been responsible for planning important festivities at the golf club for the last three years in a row. All those endless phone calls to suppliers for food, drinks and decorations.

She didn't even want to think about the hours of debates with the rest of the ladies of the club about the seating arrangements: *But you know, dear Leticia, how Vitor Marsh feels about William Stuart Jr. ever since they had that argument on the 10th hole about the missing golf ball, which is why Vitor lost the 2011 autumn tournament. To this day, he is sure that William made the ball disappear. This is typical of the Stuart family. Even old William played his way to the top of the golf club with little cheats. So, the two of them can't possibly be sitting at the same table. And while we're at it: Romario Palmeiro and William Stuart Jr. are both running for the Funchal district in the municipal elections in September. Long table talks about politics, that really doesn't have to be the case.*

Table order, wait, there was something.

"Aurelia, did you remember to give the printers the design for the invitations and place cards? I promised them they'd get it last week at the latest, so they'd have enough time to set the printing."

Aurelia threw her head back and sniffled audibly again. This time she even used a handkerchief to dab at her eyes.

"You see, Doutor Ignacio, what I mean? Leticia is always putting pressure on me. Last week I couldn't even think because she kept coming at me with, 'Did you think of this? Will you do it, please?' No wonder things get left behind with such a burden. I'm very good at that kind of thing. I'm good at planning things. But now I just can't."

Again, Ignacio patted Aurelia's knee and looked pleadingly at Leticia.

"Um, I was really hoping that you two would do the organisation together this year. Aurelia with her youthful verve and new ideas and you, dear Leticia, with your experience."

The younger one swallowed audibly again.

"The earth is scorched for me. I'm so fucked up and I just can't work with Leticia anymore." She shook her head, lowered her eyes and started picking at the handkerchief.

Leticia didn't know whether to be angry or to laugh and applaud. What a performance. She only felt sorry for old Ignacio. He really didn't know what to do next. But she wouldn't pay any more attention to that.

She cleared her throat.

"I suggest that Aurelia takes primary responsibility for the event. I have other things on my mind in the coming weeks and months." She looked meaningfully at her middle.

Ignacio did not look particularly enthusiastic, but a triumphant smile flitted across Aurelia's face.

"But dear Leticia, your experience! Surely we can't do without that." The younger girl screwed up her face at that. That was certainly not what she wanted to hear.

"Do you really think we can do this without you?" Ignacio Coelho's voice sounded worried.

"For sure." Somehow Leticia knew that this probably didn't correspond to reality. But she didn't care now. She wasn't in the mood for these games anymore. And an empty nursery was waiting at home, which she still wanted to furnish in the next few weeks.

"Can Aurelia call you if there are any problems? Maybe you could talk briefly on the phone every few days", Coelho clung to the last straw.

Leticia sighed. May God protect her from that. She looked over at Aurelia. Then she grinned. The little girl would probably drop dead sooner than ask her for help. Leticia hardly believed that Aurelia would ever call her.

"But yes, with pleasure. I will be at your side to advise you if necessary. I'll send you the addresses of the previous suppliers for flowers, food and drinks by e-mail, just in case. I'm not sure you've contacted them all yet, Aurelia." She looked admonishingly at Aurelia, who stared back angrily with narrowed eyes, but refrained from commenting further.

"We have negotiated very good conditions over the years, and I can only advise you to treat these suppliers with care. But if you'll excuse me now, I have another appointment with my doctor today. We'll be in touch." With that, Leticia stood up and walked out of the club president's office as briskly as she could at that moment.

01.08.2013–15:23

*E**s tou*?" a slightly shaky, hoarse voice sounded from the line.

At first there was silence at the other end, as if the caller had to consider whether to speak or hang up again.

Then a calm, clear voice sounded from the receiver.

"It's me, old friend."

"You? I thought I knew the number." The other cleared his throat, but the huskiness in his voice remained.

"We need to talk."

"Talk? We haven't done that for years."

"I know. But something has happened. Before I do anything, I want to talk to you about it calmly."

"What's all this about? Why are you making weird insinuations? Tell me, what happened?" He coughed.

"Do you still smoke so much? You know it doesn't agree with you. The doctor advised you to stop years ago." The other's voice had a slightly worried undertone.

"Now I want to know what you want to talk to me about. Stop beating around the bush already." The voice got louder, then the wet, heavy cough sounded again.

"Stay calm. At our age we should avoid any excitement. Someone came to me and showed me something. I had to draw some conclusions from that. And that's what I want to discuss with you."

"Showed what? Draw what conclusions?"

"It's about what happened back then. I want you to get a chance to explain it all to me face to face, and then we'll decide together what to do. Out of old friendship?"

Silence at the other end, broken by short, slightly gasping breaths.

"I still don't know what you're talking about. But if you really want to meet, then we'll meet."

"Well, first thing tomorrow afternoon around 4 pm, yeah?"

"Tomorrow afternoon? During the rally? So, you're still not a fan of fast cars, my friend? But that's fine with me. Shall we choose a place away from the hustle and bustle then, so we can talk undisturbed?"

"Yes, agreed. Make a suggestion."

"My son told me that he still meets you from time to time on the Levada dos Tornos. That's not so far for both of us, and we can easily get there by car. Shall we meet in Babosas? A few hundred metres further on is the bench from which we always enjoyed the beautiful view."

"Have you been up there lately? It looks a bit different there since the flood three years ago. Are you still sure-footed enough?"

"I know what it looks like there. Let me worry about that. We only have to walk a few metres and I'll be very careful."

"All right, let's do it that way. At least we can be sure of being undisturbed. Most people will be down at the start of the Rali Vinho. Tomorrow at 4pm in Babosas, right at the entrance to the levada. See you tomorrow, old friend." With a click, the conversation was over.

Funchal,
02.08.2013–15:34

H ow much longer does it take?" Avila looked at his watch again.

"About another hour, boss. 4:30 is the official start, and 4:41 is the launch ceremony." Vasconcellos' calm voice was not affected by the fact that he had been answering this question every twenty minutes for the last two hours.

"I don't believe it. What are they doing there for so long? When the guy at the front arrived with the lists over an hour ago, I thought it was about to start."

"Those were only the start lists that were published. They still have to be seen by the riders and their teams. Sometimes there are protests. It all takes time."

"I already know why I usually avoid this event. Last year Leticia and I went over to Porto Santo on that day. If you ask me, that's the best place to be today. Sandy beach and a wonderful peace and quiet. No car noise and especially not that stench and the crowds." Avila grumbled to himself.

Vasconcellos tried to ignore his boss's mood, preferring to concentrate on the pretty blonde tourist who had been eyeing him with interest for some time. She was standing directly on the other side of Avenida Arriaga, leaning against a lamppost. Maybe he should inspect the bin next to her more closely to strike up a conversation with her? She really did look very pretty with her half-length, light, straight hair. Two firm breasts, not too big, not too small, stood out under the tight white T-shirt.

Avila had noticed Vasconcellos' glances.

"Don't even think about it. We're here on business. Besides, I thought things were serious with you and Kate? At least that's what Leticia told me."

Vasconcellos groaned softly. It had not been a good idea for him to get involved with Kate, who frequented the same golf club as his boss's wife. Not only that, no, the two women regularly played golf with each other because they had roughly the same handicap. And so, Avila was apparently more than a little in the know about his relationship status with Kate.

"Kate and I take a more relaxed view of it."

Avila said nothing more about it. In fact, he was already annoyed that he had brought up the subject at all. After all, it was none of his business how Vasconcellos treated his girlfriends. If he were to tell him now that Kate officially called him her life partner, he would most likely trigger a discussion that could, in the worst case, spill back to Leticia. And in such a conversation he would end up being blamed for something. He already knew that.

Abruptly he changed the subject.

"What did you mean by the 'launch ceremony'?"

"Each driver and co-driver will be handed a glass of Madeira wine in the cockpit before the start."

"Excuse me? You're telling me they all drink alcohol before this race? Not only are they racing like maniacs down the switchbacks, along roads not built for car racing, but they've been drinking alcohol? Are they all crazy here?"

Vasconcellos remained silent. It was common knowledge in the presidium that Avila was not averse to pleasures, be it food or even drink. But drinking and driving was an absolute no-no for him. When Avila had the opportunity, he let alcohol offenders sleep it off overnight in the cell instead of just sending them home. Deterrence, he called it. And the rank and name of the sinner did not matter. A fact that Diretor Lobo had already had to explain a few times and that was probably also one of the reasons why Avila had not yet risen higher in the police hierarchy.

Suddenly there was movement in the crowd. All heads turned towards the small tribune that had been set up for the guests of honour.

The President had entered the tribune with his entourage.

"I really hope we won't see this image for very long", Vasconcellos said, looking at the slightly plump grey-haired man. "The old man is holding court again. It's hard to believe that I've had to endure this sight all my life now. I can only hope that the upcoming regional elections are the beginning of the end."

"Our help, Ana, has told us that his party is once again using the usual tricks to catch votes. All of a sudden, generous gifts are being handed out. For the past two months, small building permits have been issued, which had previously been languishing in the building authority for several years. There are also generous donations in his name to various associations."

"Yes, just last week he presented a big cheque, accompanied of course by an article in the Jornal da Madeira, for the children of *Bombeiros Funchal*."

"I have seen that picture too. Unfortunately, one thing has to be conceded to him, he knows how to promote himself at the right time. One can only hope that people are wiser this time and don't forget again how things are for them in the periods between election years."

Now the riders were being interviewed. A pretty dark-haired reporter with an oversized microphone tried to get one of the favourites of the race to make a spontaneous statement. Unfortunately, he proved not to be very talkative, so the interview, which was broadcasted over loudspeakers, consisted of long questions on her part and monosyllabic answers on his.

"Dear Rodrigo, we have all been following your career in the Intercontinental Rally Challenge for years. Last year you were in the leading position here at the Rali Vinho. Then the accident happened on the descent to Machico. The blood froze in the veins of everyone who watched that terrible fall down the slope. Have your injuries healed and do you feel fit to compete for pole position today?"

"Yes."

Avila listened, shaking his head, as the driver also answered the next question with a simple "yes", with her asking how far he would drive the tracks and study the set-up before the race and whether he would take notes to go through them before the start. There was an embarrassed silence, probably due to the reporter frantically looking for other questions or a way to end the interview elegantly.

"How much longer do I have to put up with this madness?" Avila knew that he must sound a bit snivelling, but he didn't care at all. He would even prefer an afternoon in the presidium writing minutes to this event.

"It's about to start, boss. In about an hour, the spook will be over, too. Then we can have another *bica* in the little café near the market halls. It should be emptier there now, because it's not market day and the traders aren't there."

"Good idea, Vasconcellos. A *bica* and a *tarte de requeijão* to go with it. That sounds good. Baroso, what do you think? Are you in?" Baroso had re-joined them a few minutes ago, after a patrol towards the mall and back. He had stood there silently and listened to the conversation.

"Oh, yes, I would love to come." Avila could clearly tell he was pleased not to be forgotten. *If the boy gains some more confidence in the next few years, he will make his way up with us.* He really was a good addition to the team.

"I think it's starting now!" Vasconcellos pointed over to the start. There, the first of the cars drove onto the ramp. A young woman in a red floral costume with a long skirt came with a tray and handed the driver and the co-driver each a glass of Madeira. A short time later, the first car drove onto the closed-off course to the cheers of the spectators.

"Do I have to look at this now for every single car? This really can't be happening!" Avila's mood had fallen to the bottom of his socks. The trip to the café with his two co-workers became a distant prospect.

The next car drove slowly onto the ramp. It would be a long afternoon, that much was certain.

Madalena do Mar,
08.01.1950

The man in the grey woollen coat adjusted the cigar in his mouth. He looked over at the small yacht, where a strawberry blonde woman in a modern bikini was lolling in the sun. Amazingly, she wasn't too cold. He shivered slightly in the wind that was slowly coming up from the sea. He put the brush aside and pulled his coat in tighter at the neck. Perhaps she saw him too and enjoyed being painted by him? In any case, her companion had been gone for at least an hour. He had taken a small rowboat and paddled towards the shore. But this did not seem to worry the redhead. Quietly she lay on the deck. She had a wide-brimmed hat and large sunglasses on. Her long hair lay over her shoulders like a shiny shawl. It would be a beautiful picture once it was finished. Now it was just a matter of capturing as much as possible, because tomorrow he would certainly not find her like this.

This day he could finally enjoy what he was doing, undisturbed. His first attempts at painting on the island had been constantly interrupted by the local press and onlookers over the past few days. Even the cheering people at the roadside had not improved his mood. Worst of all, though, was that silly parasol his assistant had to hold. Cat had insisted on it. It would now be captured in that photo for all time. It was January, he wouldn't get sunburn any time soon, even though it was a pleasant 18 degrees here.

Last night at the bar in Reid's, after three dry martinis, he had complained to Fred the bartender that he was unable to paint undisturbed.

Fred only said dryly that it might also have something to do with the Rolls Royce in which he drove across the island. A more inconspicuous car and a more secluded spot could do wonders. Fred had recommended his brother Jorge as a chauffeur and driver who knew the island. Since he also worked as a waiter at Reid's, they had become acquainted immediately.

So, they had arranged to leave bright and early the next day. Cat had turned over in bed, silently grumbling, when he got up at a little after five. She had never been an early riser, the mornings usually belonged to him alone. She would probably go in the late morning with Diana, her daughter, to the little basket-making shop in Câmara de Lobos that had been recommended to them. Cat really wanted to have some beautiful handmade wicker chairs for her drawing room at home. She should. The main thing was that he didn't have to come along.

His new chauffeur had even managed to organise a small breakfast, which they ate among the busy staff preparing breakfast for the other hotel guests. They then walked out of the hotel while it was still asleep, unnoticed by the rest of the company. Only one of his bodyguards, James, and his literary assistant Bill Deakin, with whom he was writing his war memoirs, accompanied him. If the opportunity was favourable and he could put a few sentences on paper, inspired by the surroundings, he wanted to do so.

Over narrow roads away from Funchal, Jorge finally brought them to this enchanting place right on the Atlantic. Full of pride, he told him the story of this little village. Legend had it that it was founded in the middle of the fifteenth century by a man named Henrique Alemão. Henry the German. But here the history books were wrong, Jorge explained to his attentive listeners. A completely different person was supposed to have been behind it, namely the Polish King Władysław III. The Polish king had not fallen in battle as people had thought, but had spent his remaining years here on the island. The Portuguese king at the time had granted him asylum. Bill, being dreamy, especially liked this story, as he himself could hardly imagine that a Polish king had found refuge here.

Surrounded by high cliffs, the small fishing village lay before him. The rocks looked as if a painter had painted them in stripes. Brown, grey, pale pink or almost deep black, they rose high above him. Below, the Atlantic broke on the parts of the rocks that were hidden under the water. Some of them in wild fountains, which reached towards the gradually brightening sky.

The elegant, narrow sailing ship was already anchored in the small bay at that time, but it was not until late in the morning that any movement was seen on board. First, a young man appeared on deck, tampering with the small dinghy attached to the stern with a rope. A short time later, he boarded the boat, which tilted dangerously from side to side as he courageously jumped from the top rung of the swimming ladder. But he kept his balance and a short time later rowed with powerful long strokes towards the beach. Well, beach was certainly a somewhat euphemistic term. Basically, it was an expanse of large black pebbles spread over a section of about twenty by four metres on the shore. Rounded by the force of the sea, they joined together to form an uneven surface. The young man seemed unimpressed by this. After pushing the boat onto the pebbles, he quickly and safely disappeared from their field of vision.

He started making the first sketches of the ship with the jagged background of the lava rocks when she came on deck. What a sight. Her hair glowed red and gold, illuminated by the sun that had now reached the small bay. Briefly, he had the impression that she was looking directly at him as she gazed in his direction. Would she disappear into the body of the ship again? No, she actually did him a favour and spread out in all her glory on the front part of the ship, right under the mast. Feverishly, he began to mix the tone of her hair with his colours. An almost impossible task. Brown, red, and yellow together could not replicate that golden tone. He had to settle for less, to at least make one more sketch of this sight before James or Bill reminded him of teatime at Reid's. If he missed it today, Cat would give him hell, that much was clear.

He took a deep breath. The air tasted slightly salty. He would miss that in London. Somehow, he had to manage to capture this mood, so he knew that he could pull out this image on cold rainy days. He squinted his eyes and tried to take in more details of the yacht. Who was this young couple? He wondered if the yacht belonged to them. Maybe they would even turn up at the ball at Reid's tonight. It was one of the social highlights of the year that had just begun. Everyone who was anyone on the island would surely be there. And whoever owned such a vessel was undoubtedly one of them.

Funchal Presidium,
05.08.2013–10:31

"Have you heard yet, boss?" Vasconcellos opened Avila's office door with a flourish.

He had just prepared a *galão* after a second breakfast in the form of a small *nata*. Avila had actually hoped to browse a bit more through one of the books Leticia had given him. After yesterday's annoying day–they had only finally arrived at the café shortly before 7 p.m., by which time it was already closed to make matters worse–he felt he had more than earned a longer break today.

Embarrassed, he tried to slide today's *Diário de Noticias* over the book entitled "Late fathers–how to master the challenge". But Vasconcellos had already caught on to what his boss was reading with one glance, as the laughter that now flashed in his brown eyes made clear.

"Where was I? Oh yes, did you happen to hear any news?"

Avila pointed annoyed at the daily newspaper.

"I just can't get around to finally reading them in peace."

"No, more recent news. It happened about an hour ago."

"Spit it out, what's wrong?"

"There was an accident at Rali Vinho yesterday."

"The way I assess it, it shouldn't be anything unusual, should it? When these guys drive at their breakneck speed over roads that aren't designed for racing, it isn't a surprise at all."

"That's true. But the surrounding circumstances are interesting. Do you remember Rodrigo Perez?"

"You don't mean that eloquent young man from Friday?"

"That's the one. He already had a run-off last year when he raced down to Machico. This time he got hit again. The ER201, above Curral dos Romeiros. There is a very sharp, tight curve there, clearly more than 90°. There he drove straight ahead, over the side of the road."

"Is he dead?" Avila looked dismayed. Actually, he had found himself feeling quite sympathetic towards the young driver. He himself would probably have answered the young reporter's questions with hardly any more words. After all, he could well imagine that as a driver one needed a certain amount of concentration before a race. Or before a meal. How he hated to be involved in long conversations before dinner. He wanted to concentrate on what was in front of him. And if it was the enjoyment of a good *espada com banana*, he couldn't take a joke. It had to be celebrated. And that included the silence before the meal.

"No, he got away with a broken collarbone and concussion. But when the helpers were cleaning up the last traces of the accident this morning, they discovered something. Pure coincidence. If the car hadn't taken a few trees with it and one of the helpers hadn't happened to look further up the slope towards the Levada dos Tornos, we would hardly have found him."

"Found who? Please don't make me pull every word out of your nose, Vasconcellos." Avila was irritated.

"The dead body. He must not have been lying there for long. The assumption is that it's another careless tourist who didn't understand that an inner-city levada can also be dangerous."

"That's the levada that goes down to Funchal from Monte, right?" Avila remembered darkly that accidents had happened many times in the past.

"Yes, that's the one. I don't think there's been a year in recent times when we haven't had fatalities there. One problem, in my opinion, is that it is still wrongly identified as 'easy' in some hiking guides."

"And it isn't?" Avila was not particularly interested in hiking. He preferred to leave that to the tourists.

"No, definitely not. Especially after the heavy storms of the last few years, there are some places where there are no boundaries left and the slope goes steeply down into the valley."

"Do we have any idea yet who the dead man might be?"

"Unfortunately, no. The skull was completely destroyed by the impact. Therefore, it will hardly be possible to make a reconstruction of the skull or a sketch for the search. The victim's clothing does not provide much information either. Forensics is now checking whether anything can be found out about the manufacturers. Our colleague from forensics told me that it is not typical hiking attire. Sturdy shoes, but no functional clothing like the tourists like to wear."

"Are there any other special features?"

"Not yet. The discovery is only an hour old. Everyone is pinning their hopes on forensic medicine now. That's where the body is heading right now." Avila nodded. If the dead body fell into the capable hands of Doutora Souza, there would surely be more information soon. Vasconcellos continued, "Unfortunately, the dead man had no papers on him. Only a car key. Our colleagues are now trying to find his car at the entry point, which he hopefully parked there. They are also checking to see if there are any missing persons reports that might fit."

"Are we assuming it was an accident? Or does anyone think this could be a case for us?"

"Colleagues say there is no evidence of foul play so far. But as I said, the final examination is still pending."

"Good. Keep me informed, please. Which of us is on the premises now?"

"I sent Baroso as an advance guard. He's been very observant lately and since it looks more like an accident at the moment, I thought we wouldn't make a mess of it by all being there together. If the press finds out about it, it'll be all over the papers. I wanted to take a quick look at the five missing persons cases from the last few days before I set off."

"Good idea. Please also keep in touch with Doutora Souza about the autopsy report. If it can't be ruled out that someone else is responsible, I want us to be right there in case. And if you notice anything strange, please let me know immediately."

"We will. And now I'll leave you alone to get back to your late-night fatherly pleasures." Before Avila could think of a suitable retort, the door closed behind his Subcomissário.

Garajau,
05.08.2013–11:12

The telephone invaded Leticia's dreams with its shrill ringing. Just a moment ago, she had been the radiant centre of the evening at the golf club, wearing a deep red, tight dress that showed no belly at all. Then that ringing came and brought her back to reality. Mechanically, she turned onto her left side to wake Fernando. The call was probably meant for him. But the bed next to her was empty. Again, the piercing ringing sounded. With difficulty Leticia straightened up and leaned against the headboard of the bed. Annoyed, she looked at the clock. Who could be calling so early … Shit, the clock said 11:13 am. Had she really slept for that long?

Fernando must have been at work long ago. She hadn't even noticed him doing his rounds with Urso. He must have quietly stolen out and somehow prevented the dog from barking loudly with joy at the prospect of the morning walk.

She looked around. Urso was indeed lying next to the bed. But now he seemed to be disturbed by the ringing too, because he barked softly and looked at Leticia reproachfully.

"Okay, you're right, I'll get it."

She reached for the phone and picked up the receiver.

"*Tou*?"

"Leticia, is that you?" her friend Inês' voice sounded from the receiver. "Is everything all right with you? You sound so sleepy?"

"Yes, you're right. Fernando let me sleep a little longer today."

"Poor you, I remember when I was pregnant with my youngest. I was tired all the time. But that will pass. Luckily, I had this wonderful nanny who always took such good care of the kids. Have I given you her address yet? She's quite excellent with small children."

Leticia sighed. For Inês, the wife of Avila's boss, it was easy to afford domestic help for everything. Her and Fernando also had Ana to help them keep the house in order. But Ana only came twice a week, that was all they could afford. And a nanny around the clock, like Inês had had, was out of the question. Besides, Leticia wanted to be responsible for her child herself, but she didn't want to tell her friend that.

"Yes, Inês, you've already given me the address. But Fernando and I are very happy with Ana, and our house is simply not big enough for more than one helper."

Leticia could practically see her friend's finely plucked eyebrows lift slightly in disapproval. Leticia used to care a lot about what Inês thought of her. But much had changed for her in the last year. When she thought of how she had almost put her life with Fernando on the line for that charming, good-for-nothing Lucca. Luckily Vasconcellos had saved her from Fernando finding out. Otherwise, the little bundle of joy in her belly wouldn't be on its way now either. She stroked it tenderly. Yes, she was happy with her life.

"Leticia, are you still there?" Inês' bright voice broke through her thoughts.

"Yes, I'm listening."

46

"I was just telling you about the problems this Aurelia is causing. She showed us ladies the first draft of her table arrangement. It is a disaster! This child has no understanding whatsoever of social rules. She seriously wants Romario Palmeiro to sit at the same table as Vitor Marsh. We know that Palmeiro has been trying to ruin the Marsh family with cheap Madeira wine for years. Vitor's wife told me that they have actually lost almost 20% since Palmeiro also opened his shop in Avenida Arriaga. Yet the Marsh family has been there since the century before last."

"You're right, you really can't do that", Leticia hastened to agree.

Now, with a little distance from it all, she was amused by these stories. Actually, she would love to tell Fernando this evening. But he had even less sense for these social pitfalls than little Aurelia. And when Inês was around, Fernando usually took to his heels.

"And that's not all. Have you heard what she did with the order at Blandy's? Apparently, she doesn't know which Madeira is drunk as a digestif, which as an aperitif. I can't believe this. This would never have happened with you as the organiser."

Leticia sat back and relaxed, listening to the gossip from the golf club.

Meanwhile, Inês had talked herself into a rage.

"The evening really promises to be a disaster. Aurelia has somehow managed to fall out with Sara who does the orchids. Who now refuses to deliver the flower arrangements for the tables. You came up with the whole wonderful idea with the violet orchids beforehand. I guess that's not going to happen now. Of course, the silly girl thinks she'll find someone else to deliver her orchids. How is that supposed to happen so quickly?"

Leticia had to smile. It was easy to fall out with Sara, a well-known florist who had a firm foothold in the market halls. For example, if you questioned the quality of her orchids. Or if you argued with her about the importance of the individual orchid species and disagreed with her. But one thing you had to hand to Sara, was that her orchids were always fresh, and always beautiful. It was a shame that Aurelia had messed up with the table decoration.

"So, what's the plan now?"

"I will go to the Mercado dos Lavradores this afternoon and make amends with Sara. I have a little hope that you will accompany me. I'd also pick you up from home and bring you back. What do you think, a little trip to Funchal? We could also have a *bica* afterwards upstairs in the new little café and enjoy the view over the old town. What do you think?"

Leticia thought about it. Wouldn't it perhaps be better to stay out of it completely? On the other hand, a change of scenery for a few hours would be nice. However, she had promised Fernando to cut back a bit and, as he put it, stay out of the whole "golf club theatre". It had been hard enough to persuade him to let them go to the big dinner at the club on Friday. Only the prospect of really good food and fine Madeira wine had been able to persuade him. Admittedly, perhaps the threat that she would go alone if he didn't had also contributed to him finally giving in. She felt a tiny bit guilty. She knew how much Fernando worried. At her age, pregnancy wasn't that easy either. But if it stayed as a short trip this afternoon, Fernando probably wouldn't even notice. By the time he got home in the evening, she would be back.

"Well, come and get me then." Now that the decision had been made, she realised how much she was looking forward to getting out again. It felt like weeks since her last visit to the golf club, yet it had only been three days. But time just crawled when you were home alone all day. Even though Urso bravely kept her company, it was boring as hell. She had unfortunately had to give up the idea of setting up the children's room due to pressure from Fernando and the doctor. "Too strenuous in your condition" was the men's opinion.

Inês' voice was clearly filled with relief.

"Wonderful, *querida amiga*. I'll feel better in a minute. Together, I'm sure we can straighten everything out. I already told Ignacio this morning that if our Leticia helps, everything will be fine. We'll park in the car park opposite the market halls so that you don't have to walk too far in your condition."

Leticia was not too sure whether her friend was not just being a little too optimistic. The opening dinner for the big exhibition was threatening to be more of a fiasco than anything else.

Funchal, Police Headquarters, 05.08.2013–15:01

A vila was plagued by an inner restlessness. He had not heard anything from Vasconcellos or Baroso for hours. When Vasconcellos had reported to him earlier, he had initially been happy that his Subcomissário had everything so under control.

In the meantime, however, he felt strangely superfluous. Why didn't the two of them come forward? Was the case more serious than they thought and they had too much to do? Or were they sitting with *bica* and *nata* in a café without him?

He jumped up and walked aimlessly around the room. Maybe he should call Vasconcellos? But then he would end up thinking that Avila didn't trust him. No, not a good idea. He walked another next round in his small office. Or were Vasconcellos and Baroso already back and writing reports?

Avila left his private office and walked towards the open-plan office where his colleagues' desks were located. No sign of the two of them.

"Have any of you seen Vasconcellos or Baroso in the last few hours?" he asked his other colleagues. An almost simultaneous shake of the heads was the answer.

At that moment, the phone rang at Vasconcellos' desk. Reflexively, Avila picked up the receiver.

"*Tou*?"

"Ernesto, is that you?" the melodious voice of Doutora Souza sounded from the receiver.

"No, Doutora, it's Avila."

"Ah, Comissário. Then I have the right person on the phone. It's about the dead man from this afternoon. Ernesto had asked me to get back to him as soon as possible if I could say anything that would help with the identification. He didn't want to wait for the whole autopsy report."

"So, what can you tell us?"

"Unfortunately, I have not yet been able to complete the identification. It won't be that easy either. The fingerprints are not in the system, Ernesto had already checked that. And for a jaw print, the dentition is unfortunately too damaged by the fall from the great height. Even for age determination, I couldn't use the front teeth. I had to use a maxillary molar for root dentine transparency."

Avila did not understand a word of what she was saying when it came to the technical medical terminology.

"Doutora, I beg you. For laymen!"

Doutora Souza's voice took on a slightly amused undertone.

"I used a molar from the dead man for age determination. I will spare you the details of the procedure. Although it is really very interesting, it was developed in outline as early as 1955 and has become…"

"Doutora, please!" Avila became impatient.

"Fernando, you really should be a little more patient. The dead man can't run away from us anymore. So, I estimate the age to be over 70. Unfortunately, there is a high margin of error with this method. It could be 10-20 years more or less than that. To determine the age more reliably, I now have to combine several approaches. But that takes time."

"We will start by working with the fact that we are dealing with an older victim. Thank you, Doutora Souza."

"Now we come to special features. The dead man has a darker skin colour. This is probably due to the fact that he mostly stayed in warmer climes."

"A local?"

"That could be, but it could also be a tourist from southern Europe. I would say to rule out northern Europeans for the time being."

"Other features?"

"Well-kept appearance, as far as one can judge after the fall. Finger and toenails very neat, which is sometimes not the case in older people if they are not very well off. The hands do not show any calluses. He probably didn't do any heavy work in his life. I did not find any tattoos or special markings, except for a well-healed scar on the knee. I have a suspicion about that, but I still have to wait for the X-rays to confirm it." Avila heard a door rattle in the background. "As if on order, here comes my assistant with the X-rays right now. Hold on." Doutora Souza put the phone down to the side and Avila heard only a muffled murmur.

A short time later she was on the phone with him again. Whereas her voice before had just sounded amused and quite calm, there was now a clear sense of joy in it.

"My dear Avila, we have it! The dead man had an artificial knee joint. We'll find him through the serial number in this spare part. What luck! This also confirms my assumption that the dead man comes from wealthier circles and is neither a local worker nor a farmer. They could hardly afford an artificial knee joint with our insurance system. Give me a few hours and we'll know the identity of our dead man." Without waiting for his reply, she hung up.

At that moment, Vasconcellos and Baroso came into the office. From their clothes, Avila judged that they had probably spent the last few hours on the levada and in the bushes. Baroso's black trousers had a large tear below the knee and Vasconcellos' shoes, which were usually shiny, were encrusted with mud and dust.

But as always, Vasconcellos was in a good mood and beamed at his boss.

"Baroso and I have probably found the place where the dead man fell. It is not that far from Babosas. It took us forty minutes to get there from the entry point. So, it was also before the tunnel above Curral dos Romeiros. You could see exactly where he fell from the bent branches of the bushes. There were various footprints around the spot. Unfortunately, we can't place them in time. The levada is frequented every day, and it is very likely that some hikers passed the spot later. Forensics is now on site to see if they can find out more."

"Doutora Souza has also already given us a clue about the age of the dead man. He is probably around 70 years old. But she will be able to tell us the identity shortly." Baroso and Vasconcellos looked at him in amazement.

"Yes, the dead man has an artificial knee joint and Doutora Souza can therefore…"

"Recognise by the serial number of the implant." Baroso interrupted him before he could finish.

"Exactly", Avila grumbled good-naturedly. He liked the eagerness of his young colleague. One could overlook the rude interruptions every once in a while.

"That's good. Because the missing persons cases have not turned up anything special. In part, they have already overtaken each other again. A child turned up again, not that he matched the description. And the only male missing person, a tourist, reappeared in the hotel after two days. He had taken advantage of the nice weather and spent the night outdoors." Avila had to think again of the couple he had surprised that morning at the Christo Rei a few days ago. The beautiful summer weather was really inviting at the moment. Maybe he himself could at least spend the night on the terrace tonight and look up at the starry sky.

Funchal, Market Halls, 05.08.2013–15:13

Leticia and Inês entered the Mercado dos Lavradores. As per every other time, Leticia was overwhelmed by the visual and olfactory impressions. She sniffed. Her pregnancy had clearly heightened her sense of smell. She thought she smelled the fresh, almost green-like scent of lemons, plus the fragrance of frangipani, which combined light notes of vanilla and amaretto.

The entrance hall was not as full today, on a Monday, as it was at the weekends, when the local farmers offered their products. Only a handful of traders had set up their stalls in the middle of the hall. This meant that the small brick pavilion with its roof covered in shiny red tiles finally became prominent. Leticia would have liked to stop in the middle for a moment to enjoy the play of light from the sun between the leaves of the trees growing in the courtyard but Inês headed purposefully towards the northern corridor where Sara had her stand.

When they arrived there, Sara was discussing the breeding and flowering behaviour of Venus slippers with an elderly gentleman. Apparently, a subject on which the two disagreed.

Sara's furrowed weather-beaten face was covered in a deep blush, and she had straightened her gaunt figure to full height. Which in her case was not particularly impressive, since she measured well under 5'6". But the older gentleman finally backed away, not without having squeezed a few more angry words out of his toothless mouth.

Leticia was briefly tempted to pull Inês back again. Was it really a good idea to argue with orchid Sara, who was already in a rage, about the flower decorations?

Too late, Sara had already discovered the two women. Her hard features relaxed a little and the hint of a smile, which also revealed countless gaps in her teeth, slid across her face.

"Dona Leticia, Dona Inês! How nice to see you both. You haven't been here with me for a long time." Now there was a clear reproach in the older woman's voice.

"Sara, what beautiful orchids you have again today." Inês made a sweeping gesture towards the lushly stocked stand. She was right. It was a real splendour. Spanish dancers with their little yellow-brown floral skirts, lush purple and blue violet orchids in between. Elegant white butterfly orchids were also not missing from the selection. They were Sara's pride and joy and were popular as table decorations in all the big hotels. There were many other orchids in all shapes and colours, but Leticia knew too little to name them correctly.

"Everyone knows that they get the best orchids from me. So, of course I always have to have a large selection." Sara straightened a little more, she was proud of her flowers. But she was also smart, which her next words revealed.

"What do you two want with old Sara? Is it something to do with the golf club, perhaps?" She grinned.

Leticia and Inês looked at each other. They hadn't worked out a strategy for how they wanted to broach the subject. Nor had they counted on Sara immediately guessing why they were both here.

Leticia jerked away.

"Dear Sara, we don't want to fool you. Yes, it's about the event at the golf club."

"Dona Leticia, you know that I have always done a good job over the last few years. You won't get better orchids than mine here." Sara's voice sounded slightly sad.

"Of course, we all know that. Unfortunately, I am not responsible for the organisation this year. There are other things in my life." She pointed to her belly.

"I've already heard about that! How nice for you and Senhor Avila! My Bruno and I, unfortunately, have no children. My orchids, they are my children." Now her hard features actually softened as she stroked the leaves of the purple violet orchid.

Leticia, who knew Bruno, wasn't sure if it wasn't perhaps better that the two of them didn't have children. Bruno, who earned his money as a basket sledge driver for the tourists up in Monte, was known in Madeira for liking to drink a lot. Under the influence of alcohol, he also tended to start fights with almost everyone. Whether this was the right environment for children, Leticia dared to doubt.

"Thank you very much, Sara. Yes, we are very excited. The baby will be here in about nine weeks. And as I said, that's why I'm cutting back a bit at the club now and have left the organisation to another young club lady."

Sara rolled her eyes.

"I have already had the pleasure of meeting this lady. If you ask me, she's a spoiled brat! Who does she think she is? Comes here and badmouths my orchids. Says they're not good quality. The flowers should be bigger. Pah", she spat on the floor in front of her. "She has no idea. My white phalaenopsis have the biggest flowers. Just look, isn't that splendid?" She picked up one of the largest butterfly orchids and held it out to Leticia and Inês. Sure enough, the flowers were almost as big as a pre-schooler's palms. Leticia shook her head. What was Aurelia thinking?

"Beautiful, Sara, really. And *such* big flowers!" Inês opened her eyes in search of help and looked at Leticia.

"You are absolutely right, Sara. I also think that Aurelia doesn't know much about orchids. But she is probably also a bit overwhelmed with the organisation of the whole thing and therefore...", Leticia tried to placate.

"And that's why she has to insult me? No, Dona Leticia. I know you are a good person. But that little blonde…" Aurelia had clearly and once and for all made a mess of her relationship with Sara, that was clear.

"But what are we going to do without you, Sara? Senhor Ignacio is desperately unhappy with the idea that the tables won't look as nice as usual for this special occasion. Could you perhaps make another exception for us? I promise you that Dona Inês and I will take care of everything, and you will have nothing more to do with my young club mate."

Sara swayed her head slightly back and forth, looking scrutinisingly from one to the other.

"Fine, Dona Leticia. Because it's you, and I like you, and Dona Inês. You've always been good to me, and I'll do the same for your little one who's coming." She gestured with her head towards Leticia's middle.

"You are lucky. Senhor Franco wanted twenty plants for his Quinta das Flores. But he didn't come. I phoned his *faxineira*. His help didn't know where he was either. Nor did she know anything about any flowers. So today I have twenty white ones left. You usually take those, don't you?" Leticia smiled to herself. Sara was a good businesswoman too, you had to give her that. She had probably planned almost from the start to let the two women have Cecil Franco's orchids. Actually, it was strange that he hadn't picked them up. It didn't suit the old man at all.

Inês breathed an audible sigh of relief.

"You are a treasure, Sara! We'll get everything ready with you right away, too. I have money with me, and I'll get the car right afterwards to load the plants." Inês started rummaging in her roomy handbag for her wallet. Leticia had to grin. Her friend was obviously afraid that Sara might change her mind. If that were the case then the cosy *bica* on the terrace upstairs would probably come to nothing. She looked at her watch. Should she ask Inês to drop her off at home first, or did she want to make a detour to the golf club after all?

Funchal, Police Headquarters, 05.08.2013–17:11

I'm afraid we have our dead man." Vasconcellos put the phone down with a serious look on his face.

Avila, who had just gotten back to the open-plan office to ask about the state of the investigation, looked at him.

"Who is it?"

"That was just Daria, Cecil Franco's help. He wasn't there this morning when she came to clean. At first she didn't think anything of it, but then this afternoon she noticed that apparently he hadn't been home during the night either."

"How does she know he wasn't home?"

"Because of the milk."

"Huh? What do you mean?" Avila looked irritated. Was this some Madeiran superstition? Sometimes it seemed like nothing could surprise him on this island. Portuguese people from the mainland were simply more down-to-earth in his opinion.

"She says she always gets fresh milk from the farmer for Senhor Cecil. He must like it very much and drink a lot of it. They both joke that it's always scarce on the weekend because she can't bring him a refill then. This afternoon, when

Daria took the milk jug out of the fridge to take it to the farmer to be filled, she noticed something. The milk jug in the fridge was still over half full. Which couldn't be. It's usually almost always empty on Monday mornings."

"So he had no appetite for milk for once?" It made more sense now, but Avila still wasn't really convinced.

"She says that's what she thought at first. But then she went around the house and looked for other signs of him. Everything pointed to the fact that he was indeed not at home. Later, the florist called and asked why Senhor Cecil hadn't picked up the flowers he had ordered especially for his *quinta*."

"What if Cecil Franco just spent the night somewhere else and forgot to pick up the flowers too?"

"Franco is 86 years old. Still very spry, but certainly not someone who doesn't come home at night."

"Good, we now have a missing person who could match the dead man. But until we have a clear determination with the serial number from Doutora Souza, we'll keep it to ourselves."

After clearing his throat shyly several times, Baroso took heart.

"I would also like to say something about that, if I may. *O senhor* Cecil and my grandmother know each other very well. My grandmother had problems with her hip some time ago, but didn't dare to have an operation. Senhor Franco then recommended his orthopaedist to her, who had already implanted an artificial knee joint for him."

"Hmm, o. k. You've convinced me: our dead man is probably this Cecil Franco. We're sticking to our guns, though, no information to the public. I assume one of you two also knows who to notify once the identity is confirmed?" Avila, as a mainland Portuguese man himself, was still not as well connected even after his years in Madeira as Vasconcellos, whose family had lived on the island for generations. And the young Baroso's ancestors also came from Madeira. In the beginning, Avila had always secretly made fun of the fact that everyone here knew everyone on the island. But since it had been quite useful in the past in more than one case that his colleagues could fall back on their family's memory, he was now always willing to take advantage of this circumstance.

"Senhor Cecil's wife died very young. They had no children. My grandmother always said that was just as well, because he was considered quite a Casanova in his younger years."

"Are there other relatives?"

"As far as I know, no. But I will check as soon as we have confirmed the identity with Doutora Souza."

"Did Forensics have any further comment?"

"Negative, boss. As we had already feared. The levada is very busy and it's impossible to tell if there are tracks that belong to a second person or if it were hikers who passed by the spot before or after the fall."

"What a bummer. Something tells me that the old man must have been experienced and careful enough to correctly assess the dangers of this levada. But maybe further autopsy will reveal if he had a stroke or heart attack and that's why he fell. We'll have to wait and see."

Funchal, Golf Club,
09.08.2013–19:23

Avila entered the golf club with a beaming Leticia on his arm. There was no sign of the mood of the last hours at home, when Leticia had been close to tears.

"I look like a beached whale in this dress", had been the most harmless outburst Avila had faced until shortly before their departure. His attempts to persuade Leticia to choose a suitable wardrobe item more quickly by complimenting her had failed miserably.

"The gold of this dress accentuates your brown eyes, *o meu amor*" was countered with "I could pass for one of the fat cherubs in St. Peter's". Even simple exclamations like, "You look beautiful!" were met with "You're only saying that because you love me" and tears.

At some point he had retired to the living room with a glass of dry *sercial*. Slowly he had moved each sip around in his mouth, striving to taste the different flavours of orange and nuts, and waited. A perceived eternity later, Leticia had appeared before him wearing the exact golden dress that had caused the outburst of emotion earlier. He had been careful not to make any further comment about it, but only grabbed his jacket and quickly pulled Leticia towards the car.

Avila looked furtively at his watch. It was just before half past seven. He breathed a sigh of relief, as they were still on time. The idea that they might be the last to arrive and thus attract everyone's attention was pure horror for him.

Leticia looked around.

"You can't do that! Do you see that, Fernando?" she said, pointing to the colourful lanterns hanging in the trees in front of the club.

Absent-mindedly, because he was just trying to make out at least one familiar face among the people streaming in, Avila said:

"Wonderful, dear, you're right…" He realised too late from Leticia's indignant expression that this was not the reply she had wanted to hear.

"I meant, uh, not so good?"

Leticia shook her head.

"No, not so good. We didn't want to use those lanterns at the club anymore. A few years ago, some were blown away by the wind and set fire to one of the old dragon trees here on the grounds. It was beyond saving. I don't understand why no one stopped Aurelia from using the lanterns. And it's really stormy today, don't you think? I have to talk to Ignacio right away. Not that anything will happen, again." She looked around for the club president.

Avila breathed heavily. This promised to be a great evening. Not only did he feel extremely uncomfortable among all the rich and famous of Madeira who were having a get-together here tonight. No, he would probably have to keep Leticia from redecorating all evening too.

Reassuringly, he took her hand.

"I'm sure everything will be fine. Just wait and see."

64

They came into the entrance area of the club. Ignacio Coelho was standing there and welcoming the newcomers. One look at his face told Avila that the club president was not happy with the way the evening had gone so far either. The smile on his face seemed frozen and did not reach the eyes that were now looking at them anxiously.

"My dear Leticia, how good it is to have you here. And how wonderful you look. You are positively radiant." Coelho hugged Leticia.

Avila did not receive such a greeting, a short murmured "Fernando" was enough. For the Comissário, this was not a disaster. The club president and he avoided each other wherever possible after Avila had investigated in the vicinity of the golf club a few years ago.

"Thank you again for at least solving the table decoration issue with Inês. If you hadn't gone to Sara about the orchids this week, it would look even worse in there!"

Avila looked at Leticia in disbelief.

"Went to Sara? This week?"

A blush spread from Leticia's neck to her face.

"Yes, I wanted to tell you, Fernando. Inês and I went to Funchal on Monday. But only very briefly, and Inês made sure I didn't walk too much."

Avila raised his eyebrows disapprovingly and muttered softly to himself:

"If I don't check everything all the time…"

At that moment, Leticia's friend Inês, her voluptuous figure perfectly displayed as always, this time wearing a midnight blue, tight cocktail dress with a plunging neckline, approached the small group.

"*Querida amiga*, how nice that you are finally here! You're sitting at the same table as us. Luckily, I was able to correct that just now. Little Aurelia had actually wanted to place you with Romario Palmeiro. He should sit at the same table with his party friends." She pulled Leticia away towards the hall.

Avila briefly considered whether he should take advantage of the hour to take a short walk around the golf course. *Just enjoy the view and forget about the crowd here.* Then he remembered his concern from earlier that late guests might attract increased attention. After another deep breath, he followed the two women.

They had already taken their seats at one of the large round tables scattered around the hall. Everything was decorated in bright white, even the chairs had white covers. Avila was sure that Leticia could also tell him what these things were called. He didn't like sitting on them so much, because with him these covers usually developed a life of their own over the course of an evening. In the end, everything usually hung sadly down from his chair.

He looked around. At the head of the room, directly opposite the large panoramic window that offered a view of the lights of Funchal in the twilight, a small stage had been set up. Behind it, prominent and large, hung the famous photo of the old statesman that everyone here in Madeira knew.

With the obligatory cigar in his mouth, wrapped in a thick coat and hat on his head, he sat at his easel in front of the backdrop of Câmara de Lobos and painted. Somewhat disturbing to the viewer was the small parasol held over Churchill's head by one of the attendants. At first glance, the painting on the easel made quite a decent impression. At least the painter seemed to have captured the scene in front of him well. Perhaps it would be quite nice if they were to look at some of Churchill's paintings at tomorrow's vernissage in the gallery, Avila mused. The old man seemed to have painted quite decently after all. Still, Avila thought all the fuss around it was overdone. Why did there have to be a dinner at the golf club first and then a vernissage the next day? The newspapers, too, had hardly paid attention to any other topic for weeks. One could really think there was nothing more interesting to report on in Madeira.

Only then did he notice that Leticia was waving at him from her place at the table. Surrendering, he trotted towards his wife and took a seat next to her. Fortunately, he hadn't been able to spot his boss in the crowd so far. Perhaps Inês had really come alone in the end? Then he shook his head. No, that couldn't be. Even from his deathbed, André Lobo would get up to be present at such a *major social event*, as Leticia called it. You never knew who you might meet and what new connections you might make.

"Fernando? Inês has just told me something terrible. Is it true that Cecil Franco fell to his death? You didn't tell me that."

"How do you know Cecil Franco? I didn't know he existed at all until this Monday." Avila ventured to avoid having to justify himself. But that wasn't such a clever tactic either. Inês and Leticia looked at him in horror.

"You didn't know who Cecil Franco was? Fernando, please. He was one of the great patrons here on the island. Donated a lot of money to the sailing club and to the golf club here in Funchal." Inês punctuated her indignation with a slight snort. Avila didn't know why this was so remarkable. As if there was a lack of money in the two clubs.

Leticia continued to speak:

"Cecil Franco is, was, one of the biggest producers of *aguardente* here in Madeira. We should even have a bottle of it at our house. Don't you know that?"

Thanks to Vasconcellos, Avila now knew a lot about Cecil Franco, but he preferred to keep quiet and let the women talk. Maybe he would learn a little more that way anyway.

"Who will actually inherit the factory now? It must be worth a fortune. And the quinta too! With that unobstructed view over Funchal. Not like the Stuart family quinta where they built the ring road right around it. I bet it has something to do with Colin Stuart being so disparaging about politics all the time on his blog. As far as I know, the Presidente has even taken him to a European court for it. Did you know..." Inês was already on to the next topic. Avila turned back to what was happening in the surrounding area.

He watched a young woman, perhaps in her early to mid-thirties, talking tensely with Ignacio Coelho next to the small stage. She was about medium height,had a very athletic, slim figure, and was wearing a plain, high-necked black dress. She looked very nervous and was biting her fingernails all the time as she talked at Coelho. With her large glasses on her narrow face and her severe clothes, she reminded Avila of a governess, except that she didn't wear her hair in a knot, instead it reached just below her chin in a natural reddish-blonde frizz. *I wonder if she is Scandinavian*. She seemed a little too fair-skinned for a southern European. But it could also be that her ancestors came from northern Europe.

Leticia nudged him.

"That's Teresa Ferro, who you've been staring at for five minutes. She is more or less the main character of the evening, apart from our guest of honour. She and her partner Hugo Duarte own the gallery where the exhibition of Churchill's paintings will be held tomorrow. And Inês has just told us that Teresa organised it all by herself. She made contact with the family and wrote to collectors of his paintings to get them to lend them to the exhibition."

Inês interfered in the conversation.

"Teresa has been very secretive about it for the last few weeks. Her goal was to tell the story behind every picture that shows Portuguese motifs. She has been travelling around for weeks, photographing the locations of the pictures from the same perspective, only in the present day, looking for contemporary witnesses. There's supposed to be a huge surprise tomorrow. But I've already heard it leaked: supposedly she has managed to find pictures that were previously unknown to the public."

Leticia looked Teresa Ferro up and down.

"You can tell she's been stressing herself out over the last few weeks. She has become very thin again. Let's just hope that the exhibition will be a success so that she can recover. I wonder where the announced guest of honour is now, it was supposed to start slowly." She glanced around the hall. "No one has noticed that we have all been left stranded without a decent drink. They should have handed out a welcome cocktail long ago. What disorganisation."

The large double door, which someone had closed in the meantime, opened with a loud squeak. All the heads in the room swivelled round.

Avila watched as a young, blonde woman, who looked to be barely in her mid-twenties, came in, looking visibly upset. She looked around the room, spotted the club president and Teresa Ferro and hurriedly took small steps towards them.

"Who is that?" Avila asked his two dinner partners.

"Oh her? She our big problem. Aurelia. She's responsible for the whole dilemma here." Inês made a deprecating face and Leticia nodded gravely.

Aurelia was now talking to the other two with her head held high. Ignacio Coelho and Teresa Ferro could see that it was very bad news that the young woman was about to be delivering.

Suddenly Teresa Ferro was heard exclaiming in a creaky, almost squeaky voice:

"You've got to be kidding! This is a disaster!"

"What's wrong with her voice?" Avila was irritated.

"Oh, we already know to expect that with her. When she is stressed, she becomes hoarse. Sometimes she loses her voice completely and can't talk at all. Then when you're on the golf course with her and she wants to debate with you, it always gets a little funny." *Inês doesn't seem to be a big fan of Teresa Ferro,* Avila thought.

Coelho left the two women to continue their discussion and went on stage to the microphone. Sweat was on his forehead, but his voice sounded calm as he announced:

"My dear guests, my dear friends. Unfortunately, we have bad news. Due to a mishap, our guest of honour unfortunately cannot appear today. However, we do not want to let this spoil our mood and will enjoy the evening as it is. I have instructed the waiters to serve you all an aperitif. As befits Madeira, there will be a decent Madeira wine. We always stock a Reserva Velha from our dear club mate Vitor Marsh for such occasions." Suddenly Aurelia became very frantic, jumped up on stage and whispered something in the club president's ear.

Now his face was also turning red.

"What, this can't be..." He looked down at the open microphone and then held it closed while he spoke to Aurelia, who was now completely distraught and standing in front of him with her head hanging down.

Then he reached for the microphone again.

"I'm just now hearing that this year we're deviating a little from our tradition. We are about to pour Romario Palmeiro's new Madeira wine. A Tinta Negra Mole with a completely new fermentation method. We can all enjoy being curious."

Whistles sounded from the table where Vitor Marsh was sitting with his friends.

Avila only said dryly:

"Well, the evening can hardly get any worse. Replacing a ten-year-old Cuvée Madeira with a cheap imitation of the real Madeira Wine. I think it's time to get some air. I can do without the aperitif. I'll be right back." Before Leticia could say anything, he had already gotten up and left the room.

Funchal, Golf Club,
09.08.2013–19:57

Avila inhaled the scent of freshly cut grass and salty sea air that greeted him outside on the golf course deeply.

He looked down at the lights of Funchal. From up here, the city was a wonderful sight. Avila loved this time of day. Funchal appeared less lovely, as the many pink-orange roofs that gave the city such a charming appearance during the day slowly faded. Now the city began taking on character for him. In the twilight, the shapes of some of the houses could only be guessed at. Nevertheless, Avila could make out the individual churches and larger buildings from the shadowy outlines. It was fortunate that no one had yet thought of allowing taller buildings to be built in the old city. It was bad enough that such horrible boxes had been built further west, in the hotel zone. There were some older traditional houses and quintas there, but for him, that part of town was simply blighted by the big hotels.

He noticed that he was not alone. Back there, by the putting range facing the large window in the hall, were two figures. Avila narrowed his eyes to get a better look at them. To him, it looked like a man and a woman. The man was holding the woman by the shoulder and gesticulating wildly at her. She kept shaking her head. It didn't look like the two of them were of one mind on whatever topic they were discussing. Curious, Avila stepped a little closer. Now he could also recognise the woman. It was Teresa Ferro. Avila did not know the man. He might be a lot older than Teresa though, older than Avila too. Maybe in his early fifties. But he certainly cut an athletic, if somewhat beefy figure. Under the tight-fitting jacket, distinct arm muscles stood out. Avila stroked his stomach. That one over there was clearly in better shape than he was. It was about time he did something about himself. Leticia was right about that.

"Oh Fernando, here you are!" Avila flinched, startled. His boss was standing in front of him.

"The women have asked me to look after you and to manoeuvre you back into the hall. They're about to serve the first course, and surely you don't want to miss that either?" Lobo took Avila by the arm and pushed him back towards the clubhouse.

For a moment, Avila was inclined to shake off his hand and simply walk away. Then he realised how childish his behaviour was and that Leticia would certainly be very disappointed if he spoiled her evening with it.

So, he dutifully let his boss take him back into the hall. At least someone had had mercy and opened some of the wing doors on the side so that Avila no longer had to deal with the oppressive feeling of being locked in.

A third lady was now sitting at their table, whom Avila recognised when she turned to him.

"Kate, how nice to see you." Avila liked the young woman. He had only met her a few times when he had picked Leticia up from golfing, but had taken her to his heart right away because of her cheerfully open manner. She also belonged to one of the richest families on the island, but unlike Inês, who liked to emphasise her social position in between, Kate was completely unemotional about it. Today, however, Kate was not in the exuberant mood he usually knew her for. Her light green eyes looked at him dully from under slightly swollen lids. Had she been crying? He hoped it wasn't about his Subcomissário. If he got into any more relationship drama tonight, the evening would be ruined for good. Above all, whose side was he supposed to take? He knew that Vasconcellos didn't want to commit himself when it came to women. But at the bottom of his heart he was a fine fellow and always tried not to hurt the women he was with. At least that's what Avila assumed, because he hadn't heard anything to the contrary so far.

"*O doutor* Fernando, I'm glad you're here." Kate had never called him Comissário before, very few people called him Doutor Fernando actually. Avila liked the way she emphasised it in her bright voice. In a way he could really understand Vasconcellos. This Kate was a beauty. Her long, dark hair was tied in a simple ponytail today, and she wore a tight green dress that accentuated the colour of her eyes. But her narrow face under her delicate dark eyebrows looked serious.

"I am very sorry to be so late. But my father is not very well today. For a moment I thought about staying with him, but he and my brother insisted that I enjoy myself." Avila knew from Leticia that Kate's father, William Stuart Sr. was very old. Well over eighty. Kate was a latecomer, her brothers Colin and William were teenagers by the time she arrived. At birth, her mother had died. Leticia said that this was also the reason why Kate constantly worried about her father. Somewhere deep down she blamed herself for her mother's death, and now her father was all she had.

Leticia patted Kate's hand sympathetically and looked at Avila slightly reproachfully.

"We were worried about where you were. Luckily, André was kind enough to look after you."

Lobo had taken a seat to his wife's right and was now sitting directly opposite Avila. He winked conciliatory at Avila as if to say, "Don't take it so hard".

Another guest joined them at the table and sat down on the last empty chair, directly between Kate and Leticia. Avila recognised him as Teresa Ferro's discussion partner. The newcomer made no effort to introduce himself to Avila. He scowled at the table and did not look at anyone. Kate was visibly uncomfortable with his behaviour. She cleared her throat.

"Doutor Fernando, I don't think you've met my brother. This is William."

William Stuart Jr. glanced up briefly and Avila found himself transfixed by piercing dark eyes. A brief nod, a "Pleased", then the man sank back into his thoughts.

Before an awkward silence could spread, the waiters poured into the hall with the appetiser. As if following choreography, they spread out over the crowd and a short time later a fragrant *sopa de tomate e cebola* was in front of him. With a poached egg to top it off. Just the way he liked it. He gleefully inhaled the sweet aromas of fresh tomatoes and onions. *At least with the food, I guess there has been no experimenting.* He took Leticia's hand and squeezed it tightly. Maybe the evening would turn out to be nice after all.

Garajau,
10.08.2013–10:21

Hurry up, Fernando. Otherwise we won't be there in time for the opening of the vernissage." Today he was the one dawdling.

Avila was in a bad mood. He had a headache and had slept far too little. He blamed the headache mainly on the cheap Madeira from Palmeiro, which he had drunk at the end of the evening. Simply because there had been no other Madeira. He had to agree with Leticia, the organisation skills of this Aurelia had been a disaster.

He scowled at Leticia.

"I don't know why they make such a fuss about Churchill and Madeira. Do you know how long he was here in the first place?"

Leticia looked at him with raised eyebrows. He continued:

"Not even two weeks yet. And people act as if there is a special connection between him and Madeira. I bet there are many other places he visited for longer and more often."

Leticia said nothing in reply. *She's probably waiting until I calm down to drag me to this exhibition,* Avila thought.

His mobile phone began to vibrate in his pocket.

Leticia's look, which had previously been slightly amused, darkened as he picked up the phone.

"Do you have to? I thought Vasconcellos was on call. You're off today, aren't you?"

Avila glanced at the display.

"This is Vasconcellos. If he's calling me, it must be something serious. I'm sorry, *meu amor.* I have to take this."

He picked up.

"*Tou*?"

"Something has happened, *chefe.* We have a dead body. And this time it doesn't look like an accident."

"Fine. Pick me up at home, please."

Leticia looked at him angrily.

"There is no other way. We have a murder on our hands. You understand that, don't you?"

Leticia sighed.

"I'm going to call a taxi. Don't get any ideas about me staying at home now, do you hear me? I'll ask Inês to have her and André bring me back afterwards." She reached for the telephone, which was in the hallway on the small sideboard. Briefly, Avila considered vetoing her decision. But then he decided against it; he would lose out anyway. On top of that, he had a bloody headache. No, the corpse was clearly preferable to a debate with Leticia today.

Barely ten minutes later, Leticia was on her way to the gallery in Funchal. The taxi hadn't taken long, as there were usually several standing outside the nearby hotel in Garajau, waiting for tourists.

A short time later, Vasconcellos turned into the residential street in a civilian vehicle belonging to the *brigada.* Avila, who had been waiting on the terrace, walked through the small garden and left the house through the garden gate. Leticia kept wondering why he, of all people, as a policeman, didn't think of locking the house when neither of them were there. But Avila had complete trust in his neighbours, and especially in Carlos Santos, the neighbourhood street sweeper who made his rounds every day. Always dressed in the same black dungarees but a clean white T-shirt, he walked the streets from dawn to dusk, armed with a broom and a small wheelie bin. No one really knew if he was part of the city cleaning service or how he got this job if he was. No, it wasn't even clear if it was a real job or if Carlos just did it for pleasure. Everyone in the neighbourhood recognised him from afar by the soft squeaking sound the wheels of the dustbin made as they rolled over the pavement. He knew everyone in the neighbourhood, was full of good advice and was always ready to help. Whether it was to watch a child for a housewife because she had to go into town to run errands, or to stop the schoolboys from taking cigarettes from the cigarette machine next to the small supermarket. Carlos was always there.

From time to time, Avila invited him onto his terrace in the evening and the two philosophised over everything and anything. Or they would go to one of the small, simple bars in the neighbourhood and drink a *poncha* or two. Carlos' pragmatic outlook also helped Avila to see certain things more clearly and to look at them with more calm. Under Carlos' wing, nothing could happen here in the neighbourhood, Avila was sure of that.

He closed the garden gate behind him and opened the passenger door.

Then he turned to Vasconcellos.

"So, where are we going?"

Funchal, Golf Club,
10.08.2013–10:53

Vasconcellos and Avila got out of the car. The Subcomissário had not bothered to drive into the car park, but had stopped directly in front of the entrance.

"The car park said 'members only'. So not for us, *chefe*." Vasconcellos grinned. He knew how much Avila usually avoided environments such as this golf course. Vasconcellos himself knew some of the ladies from the golf club a little closer to home, but these he never met in such public places. And, if he did, he feigned polite disinterest.

Avila was not happy to have to be in this snooty club atmosphere again, but he could not choose where he had to investigate.

On the steps stood a visibly distraught Ignacio Coelho.

"Comissário Avila, I am so glad you are here!"

Inwardly, Avila had to grin at this greeting. *Look, yesterday I was Fernando... He probably doesn't want to look too familiar with the police in this situation.*

"It is very important to me that you proceed discreetly. With all this police equipment, you will be unsettling our members. You also need to stop your staff from ruining the whole green with this equipment. We want to play a tournament this afternoon, the pitch has to be playable by then. It could be that even a very famous son of the island will drop by today. At least, he is supposed to have flown out of Madrid an hour ago in his private plane in the direction of Funchal. That's why the press will also be there. This is the chance we have been waiting for, for our club to become known. And Dona Leticia will certainly be grateful for it."

Avila could feel the anger rising in him. Why did this guy have to bring his wife into it? He already knew why he always avoided going to the golf club with Leticia. *They are all arrogant jerks. Just you wait*, he knew exactly how he'd show them.

In an emphatically serious voice he said:

"My dear *Sô* Ignacio. I am really sorry that we are causing you such trouble. It must be very unpleasant for you as president of the club." From Coelho's face, Avila could see that he was hopeful that the police would now sort out all the problems as smoothly and quickly as possible. Looking at the astonished Vasconcellos, Avila continued, "I can reassure you about the notoriety of your club. I'm sure that as soon as we hold the press conference this afternoon on the discovery of a body on your grounds, this place will be known beyond Madeira. That's the kind of thing the press loves, believe me. Even soccer can't compete with that." The club president stared at him open-mouthed. Vasconcellos made a noise that betrayed the fact that he was trying to stifle his laughter.

"Now can you please tell me where exactly the body was found?"

"At our lake." With slightly trembling fingers, a visibly shocked Coelho showed him the way.

Slowly, Avila, accompanied by Vasconcellos, walked across the green of the golf course. He noticed that the lake could not be seen from the clubhouse due to the hilly terrain and the large trees that divided the landscape. When he climbed over the crest of the hill that separated the putting range in front of the clubhouse from the rest of the golf course, he could finally make out the body of water.

All around the man-made lake, white figures in stooped postures moved forward in circles. Avila could also see a diver getting ready to climb over the bank, which was fortified with rough light-coloured stones. So, slowly he began to understand the concerns of Ignacio Coelho. One really could not call this operation discreet.

As they approached, a slender figure stretched and came towards him with long strides. Under the white bonnet, he could make out the clear oval face of Doutora Souza.

"My dear Comissário, how nice to see you. Oh, and Ernesto is with us too. How is your mother? Is she out of hospital again?" Astonished, Avila looked at his Subcomissário. The latter grinned a little sheepishly and shrugged his shoulders.

"Dona Katia, thank you for asking. Yes, *mamã* is better again. It was just a little fainting spell, the doctors say. She's back home." Avila swallowed. Was Doutora Souza's name Katia? And how did his Subcomissário know that? And why hadn't Vasconcellos told him about his mother's illness?

"*Graças a Deus!* I can imagine that Francisco was already worried that he would starve if Marea didn't cook for him."

Vasconcellos had probably noticed from the astonished expression on Avila's face that an explanation was slowly becoming necessary.

"Chief, Dona Katia, I mean Doutora Souza, is a very close friend of my mother Marea and my godmother." Avila was flabbergasted. Once again, he realised how little he actually knew about his Subcomissário.

"Yes, and I've known Ernesto since he was a baby. Even then he turned all the women's heads." Doutora Souza let out her dry laugh. "But now we have business to attend to."

Avila tried to make out something over Doutora Souza's shoulder. He saw a slender figure lying on its stomach at a point where the shore stretched flat towards the lake. Most of the head was in the water. Only a few red-blond curls at the back of the head were visible. Avila looked more closely. The dark, narrow dress, the slender figure. It looked familiar to him. Wasn't that…?

One of Doutora Souza's assistants now carefully turned the body over. Avila's suspicions were confirmed. It was Teresa Ferro, the gallery owner.

"She is still wearing the same clothes as last night, so she will not have gone home, but was rather killed during the evening or night."

Vasconcellos looked at him.

"Oh yes, I forgot. You were at that dinner last night too. Kate really wanted to take me too, but I preferred to cosy up with *poncha* and Coral at a bar on Rua Maria with friends." Avila said nothing to this. Vasconcellos knew perfectly well that if he had had the choice, Avila would also have preferred to be at the bar in Funchal's old town.

"We have to get a list of the guests from Senhor Ignacio. The area is secured with a high wall and the top of the wall, if I remember correctly, is also covered with broken glass. I would like to take a closer look at that, though. There were also a large number of security guards on site last night. I find it hard to imagine anyone getting in and out unnoticed."

"That simplifies things immensely, *chefe*. It only makes the entire high society of Madeira suspects of murder", Vasconcellos remarked ironically.

Funchal, Gallery, 10.08.2013–11:27

Leticia looked around. Was there perhaps a chair somewhere here where she could sit down inconspicuously? She felt like she had pudding in her legs. Standing was pure poison.

Why didn't it finally start? The official opening had been announced for 11 am, surely it couldn't take that long? The front sales room of the gallery was well filled, with people crowded together. Slowly the air became stuffy. Leticia felt dizzy. That was all she needed, to faint in front of everyone here. Slowly the surroundings around her turned grey, the colours faded, and a low buzzing sounded in her ears. Seeking help, she looked around for a familiar face. Wasn't Inês up ahead? She slowly pushed past the other guests towards her friend. She had now spotted her too and was heading towards her.

"Leticia! There you are. Where's Fernando? You're not here alone, are you?" It was clear from Inês' voice how she felt about Fernando not being there.

Leticia immediately rushed to defend her husband.

"Fernando wanted to come with us. But just as we were about to leave, he got a call from Vasconcellos about an urgent case. And I insisted on coming here alone."

Inês eyed her friend critically.

"Are you alright? You look so pale."

"The air is a bit bad in here, don't you think? I feel a bit dizzy."

Immediately Inês was worried.

"We need to get you outside to get some fresh air!" Without waiting for Leticia's agreement, she linked arms with her and pushed her towards the entrance.

As she did so, she made room for herself by shouting to the bystanders:

"Please move aside a little. My friend is not well."

Immediately, an alley formed, and the two women got outside. Someone instantly organised a seat so that Leticia found herself sitting on an office chair outside the gallery. God, that was embarrassing.

But still. Now she could breathe deeply and the colours around her returned.

"Stay out here for a bit. I'll get you as soon as it starts in there. But that may take a while. I just heard Hugo Duarte say that Teresa is still not here. And since she's the organiser, he didn't want to start without her." Inês stroked her friend's arm briefly and then disappeared into the gallery again.

Leticia watched as a few more guests streamed towards the entrance and showed their invitation to the doorman Teresa and Hugo had hired. She knew most of the guests, many of whom had also been at the golf club last night. One or two of the people who passed her raised their eyebrows in surprise, but none made any comment as to why she was sitting outside the gallery. Just a quick nod of greeting and then off inside. Leticia mused that this was typical of the finer society of

Madeira. They didn't care much about each other's needs, at least not in the way of offering their help. No, the caring consisted of the gossip that flared up afterwards when it came to dissecting a person's actions and demeanour with relish.

At that moment, an old couple arrived who did not really fit into the picture. He was wearing a simple grey suit, which Leticia's trained eye judged to be quite old because of the cut, very wide and with pleats. His wife was wearing a calf-length flared dark pleated skirt and a starched white blouse. They both gave the impression of not really feeling comfortable in their own skin.

Leticia was about to offer them her help when the doorman approached the two, who were standing so hesitantly in front of the entrance:

"*Hola*? What do you want?"

The old man cleared his throat and said:

"A senhora Ferro invited us. We wanted to go to the exhibition opening."

"Please show me your invitation, o senhor. This is a closed event."

"A senhora Ferro told us to report to the entrance and she would let us in."

"I am very sorry. A senhora Ferro is not here yet. Are you perhaps on the guest list? I can only let you in if you are on the list."

"I don't know." Indecisively, he looked at his wife. She pulled him by the sleeve a little away from the door and the resolute doorman. Apparently, she was so embarrassed by the situation that she would rather leave now.

"Leave it." The old man did not want to give up yet.

He turned again to the beefy bouncer who was probably on duty in one of the tourist discos in the hotel zone that evening.

"A senhora Ferro will surely be here any moment. We'll wait here in front of the door. Could you please let her know that Jorge and his wife are here?"

The doorman nodded his head. But Leticia was not sure whether he would comply with the old man's request. She was already silently planning to speak to Teresa in any case, should the two old people still be waiting here later.

Inês emerged from behind the doorman's broad back. She beckoned to Leticia, who rose cautiously from her chair.

"Is Teresa there?"

"No, still not. But Hugo is going to say a few words now, and I think it will start without Teresa."

As a precaution, Leticia stopped near the entrance in case she got dizzy again. Since the room was not too big, she could at least hear Hugo Duarte's bright, somewhat excited voice well, even if she could not see him.

"My dear friends, honoured guests. As you will have noticed, we are not quite on time with the opening." Some expressions of displeasure were heard from the audience.

"Yes, I'm terribly sorry to put you to this trouble." Leticia could well imagine that Hugo, who was slightly prone to theatrics, was now surely making a few meaningful gestures.

"My dear friend and partner Teresa Ferro, who came up with this very special event, has unfortunately not yet turned up. In order not to keep you in suspense any longer, I have now decided to open the exhibition after all. But let me say a few words about it in advance. Unfortunately, there have been problems with the printing of the catalogue, so I can't make it available to you yet. Fortunately, Teresa has at least left a few written notes, which I would like to read to you now." Leticia heard paper rustling.

"Winston Churchill was able to experience the beauty of Madeira as a young man. An impression he probably never forgot during all the years in which he devoted himself to affairs of state. In the summer of 1949, he received a request from the legendary Hotel Reid's in Madeira to be their guest of honour at the reopening of the hotel after its extensive renovation. This plan failed, but in November of the same year the Reid's received the following telegram, and I quote: 'Enquiry about warm, paintable, bathable, comfortable, flowery, hotels etc.. We are revolving plans. Keep all secret'. Apparently, the Reid's feedback was so good that Churchill and his family arrived in Funchal by boat on the first of January." Murmurs of approval were the response to this.

"Accompanying him were his wife Clementine and his daughter Diana. The company intended to stay until the sixteenth of January, however…"

At that moment, Avila, Vasconcellos, Baroso and some other officials in Segurança Pública uniforms entered the gallery. All heads turned and the rest of Hugo Duarte's speech was lost in the rising clamour of voices.

Avila briefly stroked Leticia's cheek as he passed, then walked straight forward to Hugo Duarte and grabbed the microphone.

"Ladies and gentlemen. We are very sorry that we have to stop this event now. But there has been an incident. We would therefore like to ask you to go home. Please leave your personal details with my colleague, Aspirante a Oficial Baroso, the young man over there to the right of the door. We may have to contact you again. Thank you very much for your cooperation."

Funchal, Police Headquarters, 11.08.2013–09:31

O h man, if we interrogate them all, Diretor André will be on our backs." Vasconcellos had the list of those present in the gallery in front of him.

"*Chefe*, why did you actually think we needed the list of people present in the gallery? Teresa Ferro was murdered on the golf course, wasn't she?" Baroso tried in vain to understand Avila's train of thought.

"You're absolutely right. But we can assume that almost everyone who was at the opening yesterday was also at the opening dinner the night before at the golf club. The same closed society. And one of those present will most likely also be responsible for Teresa Ferro's death."

"Hmm, so you're a suspect too then, boss?" Vasconcellos' grin crossed both cheeks.

"Haha, very funny. But it's an advantage for us that I was there. So we can reconstruct parts of the evening more easily."

"And if need be, the wolf will be able to help you." The fat grin again.

Avila still vividly remembered the reaction of Diretor André, who had also been in the gallery. Gritting his teeth, he had put his and Inês' personal details on record. Fun and cooperation looked different.

"Let's leave Diretor André out of this for now. Has Senhor Ignacio already given us the guest list from the night before last? I'd like to check it again against our list from the gallery. Just for form's sake."

Vasconcellos held up another list and nodded.

Avila took a sip of Galão, leaned back in his office chair, which answered this strain with a distinct creak, and turned to his two co-workers.

"So, now please tell me what we have so far."

Vasconcellos took the floor.

"Unfortunately, the forensic medicine report is not yet available. But forensics has already given me an interim report. They found the dead woman's handbag in the immediate vicinity of the crime scene. The contents were scattered, as if someone had rummaged through the bag in a great hurry."

"A robbery?"

"It would fit that we only found an empty wallet. The victim was not wearing any jewellery. So it could be that the perpetrator took that too. A mobile phone has not been discovered so far either."

"Was there anything else in the handbag?"

"The invitation and a Montblanc pen."

"No key?"

"No, no key. I already sent someone to her house in case the perpetrator was looking for something there. We couldn't find any traces."

"Which may also mean nothing, since he could have entered the house quite regularly during the night to get something." Avila's stomach ached. He didn't like the case at all.

"I have someone posted just in case. In case the perpetrator comes back."

"Good. What else do we have?"

"We checked the wall. I took a ladder and looked at the fuse with the broken glass. To get over there without serious injury I think is quite unlikely. Senhor Coelho also told me that they have installed additional motion detectors in many places on the top of the wall, which set off an alarm if someone gains access over it. That night, however, there was no alarm, everything was quiet. Which brings us back to the issue that only an insider who knows the terrain and the security very well can be responsible."

"In that case, it's really positive that they're guarding their golf club like it's Fort Knox."

"Yes, I see it the same way. The only way in is through the entrance gate. I asked the head of the security team to give me the videos from that evening from the surveillance camera at the gate. Baroso and I were able to match up a large part of it yesterday. So for many of the people present, we already know the time they left the premises. It's all noted on the guest list." As if to prove it, he held up the list, which was supplemented with many handwritten remarks.

"Fine, that's something for a start."

"May I make a suggestion?" Baroso raised his hand shyly.

Avila nodded.

"Go ahead."

"How about we draw the seating arrangements on the large white board in the meeting room and then start by underlining the people who we know either have a connection with Senhora Ferro or who you remember talking to during the evening?"

"I think that's a very good idea, Baroso." André Lobo had entered Avila's office where the brief meeting was taking

90

place. The three of them turned to look at him. Really, none of those present had expected to see him on a Sunday morning. That clearly showed how important this matter was to the wolf.

"I would like to offer my help. I also saw some things the day before yesterday and I'm sure, Fernando, if we tap into the memory of our two wives, a good picture will emerge. Provided my spouse and I are not among the suspects."

Very briefly, Avila hesitated about whether he should reply to this, but that would really be nonsensical. Internally, one could still check whether there were connections between the deceased and André Lobo or Inês. But he would do that very discreetly, without involving Vasconcellos and Baroso. If this came out, he alone wanted to ride out the storm.

To Avila's regret, they then left his office and went to the ice chamber, as he called the new meeting room.

Funchal, Police Headquarters, 11.08.2013–10:03

E agerly, Baroso went to the white board and began to draw up the seating plan. There ended up being six tables, each occupied by six people. Avila sighed. If you took out Leticia, the wolf, Inês, the dead woman and himself, that actually left 31 possible culprits for now. Not counting the staff and other helpers. What a horrible case.

An agent of the Segurança Pública stuck his head through the door.

"Doutora Souza is on the phone. She would like to speak to Comissário Avila. It's about the dead woman."

"Put her through, please." The agent disappeared and shortly afterwards the phone rang.

Avila picked up the phone.

"*Tou*? Avila here. I'll put you on speaker, Doutora Souza, so that my colleagues can listen in."

Doutora Souza's melodious voice rang out:

"*Hola* everyone. I'll get to the important stuff in a minute. I know how urgently you need information. Time of death: I cannot tell you the time of death yet, but I dare to make a few preliminary statements. First of all, let's look at the external characteristics that I recorded at 10:27 on the tenth of August 2013 during the first examination on the golf course: the body temperature of the deceased was 23.3 degrees. If we assume that due to the warm August night the body temperature dropped by a little less than two degrees Celsius every hour, the time of death would have been six to, let's say, about ten hours ago. This also fits with the mortuary stains pronounced on the abdominal side of the body due to hypostasis. They were reversible at the time of my initial assessment. That is, by pressing the corresponding part of the body they disappeared for a short time. This is only possible up to about twelve hours after the onset of death. They were also not yet fully developed. In a time window of four to twelve hours after death, this is the case."

Avila's head was spinning. Baroso and Lobo also looked disturbed. Only Vasconcellos seemed unimpressed as usual.

"I'll summarise again briefly. I would estimate the time of death from body temperature and livor mortis to be between one o'clock in the night and about four o'clock in the morning. I was still able to loosen the rigor mortis with a little force. That also fits into the time window I mentioned. Maybe after a few more examinations it can be reduced by another hour. But it will hardly be more precise than that." Doutora Souza continued in an emotionless voice: "The external postmortem is finished so far, and the first analyses of the blood are available. Teresa Ferro had a large amount of alcohol in her blood at the time of death. I will only be able to determine the exact alcohol content once the time of death has been narrowed down. In short, she was heavily intoxicated. Her head shows an injury with a blunt object. Not fatal, but it may have been enough to stun her and bring her down. There are haematomas on her neck. According to the arrangement, it looks like the perpetrator put his hands around her neck from behind and then pushed her head into the water. Due to her condition, she will not have put up much resistance. At least the arms don't show any defensive features that would have been expected in a struggle."

"Does the perpetrator have to have been male?"

"Unfortunately, I cannot rule out the possibility of a woman because of the external injuries. It would be interesting to know exactly what kind of object the dead woman was struck with. A picture of the impression will be enclosed with the autopsy report. So, now I have to take a look at the lady's insides. See what the stomach has to offer. I may be able to be more specific about the time of death." With a click, the conversation was over.

"One o'clock to four o'clock? That's quite a long time." Baroso looked unhappy.

"Three hours. At least. If we had found the dead woman later, it would have been even less precise. Maybe Doutora Souza will find more clues." Avila was pleased, as always, with the coroner's work. So far, she had never been wrong.

"According to Doutora Souza's statement, we will now first remove from the list those guests and staff who left the premises well before one o'clock in the morning. Vasconcellos?" His Subcomissário picked up his list and stepped forward.

He started crossing out names on the board. When he was done, Avila still counted about half of the originally invited guests.

"These here are the names of the staff who were still present." Vasconcellos wrote eight more names on the board and made a circle around them with the designation "staff".

"Why are there so few of them? Not that I'm complaining, but I saw so many waiters during the evening, I find it hard to believe." Avila raised his eyebrows in irritation.

"According to Coelho, most of the kitchen staff had already been dismissed before midnight. Baroso and I checked this out on the cameras. Per Coelho, the staff are not allowed on the premises in their private cars, so every single person had to pass the gate on foot."

Avila breathed a sigh of relief. The picture cleared a little.

Lobo nodded enthusiastically.

"Wonderful work. It looks to me as if only three tables belonged to the hard core of the evening. The table we were at, Fernando, the table with Palmeiro and his party friends, where Teresa Ferro also sat with Hugo Duarte, and the table of Vitor Marsh. But I assume, of course, that we will find our culprit not among my valued golfing comrades, but among the staff." Avila shrugged. It would have been too good to be true if the wolf had wanted to treat all people equally in this case.

"Unfortunately, we have to classify everyone as suspicious first, Diretor. We don't want to end up being accused of excluding someone just because they have a fatter wallet, *não é*? The independent press"–*of which there was unfortunately not too much of here in Madeira*, he added in thought–"would be happy to spread the word. And this before the elections. I don't think social discussions are wanted by many parties at the moment." Here Avila was alluding rather clearly to Lobo's proximity to the currently most powerful party, which had enjoyed supremacy on the island for decades. Social justice was hardly the issue of the old-established party members. Although there were now newly forming wings in the party that spoke of upheaval. But that was pie in the sky to Avila's ears.

"Uh, yes, of course. We certainly want to treat everyone fairly. Please continue, Vasconcellos!" The wolf's neck hair stood up noticeably at the subject.

95

Vasconcellos looked at Avila hesitantly. It was obvious that there was nothing more to report at this point.

Avila stepped in.

"I think this line-up and the reduction of suspects is a very good start. Before we begin the interrogations", Lobo winced at the word, "we should see what information we can find beforehand. Vasconcellos, please try to find out everything you can about Teresa Ferro. Who belonged to her private life, who to her professional environment? Were there any problems? Baroso, I want you to start checking everyone in the room for criminal records: I'm thinking mainly of thefts, but also violence against women."

Then Avila turned to Lobo.

"I suggest you and I try to identify from the board those with whom we saw Teresa Ferro talking to at the club. I seem to remember there were quite a few."

The wolf nodded eagerly.

"I can also confirm Doutora Souza's comments that Teresa Ferro had been drinking quite a bit. Inês made a remark about it several times during the evening."

"All right, then, everybody get to work. We'll meet again at 4:30, here in this room. Diretor André, is that all right with you?"

Funchal, Police Headquarters, 11.08.2013–10:27

For the sake of simplicity, Avila and Lobo had stayed in the large meeting room. The board with the seating arrangement was there and did not fit into Avila's office by any stretch of the imagination. But at least he had been able to convince his boss that they both needed a galão to think.

It now stood in front of them in its caramel-coloured splendour, and they looked at the table.

"Where do we start?" Lobo looked at Avila expectantly. As he so often did, Avila wondered if his boss had ever done real police work or if he had just been so high up in the hierarchy for too long that he no longer remembered.

"I suggest we try to reconstruct the time at the club as accurately as possible in relation to Teresa Ferro, where she was and who she was talking to. If we have gaps, we can first question Leticia and Inês as witnesses later. We will then add other witness statements to the picture in the course of the investigation and identify contradictions."

The wolf seemed impressed, he nodded gravely.

Avila continued:

"I first noticed Teresa Ferro that evening when she was standing next to the stage with Coelho. She seemed very excited and nervous, she didn't say anything. Then came the disaster because of the guest of honour. This must have been very bad for Teresa Ferro, as it diminished the whole event. I don't even want to talk about the other mistakes with regards to the organisation." Avila shook himself as he thought of the terrible Madeira.

"Inês told me, but I came later. I had to coordinate a few things with the presidente. So, there was no love lost between Aurelia and Teresa that night. What is this Aurelia's last name?"

Avila tapped a seat at Romario Palmeiro's table.

"Gomes, here it is."

"Gomes, the name doesn't ring a bell. She's certainly not from one of the long-established families here in Madeira. But that would mean that someone at the golf club vouched for her. Otherwise, she would never have joined us. I'll ask Inês about that."

Avila was not yet clear what the club's exclusivity had to do with the case. But if the wolf wanted to investigate there, he could with pleasure. Maybe something useful for the case would come to light. Avila continued to reconstruct the evening.

"Shortly afterwards I went outside to get some fresh air. As I was doing so, I saw who turned out to be William Stuart jr. and Teresa discussing something at the putting range. Unfortunately, I couldn't hear anything because you came to get me at that moment."

"Oh, and I had wondered what you were watching, Fernando! But I didn't have time to look closer, because our wives were breathing down my neck. What happened next?"

"Unfortunately, I didn't see when Teresa Ferro went back in."

"Then I'll take over: it must have been about shortly after 9 pm, we were having dessert. Then I noticed that there was a loud discussion at Palmeiro's table. I had felt disturbed and turned around to say something. Palmeiro and Teresa were involved in a loud discussion. She must have been drinking quite a bit at this point, at least he was getting upset about it. Teresa got quite indignant and made a real scene directed at him." Avila could not remember this at all. He suspected it was because of the dessert. He had been so engrossed in the meal that he had blocked everything out. Good thing not everyone enjoyed their food as much as he did.

"We should ask Palmeiro about that and also Hugo Duarte, he was also at the table." Avila drew an arrow between Teresa and Palmeiro and one from Teresa to William Stuart Jr., each with a lightning bolt.

"Later, when I went to get our wives a drink from the bar, Teresa Ferro was standing there again. But this time with Vitor Marsh. But the way they were talking seemed much calmer than her discussion with Palmeiro. I was still surprised that the two of them were talking, because Teresa had come with Palmeiro after all. And the fact that Palmeiro and Vitor Marsh can't stand each other is an open secret in the club. That's why I remember it so well."

"When was that?"

"Late, I guess just before midnight. The midnight snack hadn't been served yet. So, let's say 11:30." Now the director drew an arrow to Vitor Marsh, but without a flash.

"Was there anyone else at the bar?"

"I'm not sure. I think I saw William with his sister Kate. But perhaps this was at an earlier stage when I was trying to find something more useful as a digestif than the one Aurelia chose."

"The two of them were not at our table all the time. In between, I was also alone with Leticia." Those had been the moments Avila had enjoyed the most. Watching the people around him in amicable silence with his wife and not having to make small talk.

"This is very meagre, what we have here." Lobo looked at the board. "I hope Baroso and Vasconcellos are able to find out more that will help us. I think we need to resort to our 'secret weapons' now, dear friend." The wolf winked at Avila. "Then we'll have it over with. How does it look? You with yours and I with mine?" He reached for the receiver.

Funchal, Police Headquarters, 11.08.2013–13:21

Is this an official interrogation now?" Leticia looked critically at her husband. She was not particularly happy with how the last few days had gone. Of course, she knew it wasn't his fault that Teresa Ferro had been murdered, but since Saturday morning she had felt like she was being controlled by a dead woman. The whole weekend together that she had been looking forward to was now gone. She was aware that it was unfair. But in her condition, one had to admit that she was not always easy to take care of. Fernando looked at her unhappily. Leticia sighed. She couldn't take her moods out on him, he was really trying his best. Even if things could be better sometimes.

"All right, Fernando. What do you want me to do?" She tried a smile.

Fernando visibly relaxed.

"We must try to recapitulate Teresa Ferro's last hours. For that we need you and Inês. André is talking to her as we speak."

"Can't we have the conversation as a foursome?" Leticia noticed herself getting upset again. Wasn't that a bit much theatre?

"No, we can't. So that your perception is not distorted. If you were to hear what Inês observed, it might affect your memory. But I need it unaltered."

"If you say so. I saw Teresa Ferro for the first time that night…" Leticia confirmed Avila and Lobo's observations over the next ten minutes. Unlike Avila, she had also witnessed Teresa and Palmeiro's argument. But this also led to another interesting piece of information.

"Before Teresa got together with Romario, she had a relationship with Vitor Marsh. A lot of people in the club knew that.

"But surely he must be twenty years older than her?"

"That doesn't play a big role with her. On the contrary. She is a person who is upwardly oriented and attracted to power. Older men impress her. That's why none of us were surprised when she dumped Hugo. He was far too weak for her. Did you know he didn't work at the gallery at first? He was doing her housework. Everything was amusing when she called from the golf course and told him what laundry to do and what shopping to get. But at some point, the gallery was going so well that she brought him along. Admittedly, he was also a good hand. Got some people to invest money. Although I don't necessarily share his taste in art, but Ignacio has had him recommend up-and-coming artists."

"And then the relationship with Teresa came to an end?"

"'Came to end' sounds so peaceful. There was a heated argument between the two of them. Inês claims that Hugo already suspected that Teresa was cheating on him. It must have been Vitor or William at the time, I'm not quite sure."

"William? You mean William Stuart Jr.? With him too?"

"Yes, exactly. But maybe there was something going on with both of them at the same time. Teresa really did leave no stone unturned."

"I wouldn't have guessed that at all."

"Did she seem harmless to you? Typical. Others have thought that before. But behind the façade, she was tough as nails. Rich, older men. And they almost all put large sums of money into the gallery. Hugo eventually came to terms with the situation. I suspect the money was the deciding factor. They were both doing very well. They both bought big houses in Monte and drove nice cars."

Avila thought. The picture of Teresa Ferro he had created that evening had been so different. He had almost felt a little sorry for her when she had stood so narrowly next to Coelho and nervously worked her fingernails.

Leticia continued.

"I don't know if I saw Teresa again after the meal was over. She went straight towards the bar, even before dessert. That suits her. When she's nervous, she eats almost nothing. Then she prefers to drink. I know you shouldn't speak badly about the dead, but that's how Teresa was."

Avila leaned over to his wife and gave her a kiss.

"Do you do that after every interrogation?" Leticia laughed at him.

"No, only with special people. I'll ask a colleague to drive you home in a minute. Shall we have a bite to eat at Nelson and his wife's tonight? I'll try not to be late from the office, OK?"

"That sounds good. Just sitting up there and seeing what he conjures up for us on his grill. I'm looking forward to it!" Now Leticia was really beaming.

Funchal, Police Headquarters, 11.08.2013–16:33

Almost on time, everyone had gathered in the meeting room again. Avila had come a little earlier to put Leticia's information on the board. He was astonished to find that the director had had exactly the same idea. When he came into the room, the wolf was already standing at the board and eyeing it critically.

"Inês was able to tell me a few things about Teresa Ferro after all. She doesn't seem to have been as harmless as I always thought. I must confess, she always aroused protective instincts in me when I met her at the club." Lobo had added a heart to each of the arrows to Vitor Marsh, William Stuart and Palmeiro.

In addition, there was now a name on the board, also with an arrow to Ferro. Avila tapped on it.

"Luana Alves? Who is that?"

"Inês said she saw Teresa talking to the old lady for a long time. You should have noticed her too, Fernando. An impressive personality. Well over eighty, but still totally fit. She was sitting at the next table."

Avila remembered now. He had indeed noticed the old lady. She had sat at the table, candle-straight and with a slightly pinched mouth. The woman had tied her still blonde hair into a thick knot at the nape of her neck and had spent most of the time silently surveying those present. Avila could still remember the moment when those critical eyes had set their sights on him. He had felt like a schoolboy under her piercing gaze.

Lobo interpreted Avila's expression exactly right.

"Yes, Dona Luana can be very frightening. Woe betides anyone who does not conform to her strict moral standards. That's why I find it all the more astonishing that Teresa talked with her for so long. The two of them found a quiet spot near the bar and talked."

"Does Inês remember when that was?"

"Around midnight. I got Inês the wrong cocktail and she went back to the bar alone for her special mix. How would I know something like that if she didn't tell me? No matter. While the barman mixed for her, she watched the two women. She says she was even joking with William and Kate about what they might be talking about."

In the meantime, Vasconcellos and Baroso had appeared and silently listened to Lobo's last words.

"I can add that Palmeiro is currently Teresa Ferro's only lover. Even officially, he was her companion for the evening. The relationship with Vitor Marsh and William Stuart Jr. ended some time ago. But as far as I have heard, they still got along. At least played the odd game together at the golf club." Vasconcellos also seemed to have tapped into his girlfriend's memory.

The confirmation of Avila's suspicions followed immediately.

"I was told that Teresa Ferro was seen shortly after midnight. The witness said she heard a clock tower strike and joked that it was now the witching hour. At that point, almost half of the people present had already left the party."

Avila was still not sure whether he should be angry with Vasconcellos for involving Kate before they had started testifying. To be fair, he had to admit that Lobo and he had done the exact same thing with Inês and Leticia. He decided to look past the issue for now.

"Have you found out anything about their finances yet?"

"I have an appointment this afternoon with Teresa's financial advisor from Banco Central do Funchal."

"She's with that private bank? Then she must be doing very well. You can only become a client with assets of more than one million Euros. With a gallery, the bank would have to see a very high potential to do business with her." Lobo's voice sounded genuinely surprised. "Who are you talking to, Vasconcellos? Maybe I can do something there." Vasconcellos mentioned a name, whereupon the wolf shook his head vigorously.

"No, we have to do it differently. Wait a minute." He started going through the contact list in his phone book.

"Here, this is the one. Let me have a go." He dialled a number.

"*Caro amigo*, André here. How are you? Would you like to play a game of golf with me again? My handicap has improved a lot in the last few months. Your tip with the private instructor was really worth every cent ..." He laughed boomingly, the other seemed to have made a remark. "Yes, it's my own fault. In future I won't be a victim for you ... You've probably heard what happened? ... We are of course trying everything to find poor Teresa's murderer ... Yes, it was murder." He looked at Avila apologetically.

106

"Would you do me a favour? We'd need the background on Teresa Ferro's finances." He listened strained. Apparently, his interlocutor on the other end of the line was not happy about the request.

"Of course, I realise that you're not really allowed to do that. But look at it this way: I could also ask your colleagues from the *Serviço de Finanças* ... No?" Lobo winked at the others.

"Great. It's much better if we work together. We'll do it discreetly, I promise. My associate, Subcomissário Vasconcellos, will visit you tomorrow then. When is convenient for you? … Good. And I'll see you both on the golf course, old friend."

Diretor André looked at the others triumphantly.

"That's done. Tomorrow at 10 am you have an appointment with Doutor Tadeu Parry, the head of private banking at Banco Central. He will give you detailed information about Teresa Ferro's finances."

Garajau,
11.08.2013–19:47

Avila was in a bad mood. Since he had come out of the office, everything had gone wrong. Of course, he had left much later than planned. There were just too many things to do with this case that needed to be looked at. And even if he didn't want to admit it in front of the wolf, the fact that a large part of Madeira's upper class were among his suspects made him feel sick in the pit of his stomach. Not that he had ever found it difficult in his career to treat everyone equally. No, whoever committed a crime had to be punished. But he knew, if indeed one of the distinguished company was accused of murder, what that meant. The best lawyers would start taking his case apart. This would take time and grate his nerves. And now, when he was preparing for the most important task of his life. What a bummer.

Completely lost in thought, he had been driving through Funchal towards the motorway. When he was almost in Garajau, he saw the red warning light on the fuel gauge. Had it been on in the morning? He didn't know for sure. It was not an option to break down with Leticia later because of lack of fuel. It was no use. He had to drive to Caniço to the petrol station. As expected, he was not the only one who had the idea of filling up in the evening.

There was a long queue in front of him and again time he didn't have passed by. He nervously tapped his fingers on the steering wheel. Finally, the tourist in front of him managed to manoeuvre his rental car away after what felt like an eternity. Why did they all have such problems driving here? You'd almost think they only walked at home.

To make matters worse, the EC card terminal at the petrol station had failed and he had to pay in cash. Exactly the amount of money he had planned to use for the restaurant in the evening, because only cash payment was possible there.

Cursing, he stopped on the way home in front of the small vending machine in the main street, right next to the supermarket. Again, time away from dinner with Leticia. Something growled. Was it his stomach or his anger? Probably both. He stepped on the gas and turned far too quickly into the bend in the subway to their residential street. He almost expected to hear the crunching screeching sound as the side door touched the boundary bars. It remained quiet. Thank God, that was all he needed. The car was fairly new. He had swapped his little Honda for a more family-friendly one a few weeks ago. Now he was constantly worried that he would scratch the coating. Life with an old car that was already slightly rusty was much more relaxed. Especially here on Madeira.

Leticia was already waiting for him, booted and spurred, at the garden gate. Judging by her expression, she had been standing there for some time.

"Couldn't you have called in between to let me know you were running late?" she grumbled.

Avila knew that any kind of justification was counterproductive now. With the words "You look fantastic" he held the passenger door open for Leticia.

On the way up the hill to the restaurant, he asked:

"Did you let Nelson know we were coming?"

"No, I didn't. You usually handle it, don't you?" Avila suspected something bad was going to ensue.

"Bloody hell. If I don't do everything myself." It wasn't fair to Leticia, he knew that. But it was all just too much right now.

Fortunately, Leticia did not react to this, otherwise there would have been a heated argument in the end. They drove up the serpentine hill in silence. Furtively, he looked at his watch: 20:26. They would arrive at the restaurant right at rush hour. The little turnaround where they usually parked was already full of cars. Were all those people sitting with Nelson and his wife? After a few turns, he finally found a parking space down a side street.

"Is that really OK for you? We still have to walk a little way." His anger was gone, now he was worried.

"No, Fernando. It's all right. A little exercise won't hurt, and I can lean on you if it gets too tiring. It's not like I'm sick, just pregnant." Leticia smiled at him.

When they arrived at Nelson's, his fears came true. The place was packed. Good for Nelson that it was buzzing, but bad for them.

When Nelson saw the two of them, he came right up to them.

"Leticia, Fernando, why didn't you call? I would have saved you your favourite table right by the barbecue." Concerned, he looked around the small backyard, which was full of tables. There were people at every table, and judging by the babble of languages, most of them were tourists.

"It's no use, if you don't want to come back another time, I'll have to see if I can put you with someone at a table." Normally, that was not an option for Avila. He hated sitting at a table with complete strangers and possibly having to have a forced conversation. But after today's exhausting day, he was in eating mode and doing without food now was out of the question.

"Would you like to sit over there with the single gentleman? I think that's the best option." Nelson pointed to a table just inside the entrance to the street. With a glance, Avila saw that this meant he was sitting with his back to the street and couldn't see who was coming in behind him. He hated this. How was he supposed to enjoy his meal like this? Leticia watched her husband, she knew his habit of preferring to sit in the restaurant with his back to a wall, with a good view of the room. He had explained it to her once: "So that I can keep an eye on what's happening and react in case I need to." Was that typical policeman or typical man? She had given up trying to understand.

Leticia pointed to a second table, more sheltered in the corner, where a couple was sitting.

"Thank you, Nelson. But we'll ask that couple over there if we can join them."

Two minutes later, Avila was sitting with his back to the small wall of piled-up logs that bordered the courtyard on one side. From here he had a good view of the entrance to the street, but above all he had a view of Nelson's barbecue. He slowly relaxed again. The cat of the house had made herself comfortable on Leticia's lap, and there was something reassuring about her purring.

The host came to their table.

"I'd like the usual, one of your famous *espetada*. With the house wine, *milho frito*, potato wedges and salad."

Nelson shook his head.

"I'm sorry, Fernando. There were two busloads of tourists here today, I'm actually out of beef."

"This can't be happening!" The day was ending as disastrously as it had begun.

Reassuringly, Leticia put her hand on his arm.

"Then we'll have fish, or you can have pork. I'm sure Nelson has some of his wonderful *carne vinho e alhos* there too, right?"

Still grumbling, Avila finally ordered two thick tuna steaks, Leticia opted for *espada*, the fresh scabbardfish that was touted as the catch of the day. While Nelson prepared their food on the lava grill and the smell of the tuna seasoned with oregano and garlic wafted over to them, the other couple finished their meal. When they had their table to themselves a short time later, the plates with their steaming food were already on the way.

Already almost reconciled, Avila carefully loosened his first bite with the knife and admired the rich dark pink of the tuna. Just as he was about to bring the piece to his mouth, a voice called out:

"What a surprise! Surely you don't mind if I join you?"

Annoyed, Avila put the fork with the tuna aside and scowled at the newcomer. Ignacio Coelho greeted Leticia with a kiss on the cheek and sat down at the table. Avila suddenly lost his appetite.

Funchal, Banco Central, 12.08.2013–10:00

At ten o'clock on the dot, Vasconcellos entered the Banco Central building.

The bank was housed in an old town palace in the city centre. The windows on the ground floor were fitted with sturdy iron bars, which was quite common on the island for 18th century buildings and was not due to its function as a bank.

The reception room, for that was what it was, had a cream-coloured marble floor. A sprawling leather settee was centrally placed in the middle of the area. Very discreetly at the end of the entrance hall, on the left, there was a counter of sorts made of dark, shiny mahogany. Vasconcellos was about to walk towards the counter when a voice from the right asked him:

"O senhor? What can I help with?"

Now he saw a young lady coming towards him, who had been standing on the right side of the hall at a second counter half hidden by a large column. She pointed with a punishing look at a sign that read in large letters: "*Por favor se registre primeiramente na recepção.*" OK, how could one register at the reception desk when it was so discreetly hidden behind a column?

He walked towards the young lady with a smile.

"*Desculpe-me, a senhora*. My name is Ernesto Vasconcellos, I have an appointment with Senhor Tadeu." He avoided showing his identity card, because the wolf had once again impressed upon him to be as discreet as possible.

The young lady scrolled through the large calendar that lay in front of her.

Then she picked up the phone.

"Hola? Could you please tell Doutor Tadeu that his visitor, Senhor Vasconcellos, is here? *Obrigada*." She hung up and looked at Vasconcellos more kindly now. "Doutor Tadeu's assistant will be with you shortly to escort you up. Why don't you take a seat until then? Would you like a bica or a water?"

Vasconcellos declined with thanks and let himself sink into one of the deep sofas in the middle of the room. He did not feel as if he were in a bank or financial institute. There was old furniture all around him. But not like the comfortable and slightly worn pieces in Avila's office, no, even he as a layman could see that they were real antiques. Opposite him on the wall was an old, almost black buffet, above which hung two oil paintings in impressive gold decorated frames. They showed two elderly gentlemen in old-fashioned suits. These must be the founders of the bank, Vasconcellos assumed.

He briefly considered standing up and stepping closer, when a bright voice sounded behind him.

"O senhor Vasconcellos?" He turned around and in front of him stood a young blonde woman with a slightly chubby face that gave her a childlike expression. She looked familiar, but he could not place her.

"Doutor Tadeu is expecting you. I will take you upstairs, please follow me." Her voice was very high, almost squeaky. *Fits the exterior*, Vasconcellos thought.

He walked slowly behind her up the wide staircase to the first floor. He would also have expected the staircase to be in a stately quinta rather than a bank. Exuberantly adorned with a gold-embellished banister, it dominated the back of the hall. But in a private bank, one probably had to attract the appropriate clientèle through external splendour. People like him were certainly not among the desired customers.

On the first floor, they first had to pass through a security door, which the young lady opened with a card. *So, there ismuch modernity to be had here after all*, he thought.

They went down a long corridor lined with dark oak doors emblazoned with the names of mountains in Madeira.

At his questioning look, the young lady enlightened him: "These are our meeting rooms. The biggest room is Pico Ruivo and then it goes on according to the height of the mountain and the size of the room." *What kind of ideas they come up with in banks nowadays*, Vasconcellos mused, shaking his head.

At the end of the corridor was another door. His chubby-cheeked guide opened it and revealed a kind of open-plan office that was bustling with activity. As they both entered the room, the men and women behind their screens fell silent and looked up intently. Without a word of greeting, the young woman went on to a room partitioned off with glass, on which she knocked politely, although the occupant had long since seen her.

With a brief nod, the middle-aged, slightly stocky man let them in. Vasconcellos suspected that he was now looking at Tadeu Parry.

The next words confirmed his assumption.

"Ernesto Vasconcellos? I've been expecting you. Please come in." When the young lady also made an effort to enter the office, she was turned away with him speaking in a cold voice: "Aurelia, that's all. Thank you very much. Please see to the preparation of dinner with Doutor Marsh and consort. We are expecting them at about one o'clock. I don't want there to be any problems again."

An assistant at the bank who organised meals? Kind of strange. Vasconcellos frowned.

Tadeu Parry interpreted the expression on Vasconcellos' face.

"You are surprised? That is also part of a private bank. Our wealthy clients want very special care. Business is gladly transacted over lunch together in our rooms. For this we also have a casino that prepares the meals fresh for us. But let us now come to your request. Diretor André told me you needed information on Teresa Ferro."

Vasconcellos nodded.

"Yes, we need those details. Information on her finances, did she have partners, maybe debts, things like that."

Parry cradled his head and folded his carefully manicured fingers.

"You can certainly understand that it is difficult for me to talk about it. After all, we have banking secrecy. But we'll see what I can tell you that will help to clear up the case." Vasconcellos was on the verge of telling him that there might well be other means of getting him to hand over the information, but bit his tongue. Let's see what they find out this way before he goes in with more powerful weapons.

"Teresa Ferro opened her gallery two years ago. Throughout the opening process, we advised and supported her."

116

"Is that usual for such a small company? I would have thought you only looked after the bigger fish."

"Fish? Nicely put. No, we saw the potential in Senhora Ferro's gallery. We as a bank also have assets in paintings, and our art department advises our clients to offer this investment opportunity as well."

That was new for Vasconcellos. There was an art department in the bank? This was definitely not his world.

"What exactly does it mean that you saw potential in the gallery?"

"We drew up a business plan with Teresa Ferro. A lot of money has to be invested in a gallery at the beginning. Designing and furnishing exhibition spaces, insurance and a lot of advertising. We had to work with her to see exactly when the return on investment would be possible."

"Anything else?"

"With our art department, she checked which artists here in Madeira might be interesting for the clients." Ah, so that's how it went. The bank probably even received agency fees.

"That was it?"

Parry slid slightly back and forth on his chair. Vasconcellos could tell he was becoming more uncomfortable with the conversation.

"Well. It was also about possible investors in the gallery. Silent partners, so to speak."

Vasconcellos moved closer, slowly it became more interesting.

"And did you find anyone?"

"Does it really matter?"

"Please answer my question."

"We found two investors who also saw the potential of this gallery. But I don't want to tell you the names." Vasconcellos briefly wondered whether he should put more pressure on his slick counterpart. But he was sure that they would find out the names of these two investors. Perhaps he could find out something else today in a direct conversation, that was more important.

"How has the gallery been doing in the meantime? You said it opened two years ago. Has the return on investment, as you just called it, already been achieved?"

Parry did not seem to like this question either. A shadow briefly flitted across his face, but then he regained his composure and continued in an emotionless voice.

"I'll put it this way, we were close to breaking even. Teresa, I mean Senhora Ferro, had prepared everything very well. And even managed to find a picture of Churchill to sell in the gallery. The exhibition and the sale of the Churchill painting were supposed to be the turning point. It is tragic that she will not live to see it. I am sad to say that Teresa Ferro's death comes at the worst possible time. I can only hope that her partner, Hugo Duarte, will continue to run the gallery on our behalf and that of our customers." Vasconcellos found the other man increasingly unsympathetic. It was clear that the banker was only interested in his capital investment, not in the deceased.

Vasconcellos stood up.

"Thank you very much, Senhor Parry, for the interview. We will be coming back to you in the next few days, as there will certainly be some more queries." A disgruntled frown: the banker had clearly hoped that this would be the last encounter with the *brigada de homicídios* for him. A brief curt nod in Vasconcello's direction, then he turned to the documents on his desk, emphatically interested. The audience was clearly over.

With a smile, Vasconcellos left the office. Parry would realise that he was not getting out of the act so easily. *Now I just have to find out as quickly as possible who the gallery's two donors are*, Vasconcellos thought. He already had an idea of who could support him.

Funchal, Forensic Medicine, 12.08.2013–10:30

Avila entered the *Médico-Legal e Forense da Madeira*, which was housed in one of the buildings of the "Hospital Central do Funchal".

He was in a bad mood, last night had not gone in any way as he had imagined. All Coelho had wanted to do the whole evening was talk about the murder. But the talking consisted mainly of a never-ending litany about the bad publicity for the golf club. Avila had not even been able to extract any useful information for the case. In the end, he had practically gobbled down his tuna just to finally get away. A shame with such a nice meal. He had even foregone dessert in order to spend as little time as possible with the club president. To make matters worse, he had then developed reflux during the night and had not slept for most of it. It was only in the morning that a restless sleep, peppered with nightmares, had come over him.

Now he was here almost an hour later than he had actually planned, because naturally he had slept through the alarm clock. The day was already off to a good start.

The acrid smell of formaldehyde rose to his nose and his damaged stomach reacted immediately. Hopefully he wouldn't throw up right away. He concentrated on breathing deeply and slowly and ignoring the smell as much as possible. That's how Doutora Souza found him a short time later, when she stepped out of the section room he had been waiting in front of.

"Comissário, why didn't you come in? I could have shown you a few things about the victim right away. Now I've repackaged her and put her in the cooler." Avila felt the acid rise in his stomach at the thought. He had to pull himself together to keep from shaking.

Conciliatorily, the Doutora patted him on the shoulder.

"My dear, you don't look well at all today. Almost as pale as my clients in there. Let's go to my office. I've recently got an espresso machine like you. I think a bica will do you good now." Gratefully, Avila followed her into her office.

As he sat in front of her with his bica, his spirits slowly rose.

"Are you feeling better now? I was almost worried you'd keel over just now. Not that I'd end up having to lay you to rest next to my corpses." Doutora Souza let out her deep full laugh.

"So, you want to know what else Teresa Ferro told me. Something in any case. The lady had sexual intercourse, probably shortly before her death. The phosphatase test of the vaginal swab was conclusive. Since the female vagina is a very inhospitable place, the sperm is quickly decomposed by the bacteria. But here we still found usable traces."

"Does this mean we can use it to determine the perpetrator?" Avila slid forward in his chair tensely and set the espresso down on the desk with a flourish. Too briskly, a small brown puddle spread.

Wordlessly, the Doutora handed him a paper handkerchief and continued calmly.

"Unfortunately, we cannot go that far. Teresa Ferro could have had intercourse twenty-four hours, even earlier, before her death. But since we could still detect some sperm activity, it's possible that the act occurred that evening. In any case, I have a DNA sample that we can compare."

"Do we have anything else?" Avila had cleaned up the mess in the meantime and was now thinking about where to put the wet handkerchief.

Just as he was about to let it discreetly disappear into his trouser pocket, the Doutora held out her hand to him. He dutifully gave her the hankie and she dropped it into the wastepaper basket next to her desk.

"As I told you on the phone, unfortunately we could not detect any defensive injuries. In all probability, she did not put up much of a fight. Neither did she scratch the perpetrator, which might have left scraps of skin under her fingernails. Nor torn off pieces of his clothing that we could have found at the crime scene. The perpetrator must have been wearing gloves, nor is there any foreign DNA detectable on the strangulation marks around her neck."

"But he had unprotected intercourse with her?"

"Yes, I see you think like me. It doesn't make sense. Why would he be so careful in the act of killing when he left his mark in her beforehand? I wouldn't understand."

"Nevertheless, it could still be the perpetrator if the sexual act took place far before and the decision to kill her was made later", Avila thought aloud.

"This is your playground now, dear Comissário. I only provide the facts."

"Do you have anything else on the imprint of the weapon she was knocked down with?"

"Did I say imprint? I was a little imprecise there. She has a severe bump on the back of her head. It could have come from any blunt object. A piece of wood, a branch, for example, although we found no traces of bark in the hair, which is what one might have expected. But it could also have been a baseball bat."

"A golf club too?"

"That is quite possible. And would be a logical choice of weapon on a golf course. But the imprint is too non-specific to identify the murder weapon. Sorry."

Avila stood up.

"Thank you, you've helped me a bit again. We have to make the breakthrough now."

He was about to leave the office when Souza's next remark stopped him.

"Are you interested in my other client?"

"I don't understand. Who are you talking about?"

"Cecil Franco has been with me for a week. I did some more blood tests. During the analysis, I came across a high concentration of betahistine. I then phoned Senhor Cecil's family doctor, who confirmed my suspicions."

"And that would be?"

"That Cecil Franco suffered from Meniere's disease."

"What exactly is that?" Sometimes it was really exhausting to talk to the coroner. And Avila knew that she was secretly having fun putting him on the rack.

"It is a disease of the inner ear. In addition to tinnitus, ringing in the ears, it can also lead to vertigo." She grinned.

"Doutora!"

"Let me have my fun. A vertigo is a dizziness. The sufferer can be afflicted by sudden spinning and dizziness."

"If this happens on a difficult descent of a levada…"

"He could lose his grip and fall", Doutora Souza finished the sentence.

Funchal, Police Headquarters, 12.08.2013–12:13

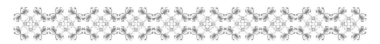

Y ou seriously claim that they serve lunch to their customers there? That's not true." Avila shook his head. Vasconcellos was talking about his experiences at the Banco Central.

"Seems to be part of the special care for rich people. Something we will probably never know with our salary. You should have seen the inside of this bank. The entrance hall with the antique furniture and the polished marble floor. No wonder they only take rich clients. You have to pay for that kind of equipment first."

"Other than knowing what it's like inside a private bank, what did your trip do for us?" Avila returned to the real reason behind the conversation.

"The gallery was not doing as well financially as one might have thought after the appearance of Teresa Ferro and Hugo Duarte. The exhibition of Churchill's paintings was therefore immensely important for them."

"That would also explain why Senhor Duarte has already called twice today. He wants to know when he can finally reopen the gallery", Baroso hastened to add.

"Oh, did he? That gives me an idea. I'd like to open the round of witnesses with him. I'd like him to tell us about the night at the club and also shed some light on the gallery's financial situation." Avila rubbed his hands together. At last, there was some movement.

"Maybe he'll take the opportunity to tell us who the two investors are."

"Investors?"

"Tadeu Parry mentioned that there are two investors who are looking at the gallery as a cash investment, so to speak. He wouldn't give their names to me."

"All right, we'll ask Duarte. But at the same time, we'll ask Diretor André to check with Parry again. Otherwise, there will have to be a decision made by the public prosecutor's office so that we finally get the complete insight. I'm really fed up. This is a murder investigation and these fine gentlemen think they can make our job difficult." Suddenly, Avila banged his fist on the table.

Baroso winced, but Vasconcellos took his boss's little outburst calmly and continued quietly.

"By the way, I also checked up on where I knew Parry's assistant from. It was Aurelia Gomes, who had also been responsible for organising the evening at the club. Doesn't have to mean anything, of course, but at least we also have a relationship here in the golf club."

"Parry's in that bloody club, too. Who isn't, for that matter?" Avila growled.

As if on cue, at that moment André Lobo opened the door to the office with a flourish. All heads turned to him.

"I wanted to hear about the appointment at the Banco Central. Was my friend Tadeu helpful?"

Vasconcellos briefly described what he had learned.

126

"The old fool. He really should have been more helpful. I'm still trying to get something out of him. But it's no use, I'll also call the public prosecutor's office to get an order to see the financial records." Shaking his head, he disappeared again.

"So, what did your visit to Doutora Souza turn up?"

Avila briefly told them about the DNA traces and that the wound on the head would most likely not help them. He also did not omit the observation that Cecil Franco had suffered from vertigo and had probably fallen because of it.

"Poor Senhor Cecil. I liked the old man. My grandmother knew him quite well from the old days. She was friends with his old housekeeper."

"The one with the milk?" Avila remembered the strange anecdote.

"No, the one before that. Daria is still quite young. She's only been with Senhor Cecil for a few years."

"At least we can tick off that subject now and concentrate fully on Teresa Ferro." Avila turned to his young Aspirante.

"Did you get anything else out?"

Baroso blushed again.

"Yes, there is indeed something. Vitor Marsh was reported for domestic violence by his wife last year. I found photos in the files. Not a pretty sight. The lady had a black eye and strangulation marks on her neck."

"On the neck? Interesting."

"She had then also obtained a no-contact order and he had moved out of the shared quinta. A few weeks later, however, she withdrew her complaint. Now the two are living together again."

"He must have had to pay dearly for this change of heart." Vasconcellos looked thoughtful.

"We will definitely raise the issue at the interview. We saw Vitor Marsh that night with Teresa Ferro. If someone was violent once, he may well be so again. Good work, Baroso. Anything else?"

"The barman, Otavio Jesus, has a criminal record for theft. He served two years in prison in Lisbon before coming to Madeira four years ago. He has not committed any offences here so far."

"At least we don't know anything about it", Vasconcellos added dryly. "Then my suggestion would be that we start this afternoon with Hugo Duarte. Tomorrow we'll call in Vitor Marsh and Otavio Jesus."

Avila nodded in agreement, that sounded like a plan after all.

Funchal, Police Headquarters, 12.08.2013–16:24

A visibly distraught Hugo Duarte entered the presidium. If last week he had given Avila the impression of a smug snob, today there was no sign of it. He was still wearing the same light grey suit he had worn to the opening of the exhibition. Only it now showed clear signs of wear in the form of creases, folds and even mud splashes on the legs. The shirt also appeared not to have been ironed, or at least had been worn for a few days. The formerly clean-shaven face was now darkened by a distinct shadow of beard. Hugo Duarte no longer looked in any way like the successful owner of a well-run gallery.

Avila almost felt sorry for him as he led him into the interrogation room where Vasconcellos was already waiting for him. Avila said goodbye and went into a side room to listen to the conversation from there, unseen.

"*O senhor* Duarte? We would like to take your testimony. It's about the evening at the golf club and your professional and private relationship with Teresa Ferro."

"Do I… need a lawyer…?" There were little squeaks in Duarte's quiet voice, almost as if he had the hiccups.

"That is for you to decide at this time, *o senhor*. All we are interested in at the moment is reconstructing the evening and getting an impression of Senhora Ferro's life. For a better logging, we will record the conversation, if that is all right with you." Vasconcellos answered emphatically, calmly.

"All right, I will tell you what I remember." Duarte spoke so softly that Avila had difficulty understanding what he was saying. Hopefully the recording would be useful later. Duarte continued, squeaking, "It's already been a few days, after all, and my memory has never been very good."

"Then let us begin." Vasconcellos looked at his watch, then started the recording.

"Funchal, 12th of August 2013, 16:37. Start of the questioning of Hugo Duarte. Senhor Duarte, first of all, I would like to briefly establish your personal details. You are Hugo Duarte, born on the 10th of May 1975 in Funchal, residing in Monte?"

In reply, Duarte nodded.

"The witness confirms the information by nodding. Senhor Duarte, would you please be so kind and not answer the questions by moving your head so that we also have the answers on tape? *Obrigado*. First of all, I would like to talk to you about your relationship with Teresa Ferro. Could you briefly describe it for me?"

"Uh? My relationship with her? We used to be a couple. But surely you know that?" He hesitated for a moment and looked uncertainly at the tape recorder. "But we broke up on good terms, really. You can tell that by the fact that we still work together. Not everyone can do that."

"How exactly did you divide the tasks in the gallery?"

"Teresa is, I mean was, responsible for acquiring new client business and planning exhibitions and their openings. I took care of the existing clients and looked after the artists we have under contract."

"That means new money was basically raised by Teresa Ferro? So, she had the most important share in her business?"

"Well, I wouldn't call it that. It's also important to keep your customer base. Besides, Teresa's great weakness was that she quickly lost her desire for everything. Everything always had to be new."

"Was that also true of her men?"

Hugo Duarte swallowed audibly.

"I don't know, maybe."

"Senhor Duarte, we are well aware that Senhora Ferro has had various male acquaintances. Our latest information is that her current boyfriend is Romario Palmeiro. What was your relationship with him?"

"My relationship? Well, yes. We saw each other from time to time. When he picked Teresa up at the gallery. Or on Friday night. She was his companion and we sat together at the same table."

"Have you noticed anything about Senhora Ferro lately? Did she feel threatened by anyone?"

"She was under a lot of a pressure because of the exhibition. She invested a lot of time to get the pictures. And then that silly little goose messed up with the guest of honour and the evening at the golf club. The only thing Teresa handed off because it was too much for her."

"So, Teresa Ferro was mad at Aurelia Gomes?"

"You could say that. I saw the two of them arguing. The little blonde burst into tears and ran away. Teresa then went straight to the bar and had a rum first."

"A rum? Were you at the bar at the time?"

"I didn't have to be. I know what Teresa does when she's angry. She drinks rum. And gladly more than one."

"Were there any other arguments that night?" Avila knew exactly what Vasconcellos was getting at. Duarte must also have noticed the argument between Palmeiro and Ferro.

"Well. Teresa and Romario had a bit of stress between them. But that's quite normal under the circumstances."

"Under what circumstances?"

"I already told you, Teresa has been working so hard for this exhibition for the last few months and was totally nervous on Friday. That got on Romario's nerves at some point that evening. Also, that she was the centre of attention, and they hardly had a quiet minute."

"Does this mean that Palmeiro begrudged Teresa Ferro her success?"

"I wouldn't want to go that far. But as an aspiring politician, he is usually used to being in the public eye. And on Friday, for once, that was not the case. The attention belonged to someone else ..." A hint of a smile appeared on Duarte's tense face.

"Did you see who else Teresa was talking to?"

"With Vitor Marsh, which didn't surprise me though. They still get on very well. Otherwise, all I can remember is that she was at the bar quite often. That's all I know, unfortunately."

"When did you leave the golf club?"

"Just before midnight, I guess. I can't tell you exactly." Avila briefly looked at Vasconcellos' list, 23:41 was noted as the departure time. So, this statement fitted.

"Did you see Teresa Ferro at that point?"

"I waved goodbye to her, she was standing at the bar again. Alone, I think."

"Let's come back to the gallery. Are you and Teresa Ferro the only owners?"

Duarte startled.

132

"How the hell? How do you come up with that question?" Beads of sweat formed on his forehead.

"Please answer the question."

"We have some clients who regularly purchase art through our gallery."

"That's not what I'm talking about. I mean investors who own shares in the gallery."

Hugo Duarte slid back and forth on his chair. He reminded Avila of a fish trying to wriggle out of a fisherman's net. But Vasconcellos kept hauling the net in.

"We know that there are two investors. Please tell me the names."

"Do I have to?"

"In any case, it would be better for you to cooperate. So far this is just a witness statement, you don't want us to get the idea that you are hiding something from us. Do you? And this in a murder investigation, remember?" Vasconcellos put on his widest grin.

The fish stopped wriggling.

"I want to be cooperative, believe me. It's Vitor Marsh and William Stuart Jr."

"Do these two also have shares in the gallery?"

"Teresa owned 50%, I own30% and the two gentlemen each own 10% of the gallery."

"Who gets Teresa Ferro's share after her death?"

Hugo Duarte turned dark red.

"That's me."

And already we have someone with a motive, Avila thought. But how did he do it? He had clearly disappeared from the scene too soon. Or had he managed to come back unobserved?

Vasconcellos also seemed to have this train of thought, which was revealed by his next question.

"Do you have any witnesses who can confirm where you were between one and five in the morning on Friday night?"

"Is that the time when…? I have to think. Wait a minute." Hugo Duarte trembled slightly. Apparently, he too had now realised that he had a solid motive for Teresa Ferro's murder.

"I was talking to friends on the phone from home late that night. Yes, I do." With a sigh, Hugo Duarte leaned back.

"Good, please let us have the phone numbers for verification. That will be all for today. If you think of anything else, here is my card. Just call." Vasconcellos switched off the device and rose.

"Wait, there's one more thing!"

"Did you think of anything else?"

"No, it's about the gallery. When can I open it again? The paintings are only on loan and we pay a lot of money for insurance. Besides, Teresa had another auction planned."

Vasconcellos sighed.

"I will talk to my supervisor. If he gives the green light, you can open up again."

"Thank you very much. Do you think it could be in the next few days?"

"I can't promise anything, but I'll ask right away, I promise."

Garajau,
12.08.2013–20:49

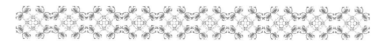

The sun was just setting, painting orange-red fires across the sky. Towards evening, some clouds had come down from the mountains and were now spreading like grey dust bunnies across the pink sky.

Avila stopped briefly at the stairs down to the Christo Rei and let Urso inspect the area. There was always a lot for him to sniff out here. It was a kind of news exchange–or "Facebook" as they call it nowadays–for dogs, Avila imagined. Each dog left his messages for the other dogs and they read out with his or her nose who had been there before.

Still frustrated, Avila thought about the case. They were not really moving forward. This afternoon's interview with Duarte had provided a solid motive, but it didn't really fit in Avila's head yet. Why would Duarte choose this time and place to murder Teresa Ferro and not wait until the gallery was financially secure through the exhibition and sales? Hugo Duarte seemed to be under quite a bit of pressure now, which also suggested that the gallery was not doing so well. Avila hoped that the wolf would be able to get the resolution for an exact review of the finances as soon as possible. Then they would finally have clarity on that point.

Yesterday, he had still obtained approval for the gallery's reopening from the public prosecutor's office. The reason for his intercession for the reopening was less the desire to help Hugo Duarte financially than the possibility of being able to observe those present at the new edition of the exhibition opening more closely.

His intuition told him that it was less about finances than about feelings. The nature of the murder, the location. It all pointed more to passion for him, perhaps jealousy? With Teresa Ferro's long list of lovers, that was entirely possible. Hugo Duarte had not given the impression of a jealous ex-lover. How would it be with the others?

Behind him he heard a soft squeak. Urso stopped reading his "dog news" for a moment and lifted his head. The creaking sound came closer.

Slowly, Avila turned around.

"You won't become a real criminal, Carlos. Even Urso has already noticed you."

The street sweeper let out a gurgling laugh.

"Yeah, I guess I'll have to learn from you on that one. I bet you're the expert at sneaking up on me." He pulled his dustbin closer, which had made the squeaking noise with its tyres, and leaned his broom against it.

Avila grinned.

"At least I'm getting better at sneaking out in the morning because I don't want to wake Leticia."

"How is she doing? I only see her sitting on the terrace in the afternoons when I do my rounds."

"Actually, she's doing quite well. She needs to take it easy, the doctor says. Having your first child in your early 40s is not so easy." Avila noticed the pressure in the pit of his stomach again. He swallowed.

Carlos patted his friend on the shoulder.

"Must not be so easy for you too, *caro amigo*. How are you doing with all this?"

Avila sighed.

"Honestly? I'm scared. With my job, how am I supposed to find the time to take care of the little worm? You know the problems Leticia and I always have because I work too late. What if something happens to me? We just bought this little house and my savings are almost gone. Sometimes I feel like I have a stone in my stomach just thinking about it." Urso nudged him with his muzzle. He sensed his master's worry. Absent-mindedly, Avila scratched the retriever's head and looked down at Christo Rei, who was slowly disappearing into the gathering darkness.

"You worry too much, Fernando. You and Leticia will make it. That's the problem with getting older. We lack the carelessness of youth. So we take apart every problem, no matter how small. Dissect it, put it back together, and in the end it's not smaller, but bigger than before. It's as if we include hot air in the analysis and inflate it. You have to deflate it. Like a balloon that's too big. So it doesn't burst. But make sure there's enough air left in it to make the balloon fly. Do you know what I mean?"

Avila nodded.

"A good picture. Deflate the balloon. Make the balloon smaller. Yes, I must do that." He nudged a pebble down the stairs with the tip of his foot, which tumbled down the steps towards Christo Rei with an irregular clack. For Urso, this was the prompt to pull on the leash to leap after the pebble. Avila would have fallen down the steps due to the sudden jerk in the leash if Carlos hadn't had the presence of mind to hold him.

"Thank you. That was a close one. Urso, you stupid animal." Urso was not conscious of any guilt, but wagged his tail when he heard his name.

"Were you going down to Christo Rei?"

"We can go for a short walk together. I don't want to put you through the steep steps down there with your dustbin." *And besides, I don't really feel like the long climb back from Christo Rei today*, Avila added quietly.

"But I don't want to restrict your urge to move." Carlos let out the chuckle again. He knew his friend pretty well.

We must make an odd couple, Avila thought to himself as he walked down the street with Carlos. *Me with my rumpled suit, the shaggy dog on a leash and Carlos with his blue overalls, white T-shirt and the dustbin he drags behind him.*

Carlos interrupted the silence.

"I heard there was another murder. Your riddle for today?"

The two friends never talked about the details of Avila's cases. But they had got into the habit of philosophising abstractly about the puzzles of the case. The street sweeper's way of approaching complex questions in a completely different way helped Avila to sort out the thoughts in his head.

"Isn't jealousy there when you can't see it? Or does it seethe in secret and explode at some point?"

"You mean like a volcano that can erupt at any time? Before a volcano erupts, the magma inside rises, there are fissures and cracks. Little quakes. Did you see fissures? Did you feel a tremor? You have to find the quake to know where the volcano is erupting. And look for the fine cracks."

Funchal, Police Headquarters, 13.08.2013–09:04

Avila had spent half the night thinking about Carlos' words. Had he seen cracks? Felt a tremor? No, not with Hugo Duarte. If he had killed Teresa Ferro, it was more likely for financial motives. But the sequence of events and the motive just didn't fit. The murderer must have decided to kill on the night of the crime. There had to be a reason why it had happened that very evening. A reason that was worth the risk.

There was a knock on his door. Vasconcellos entered before Avila could say anything.

"Chefe, Vitor Marsh is here now. He insists on speaking to the Comissário in charge. Otherwise he said he would leave right away. I showed him into the small interrogation room and told him you'd be right there." Shaking his head, Avila rose from his chair. That was what he disliked most about this case, that he had to deal with so many people who thought they were something better.

Before Avila entered the room, he first eyed Vitor Marsh through the mirrored window. They had met a few times at the club when Avila had accompanied Leticia to an event. The encounters had usually been very brief however, because they simply weren't on the same wavelength and didn't have much to say to each other. In the interrogation room, Vitor Marsh had sat down with his legs crossed on the chair directly opposite the mirror. He sat perfectly still and looked in Avila's direction. It was as if the dark grey eyes could pierce the mirror and look directly at him. Marsh raised an eyebrow slightly, which reinforced the impression.

There was no point in waiting any longer. He would not see a crack in this snob like that. Avila entered the room.

"Comissário." It was remarkable how much arrogance his counterpart could put into that one word. Avila took a seat.

"*Bom dia*, o senhor Marsh. We have asked you here today because we want to get a picture of Teresa Ferro, who was murdered. This includes her last hours, but also her relationships, both professional and private. So that we can better evaluate your statement, we would like to record it. Is that all right with you?"

"What happens if I say no?" Vitor Marsh appraised Avila.

He is looking for my cracks, Avila thought. Emphatically calm, he replied:

"Then I will ask my Aspirante a Oficial to make a written record. However, this means for you that it will take longer to record the testimony. You would have to carefully read through the entire protocol again at the end and sign it. Would you like to do that? Then I will ask the Aspirante to come in." Avila indicated a hand gesture towards the mirror, behind which, he was sure, both Vasconcellos and Baroso were standing.

"No, that won't be necessary. Turn on your recorder." Vitor Marsh made a dismissive hand gesture and leaned back in his chair. His whole posture signalled indifference and arrogance. If there was a volcano beneath this façade, it was well sealed.

Avila pressed the record button and looked at the clock.

"Funchal, 13th of August 2013, 9 am and 14 minutes past. I will begin by taking the testimony of Vitor Marsh, resident of Monte. Born on the 4th of July 1958 in Funchal. Is that correct?"

Vitor Marsh let out a curt "yes".

"Can you please describe to me the nature of your relationship with Teresa Ferro?"

"Is this supposed to be a witness statement or an interrogation?" Vitor Marsh crossed his arms and looked at Avila piercingly.

"As I explained at the beginning, we are interested in getting a comprehensive picture of Teresa Ferro. Since you were at the golf club on the evening of her death and were acquainted with her, your testimony is very important." Avila made every effort to reassure the other man. It would not serve them if Vitor Marsh pulled the lawyer card now.

Vitor Marsh lifted his chin slightly, and there was the raise of his right eyebrow again.

"Good, I don't want to be accused of not supporting the police. You also probably already know that Teresa and I had a, how do I put it best, more intense phase of acquaintance a long time ago."

"You had an affair?"

"Yes, let's call it that. But we broke up pretty much exactly a year ago, and in the meantime dear Teresa has turned to someone else. But surely you know that too?" The grin that now crossed Vitor Marsh's face did not reach his cold grey eyes. Avila could hardly imagine that such a person could commit an act of passion. Out of wounded pride, perhaps?

"You probably mean Romario Palmeiro? What is your relationship with him?"

"I thought this was about Teresa? But if you must know, Palmeiro and I don't like each other very much. He's an

141

upstart who's trying to break us old-timers with his cheap Madeira. If he were the victim, I'm sure I'd be one of your prime suspects. But to my regret, this gentleman is still alive and kicking." That unpleasant grin again.

"When exactly did you last see Teresa Ferro on 9th of August?"

"Let me think. It must have been quite late, well after dinner. We were talking at the bar and Teresa was downing rum after rum, as she often does."

"What did your wife actually say about your affair with Teresa Ferro?"

"We are still together. That says it all. Or it says something about the size of my wallet and my wife's willingness to spend that money." Vitor Marsh shrugged his shoulders.

"So, your wife wasn't bothered by the affair?"

"No, but ask her. She also has fun outside of our marriage in between. We are relaxed about it."

"Was it also this relaxed when your wife reported you for domestic violence at the end of July last year?"

There was the crack. Vitor Marsh sprang forward from his chair and suddenly his face was only a few centimetres away from Avila's face. Now it was Avila's turn to lean back, forcefully relaxed, and grin at the other.

"My wife withdrew the complaint a short time later. You shouldn't have anything more in your files about this." His voice trembled slightly with suppressed anger.

"It was also just a little curious question on my part. But you're right, we don't want to go into the subject any further. I just have one quick question. Is it a coincidence that the separation from Teresa Ferro a year ago and the little story with your wife happened around the same time?"

142

Vitor Marsh clenched his fists briefly and his lips narrowed. Avila was already expecting an outburst of rage, but Vitor Marsh relaxed.

"I think I have now told you everything about the evening in question. By the way, my wife and I left the event together shortly after midnight. But you surely already know that from the cameras at the entrance gate. I then stayed at home all night, my wife can also testify to that. Now if you'll excuse me, I have some pressing business to attend to." He pushed back the chair and stood up.

Avila also rose after he had finished the recording. He was quite satisfied with the conversation, as it had shown that this volcano under the arrogant shell was quite active. Active enough to kill Teresa Ferro? He would see. It was interesting that Vitor Marsh was well aware of the cameras at the entrance gate. He wondered if Mash was also aware of the motion detectors on the wall. Avila wanted to put Baroso on it. He should check whether there were ways to enter and leave the compound unobserved.

Shortly after Vitor Marsh left, Avila remembered that he had wanted to ask about the investment in the gallery. Did it make sense to call him back again? *No. Let the snob think we haven't figured that out yet. Who knows what other cracks will open up,* Avila reflected.

Funchal, Police Headquarters, 13.08.2013–12:31

The demeanour of Otavio Jesus, the club's barman, was in stark contrast to that of Vitor Marsh.

Just like Marsh before, Baroso had led him into the small interrogation room with the mirrored windows.

Jesus had sat down quietly at first on the chair Baroso had offered him. But as soon as the Aspirante had left the room, Jesus had jumped up and started pacing up and down the room. As he did so, he had kept passing by the large mirror behind which Avila and Vasconcellos were standing and watching him.

Unlike Vitor Marsh, however, the look towards the mirror was not piercing and challenging, but seemed uncertain.

"I don't think he's sure we're watching him. How long are you going to keep him in suspense, boss?"

"Give him a few more minutes." Silently they looked at the young man who was now sitting down again, but all the while he could not keep his hands still. Sometimes he ran his hands through his curly hair, then he nibbled at individual whiskers that had apparently been missed during the morning shave. All the while he nervously rocked his feet.

At some point, Avila nodded to Vasconcellos. He had seen enough. Vasconcellos, who was to conduct the interrogation, left the room and shortly afterwards entered the room where Jesus was sitting.

"*Boa tarde*, Senhor Jesus. I am Subcomissário Vasconcellos, I will be having the conversation with you today."

"What's it all about anyway? I don't have that much time because I have a job at Reid's later. A barman has dropped out there for the evening. I can't mess up that job at all." Jesus was talking very fast. Vasconcellos responded to his counterpart's uneasy breathing.

"Calm down. If we start right away, it will be over quickly and you will be on time for your job at Reid's."

Jesus breathed an audible sigh of relief.

"If it is all right with you, I would like to record our conversation."

"Yes, of course, no problem."

"Funchal, 13th of August 2013 12:47. We start the interview with Otavio Jesus, resident of Câmara de Lobos. Born on the 12th of May 1985 in Braga, Portugal. Is the information correct so far?"

Jesus swallowed, then followed with a short hoarse "Yes".

"You've only lived in Madeira for a few years?"

A nervous torrent of words poured over Vasconcellos:

"That's right. I moved here in 2009. It's difficult to find jobs in northern Portugal, and a distant uncle of mine said I should try Madeira. There are more hotels and maybe work for me. My parents have seven children, I am the youngest. They were happy that I got a chance here."

"How long have you worked at the golf club?"

"For two years now. It's not a full-time job, so I need opportunities like the one I have today at Reid's. If I could make it as a barman there, I'd be rid of my worries." Again, the nervous tugging at his chin.

"How well did you know Teresa Ferro?"

"Er, you mean the dead woman? I only met her very briefly. Just a brief conversation at the bar when I served there in the evening. Nothing more." He grabbed at his neck for a moment.

"Then you also talked to her on the evening of the 9th of August?"

"Was that the night of the opening dinner? I'm not so good with the calendar."

"Yes. That very evening. Did you talk to her then?"

"She must have been at the bar a few times. But there was a lot going on, so I can't tell you if I spoke to her."

"Really? I was told that Teresa Ferro was at the bar a lot that night. You must have noticed her there."

Jesus looked at the table.

"Come to think of it, it may be that I spoke to her."

"It may be? Or did you?"

The barman raised his head and looked directly at Vasconcellos.

"Yes, I spoke to her, satisfied?"

"If you tell the truth, I am always satisfied. So, how often and how long?"

"Damn, I don't know. Twice, three times a few sentences." If Jesus had only been agitated before, Avila now clearly saw the cracks. The boy was hiding something, clearly. Vasconcellos had also picked up the trail.

"So now you know again. What was your conversation about?"

"We… We were talking about the evening, I think. About the weather."

"About the evening or the weather?"

146

"Both. I don't really remember anymore. Do you always know what you were talking about with someone from days ago?"

"Since I am a police officer and I know that someone was murdered, it would also be in my interest to reconstruct the evening as quickly as possible. So, help me. Can you remember who Teresa Ferro was talking to at the bar?"

"I saw her with Senhor Marsh at the bar, they talked for a while." Avila glanced at the transcript of the conversation with Vitor Marsh, written out by now by the industrious Baroso. It fitted.

"And, yes, now it comes back to me. She spoke to Dona Luana for a very long time. I had wondered about that. I have never seen the two of them together before. But the old lady hasn't been to the club for a while either, since William Stuart Sr. and Cecil Franco stopped coming too." He crossed himself. "Poor Senhor Franco. He was really a nice old gentleman. I had a lot of conversations with him. And he was generous with his tips too." He looked up at the ceiling.

"Let's get back to the evening", Vasconcellos brought him back from his thoughts.

"Other than that, I don't remember ... wait. Maybe she was talking to Kate Stuart, too. Or was it the brother? I'm not sure."

"Did you notice anything else unusual? When was the last time you saw Teresa Ferro?"

"It must have been around midnight. Come to think of it, probably shortly after. Usually, many guests sit down again when the midnight snack is served. Then I usually use the time to clean up a bit behind the bar and replenish supplies. That's what happened that night. I went downstairs to the cellar for a while. When I came up, it was still quiet. But a little later there was a big crowd again. It must have been around half past twelve, I guess. I think Teresa was at the bar then, too." He shrugged his shoulders.

"How did the evening go then?"

"Around one o'clock, the last guests left. I went outside for a moment and smoked a cigarette. Then we tidied up. There weren't so many of us left, so everyone had to lend a hand. It must have taken two hours. Shortly after that, I left with two of the waiters."

Avila looked at the plan Baroso had drawn up. At 2:31 am, a group of three employees had walked past the surveillance camera. They had to check if one of them had been Jesus. From the time window for the murder, it might fit, but it wasn't enough to arrest the young man. They needed more. Vasconcellos also seemed to think so: he prepared to end the conversation.

"Senhor Jesus, I will end the conversation for today. Please get in touch if you have any further thoughts about the evening. I would like to ask you not to take a trip in the near future and not to leave the island."

"Why is that? I didn't do anything!" Jesus was about to jump up.

In a calm voice, Vasconcellos continued:

"It's just routine. Don't worry about it. You see, it's now 1:23. I assume that's still enough time for your job at Reid's. Our conversation is over now, Senhor Jesus. You can go." He pressed the off button.

With a short muttered "*Adeus*", the barman disappeared.

Funchal, Gallery, 13.08.2013–14:21

I can't believe I'm doing this to myself again", Avila muttered into his carefully trimmed beard this morning.

"What did you just say?" Leticia paused briefly in her contemplation of one of the pictures, which showed a small piece of lake, and eyed her husband with raised eyebrows.

"Nothing, *meu amor*, nothing." Avila, too, turned to the piece of lake, only to continue ranting: "You can't tell me that's in Madeira."

"If you'd finally get into the habit of putting on your reading glasses, you'd see that nobody says that either." Leticia pointed to the white plaque that clearly read "Black Swans in Chartwell".

"I thought this exhibition was about Churchill in Madeira", Avila continued to grumble. He heard for himself how silly it sounded, but he would much rather listen to what Vasconcellos was getting out of Palmeiro than look at pictures here among all the silly snobs. *Pull yourself together, Fernando. It was your idea to watch the people at the exhibition, so do it now*, he reminded himself silently.

Leticia had obviously not forgotten this aspect of the story either.

"I've had enough, Fernando. You yourself suggested that you accompany me this afternoon. I quote: '*Meu amor*, let's go to the exhibition together this time. Then you can hold on to me if it gets too tiring again'. Hah, remember now?" She put her hands on her hips and stood before him in all her glory.

Fernando looked down at the floor in embarrassment.

"I could have had a nicer time by coming here with Inês instead of my bad-tempered husband. We would have had fun, enjoyed the beautiful pictures, people-watched and enjoyed teatime at Reid's afterwards."

"We can go out for dinner afterwards, too."

"It's obvious again, if it's about food, you're in." Leticia turned around and turned her back on him.

Avila decided to leave his wife alone for a bit to calm down and trudged off in the other direction.

The exhibition was not very crowded. His idea to see who was hanging around on the first day had failed. Now that there was no official opening, the visitors got lost during the day. Avila looked around, no familiar faces. There were a few English women, easily recognisable by their thin cardigans and long trousers. No local would dress so warmly in August. Leticia was wearing one of her colourful summer dresses again and looked simply stunning in Avila's eyes with her round belly. Yes, she was the most beautiful woman in the whole room. He sighed. What would her life be like when the child was born? It had been crazy of him to think he could spend enough time with a child when he was already having trouble being there for Leticia.

Deflate, slowly deflate the balloon and let it rise, he thought of Carlos' words. *It will be all right.* The main thing was that his mother-in-law didn't get the idea of coming to

150

them for the first few months. Or worse, his father-in-law accompanied her. The old Catalan still scared Avila a little. He would feel constantly haunted in his own house by the old man's critical gaze. In his mind he made a little note: *by all means clarify with Leticia that her parents need not come.* But how he was supposed to justify this without arguing was still a mystery to him.

Absent-mindedly, he had moved on and was now standing in front of a larger white board on which the statesman's life and his time in Madeira were briefly sketched. Stealthily, he slipped his hand into his trouser pocket and took out his reading glasses. As he put them on, he was annoyed again that he had picked up the cheap pair from the drugstore, as the temples were much too short. Leticia had wanted to drag him to the optician right away when he started holding the book further and further away from him. But he had wanted to save money first and see if the problem with headaches while reading was really due to a lack of glasses.

Hah, that's better. He read the text with interest. Churchill had had children too? Yes, it said so. Five children. But there had certainly been plenty of staff to look after the little ones. Avila could hardly imagine that the man with the cigar had sat on the floor and played with miniature trains with his son or whatever else children had played with in the past. Or had they not spent time with the children at all in the end? Some because they were too rich and had staff for the children, others because they had spent the whole day out earning money. It really wasn't that bad with Leticia and him. They weren't rich, but they could live well on his salary in Madeira. And their little house was a real gem. He really had to plant a few more trees with Carlos. Maybe a frangipani? Leticia loved the scent of the blossoms. But it had to be a red one, her favourite colour.

He came back to the text. When exactly had Churchill actually been in Madeira? It had only been for a short time, he already knew that. It said from the 1st of January 1950 to the 12th of January. That really wasn't very long. Avila read on. The wife, Clementine Churchill, had stayed four days longer with her daughter. Churchill had had to cut his trip short because of the British elections. Had Leticia already seen the panel? He looked around searchingly. She was standing over there. And who was the man next to her? Both their backs turned on him, they were standing at the head of the gallery in front of another painting.

When Avila came closer, Leticia turned around. How was it that she always sensed when he was near? Was it his smell? Instinctively, he wanted to smell under his armpits, but remembered he was in public just in time when he saw Leticia's eyebrows slowly lift towards her hairline.

"I was just saying to Hugo that I find the arrangement of this painting a little strange, what do you think, Fernando?" She took a step to the side, clearing the view of the painting and her companion, Hugo Duarte, who was now full of style again. Nothing about him reminded him of the heap of misery they had interrogated a few days ago.

"It's not quite hanging in the middle. Is that what you mean?"

"Yes, exactly. Why do you hang the picture like that?"

"Comissário, I have already said to Leticia that I don't know why Teresa chose such an arrangement." Avila still had to digest the fact that his wife was on a first-name basis with this Hugo Duarte. That damned golf club was certainly to blame again.

"Hugo suspects that Teresa left space for the auctioneer to stand right next to the painting."

"Auctioneer? Is it possible to buy the painting?" Now Avila looked at the picture more closely. It showed a scene in a bay. Now this could actually be Madeira. There were plenty of rock formations like that here. A sailing ship was clearly visible in the bay with a woman sunbathing on it. The painter had also used the red of her hair for parts of the rocks and the sky. A beautiful picture, Avila had to admit. "Sunbathing in Madalena do Mar". So, he had been right, this picture showed Madeira.

"Yes, the painting is the main attraction. It took Teresa a long time to get it to the point where we could offer it for sale here. Don't you want to bid? The time will come at the end of the month. But before that, anyone interested can already make me an offer in person. The starting price is 800,000 Euros." A malicious grin spread across the now clean-shaven face.

Avila was about to say that it was hardly compatible with the salary of a Comissário. But he refrained from commenting, as it was obvious that Duarte was only making fun of him.

Instead, he growled:

"Well, then I hope it's worth the effort for you. I wanted to show you something else, *meu amor*. Senhor Duarte, excuse us." Avila took Leticia's arm and pulled her away with him.

Funchal, Police Headquarters, 13.08.2013–16:01

E rnesto, do I really have to answer this question? You know the answer." Vasconcellos was annoyed. He should never have agreed to interrogate Romario Palmeiro. His boss should have handled it. Romario was a few years older than Vasconcellos, but the two knew each other through their shared sport, running. For years, they had both been members of the running section of the Madeira Mountain Club, and they met from time to time to prepare for a competition or on the day of the competition itself. This year, they had even trained together in a joint running group for the marathon until April. They usually didn't talk much during the training, but they did drink one or two non-alcoholic Corals together afterwards.

Vasconcellos knew that Palmeiro did not have many friends in Madeira. To a certain extent he could understand it. Palmeiro was insanely ambitious and tried to use his Madeira wine to get a piece of the pie that had long been divided among a few well established families. They grumbled that he was destroying Madeira wine's reputation with his modern wines, on which he tried new and shorter fermentation methods. Vasconcellos was no expert on Madeira, preferring to leave that to his boss, but he thought Palmeiro's wines were quite tasty. And above all, they were more affordable, even for a Subcomissário's salary.

"Please, Romario. I told you that we would record our conversation so that it would be correctly recorded later."

"Okay, yes, I was with Teresa Ferro. For just under a year, to be exact." Vasconcellos eyed him. Sad looked different in his eyes. Palmeiro made a slightly relaxed impression, but this could also be due to the election campaign that had been raging on the island for a few months. For the first time, it became clear that not everything would be the same in the regional elections in September as it had been in all the years before.

As if the other had guessed what was going through Vasconcellos' mind, Palmeiro continued to speak.

"It's a strange feeling that she's no longer here. I don't want to fool you, it wasn't love. But we both benefited from our relationship. I had an attractive woman who also cut a good figure at an election event. And Teresa had a man by her side with whom she could show herself in public. Which, as we know, was not always the case with her."

"While we're on the subject: how about the fact that two of her exes are your biggest competitors, in business and in politics?"

Palmeiro grinned.

"Since I was the last in the chain, I could only profit from it, what do you think? A satisfied woman tells you what the weaknesses and vices of your predecessors are. So, I have a good idea of how I can score points against William Stuart in the election campaign. Or whether Vitor Marsh might play a few dirty tricks with his Madeira. You see, it's all in my favour. So why should that upset me?" Pointedly relaxed, Palmeiro leaned back.

"So, everything was fine between you?"

"Told you."

"Then how come several witnesses observed an argument between you and Teresa that night at the golf club?"

Romario did not bat an eyelid.

"A little spat. Don't tell me you don't fight with Kate from time to time. Speaking of which. I imagine you two had some stress that night too. Dear Kate seemed rather disgruntled because she only came accompanied by her brother." Silently, Vasconcellos had to agree with Palmeiro. He and Kate had had a big fight because he had not wanted to come to the event. He had not wanted to be paraded like a trophy. And certainly not on an evening when his boss and the wolf were sitting at the same table as him. That would have been a nightmare. The evening in the pub with his friends had been much more relaxed.

"I'll leave it at that. But then how do you explain to me that you left just before one o'clock without Teresa?"

For the first time, the other showed a hint of nervousness by blinking his eyes several times. But he quickly regained his composure.

"Teresa had already told me shortly after twelve that she was not yet tired. But I finally wanted to go to bed, because I had another important appointment with clients from overseas on Saturday morning because of my Madeira. We said goodbye around half past twelve and then we were going to meet at the gallery for the vernissage."

"That's when you just left her?"

"Man, what was the big deal? She could have taken a taxi or maybe Hugo would have given her a lift."

"He was gone by that time."

"Really? I can't even remember. But there must have been someone else she could talk to." That was precisely the problem. Vasconcellos glanced at Baroso's notes of when each guest had left the club. Who had actually still been there at one o'clock, apart from Teresa? Everyone had left the premises before one o'clock. Only the staff remained, but Teresa didn't want to see them after one o'clock. Was she already dead by then? Then Palmeiro would also be a possibility.

"Is there anyone who can testify that you were home all night?"

"What are you doing? I told you I went home without Teresa. Maybe I woke up my housekeeper when I got back. That's possible. She would most likely have noticed too if I had gone out again. The garage is adjacent to her bedroom." Vasconcellos made a mental note to ask Romario's housekeeper about it.

"Before we end this conversation, I need to ask you one more thing."

"And that would be?"

"Did you and Teresa Ferro have intercourse that night?"

"You mean sex? Of course we did. What do you think? Before we left, at her house. And later at the club."

"At the club?"

"Yes, there are some rooms that are empty during such an event. If you know your way around a bit, it's no problem."

"Where did you go?"

"In old Ignacio's office. Teresa was pissed that he didn't organise the evening better with his little blonde slut and wanted to do it right on his desk." Vasconcellos had to grin inwardly. He was just imagining Ignacio Coelho's face when he would find out what had happened on his desk like that. He would probably have the office completely redecorated.

"Since you're so open about it, surely it's not a problem for you to give me a DNA sample so we can clearly match the sperm we found?"

"Do what you want."

"Thank you. Then I will end our conversation now and send Aspirante Baroso in to take a saliva sample." Vasconcellos stood up.

"All right. Maybe we'll see each other again soon at training. I really need to do something. But this election just takes time." Nonchalantly, Palmeiro patted his stomach, well aware that there was not an ounce of fat on his well-trained body.

Vasconcellos raised his hand briefly in greeting and left the room. The conversation had hardly gotten them anywhere.

Garajau,
13.08.2013–18:11

"Are you sure you're not mad at me for not having dinner with you anymore?" Leticia was lying on the sofa in the living room.

Avila looked at his wife. Her face was pale and small drops of sweat had formed on her forehead and upper lip. At the same time, however, she was shivering and had wrapped herself in the blanket that was mostly just for decoration on the sofa.

"No, I'm not angry with you at all. Are you really alright? Would you like a galão or a bica?" For Avila, almost any problem could be solved with a good coffee. If that didn't work, food usually helped him.

"Maybe a glass of water. Thinking about coffee makes me feel sick right now." Leticia rubbed her stomach.

Avila hurried to the kitchen to bring Leticia a glass of water. When he returned to the living room, Leticia was even paler.

"I don't know, Fernando, something is wrong."

"Didn't I tell you that this exhibition thing was too exhausting for you?"

"It really doesn't help me now if you scold me. Owuuuu…" Leticia cringed.

"Are you in pain? Is it the child?" Now sweat was on Avila's forehead too. This was much too soon.

"I'm not sure. I hope not…" Leticia left the sentence unfinished.

"But the child can't come yet, it's not ready." Avila paced up and down the room.

"No, it shouldn't come yet. Will you help me, I need to go to the toilet. I'll be fine." Carefully she got up and let Avila take her to the bathroom.

He paced restlessly up and down in front of the door.

A short time later he heard Leticia calling:

"Oh, *merda*! Fernando!" Immediately he rushed into the bathroom.

"I think you should take me to the hospital after all."

"Why, what is it?"

"I'm bleeding." Avila's heart almost stopped as he tried to remember what to think about now. Hadn't he read something about this in the books Leticia had given him? This damn case, he had the books on his desk in the office because he had always hoped to find time to look inside them.

"Fernando, stay calm. I'm sure it's nothing. You take me to the hospital now and I'll try to reach my doctor."

After what felt like an eternity, they were finally in the car. Avila had had to run in twice more because he had forgotten the car keys and the siren.

"You're overreacting", Leticia said as he attached the siren to the roof.

"Let me. I know what I'm doing." With siren blaring, he roared up their street against the direction of travel and shot through the archway of the hotel. He took the ensuing steep right turn onto the main road with too much momentum. A

160

deafening screech was the response as the boundary posts designed to prevent parking on the pavement ate through the paint along the passenger side.

"Fernando!" Leticia clung to the handle above the door with her right hand.

"Nothing happened, just a bit of varnish. I'll report it later. Now we have to move." The adrenaline was rushing in his ears. He didn't even want to think about his new car now, the main thing was that Leticia got to her doctor as soon as possible.

"What did the doctor say?" Avila asked Leticia for the third time since they had left the house.

"I'm supposed to stay calm and we'll meet at the hospital in Funchal. But how am I supposed to stay calm when my husband is speeding around like a rally driver?"

The sound of Leticia's throaty laughter eased Avila's tension. He too had to grin now.

"Maybe I should sign up for the Rali Vinho da Madeira next year."

"If you don't wreck the car first or can't find your car keys before the start, I'm sure you'd have a good chance." She giggled.

Avila reached over and patted her knee. The car lurched briefly because he was still driving too fast on the motorway towards Funchal.

"Please concentrate on driving, Fernando. You have important cargo. Our first child, don't forget that. So, both hands on the wheel." She stroked his hand briefly and then placed it on the steering wheel.

They would be at the hospital in a quarter of an hour at the most. He only hoped that everything was all right with Leticia and the child. He thought briefly of his friend Carlos. He could hardly get rid of as much air as he would have to if he wanted to release from his problem now. The balloon was about to burst. Avila squinted his eyes and concentrated on the road.

Funchal, Police Headquarters, 14.08.2013–08:07

Y ou've got to be kidding!" Avila banged his fist on the table.

Baroso spilled his bica, which he had just prepared with Avila's espresso machine. Immediately, a brown stain appeared on the chest of his formerly white shirt. Embarrassed, he tried to remove the stain with a handkerchief, avoiding looking in the direction of his angry boss.

Avila started pacing frantically up and down the room.

"Are we quite sure? It's not Palmeiro?"

Vasconcellos, who had been sitting quietly in his chair during the outburst, slowly drinking his galão, nodded his head.

"Yes, Doutora Souza is quite sure. Teresa Ferro had sex with someone else later that evening. Only this residue was still detectable in the vagina. But she is in the process of checking the victim's clothes because sperm is detectable there for much longer. We should get the results in the next few hours."

"And what good will that do us? Then we will probably only get confirmation that she also slept with Palmeiro.

Something he's already volunteered to tell us. We need to find out who she had sex with last, damn it!" Again Avila's fist struck, this time hitting the filing cabinet he was passing.

"But we had said that a murderer who was otherwise so careful would not leave such traces", Baroso interjected cautiously.

Avila stopped short and looked at his Aspirante. The latter ducked his head in anticipation of another outburst. When Avila saw this, he immediately felt bad for his behaviour. It really wasn't right to take his temper out on the two of them. Vasconcellos was made of sterner stuff, he was probably even secretly amused by him. But Baroso? He looked completely unsettled as he made himself as small as possible next to the sideboard.

"I'm sorry I raised my voice. I had a pretty rough night at the hospital, although that's no excuse."

Now a clear expression of concern flitted across Vasconcellos' face.

"Is everything all right with Leticia, Fernando? You could have called and we would have taken care of everything today." He stood up and patted Avila on the shoulder.

"Thank you, Ernesto. No, it'll be fine. But we had quite a scare yesterday. Leticia went into labour early and we had to go to the hospital right away. That reminds me, I still have to report damage to the boundary posts in Garajau." Baroso looked irritated, apparently not understanding the connection between the stakes and the premature labour. "At the hospital they were able to stop the contractions. But the doctor said it could happen again at any time and we were very lucky there was no premature birth." Avila stroked his eyes.

"And what happens now? Is Leticia still in the hospital?"

"Today, to be absolutely sure that the contractions don't start again. But I can take her home again tonight. She will then have to be on strict bed rest, as the doctor put it. And that's for the next two months, until the due date."

"Do you have someone to help you? Or do you want to take a holiday?"

"Until the murder is solved, I can't take a holiday. You know me. I'd go crazy at home. Leticia knows that too, she's already given me the green light. And for the last few weeks I've been going home at lunchtime to walk Urso. Nothing will change. Ana is so sweet and looks after her in the mornings when she is around. She also cleans our neighbours' houses. Then Leticia doesn't feel so alone either."

"If you need our help, let us know. We can also drop in from time to time and make ourselves useful."

"That's very kind of you. At most, I might ask one of you to take Urso for a walk at lunchtime if there's no other way."

Someone knocked on the door. The wolf entered. It was not at all like him to knock first. Everyone looked at him in amazement.

"I heard about Leticia, Fernando. If you need Inês' or my help, please let me know." *The news spread quickly,* Avila thought. So much helpfulness, he was touched. Again, he unobtrusively stroked his eyes, which to his astonishment became slightly moist. *I wonder if expectant fathers also have hormonal fluctuations?* Otherwise he wouldn't be so weepy.

He cleared his throat.

"Thank you, André, that is very kind."

"Are there any new findings? Please bring me up to speed." Lobo sat down in the only seat still available, an old armchair covered in grey corduroy.

Unlike the other offices, which had modern but, in Avila's eyes, terribly uncomfortable and ugly office chairs, Avila's office was furnished almost like a living room. There were several comfortable chairs and even this armchair, which

Avila, when not pacing up and down to think better, used most of the time. He could sit in it for hours, pondering the cases and looking out the window. While doing so, he could let his mind wander and look at the current case from all angles. Now the wolf sat in Avila's thinking chair and looked expectantly around.

Vasconcellos looked briefly at Avila. He nodded in agreement and had his Subcomissário bring the director up to speed.

"We have the result of the DNA match between the semen trace and Palmeiro's DNA sample. Unfortunately, no match."

"This is not good. I was hoping we could put this issue to rest." The wolf turned to Avila, who was still pacing the room.

"Please sit down, Avila. You're making us all very nervous with these ups and downs."

Avila let himself sink into his desk chair, grumbling quietly.

"What do you want to do now?"

"We also need to get DNA samples from the other suspects to match them."

Lobo sighed.

"I was afraid you were going to say that. Spit it out, who in particular are we talking about?"

Again, Vasconcellos took the floor:

"Strictly speaking, we would have to check all the men present. Unfortunately, it is not clear if the one who had sex with Teresa Ferro is really the murderer."

"Can't we dispense with it altogether then? I don't want to deal with the Marsh and Stuart lawyers. They'll get on our backs. Haven't we got anything else?"

"We are trying to get the call records from the phone company for Ferro's missing mobile phone."

"Does that mean we are sure that the mobile phone was also stolen?"

"Yes, several witnesses have testified that Teresa Ferro was talking on a mobile phone that evening. The perpetrator must have taken it, as well as her jewellery and cash."

"But if it was a robbery-murder after all, why isn't this barman in custody yet? He's the one who has a record for theft. A Vitor Marsh or a William Stuart Jr. don't need that type of crime."

Now Avila intervened in the discussion.

"Who's to say that the killer didn't speculate on that very thought process of ours, and that's why he faked a robbery?"

"If he's so smart, why would he leave his genetic fingerprint in her?"

"Yes, that is our problem. It just doesn't match up. But at least to move forward, we have to match the sperm."

Another wolfish sigh.

"I don't like it at all. But I'm trying to persuade the prosecution. It won't be easy. Even if you don't like it, Avila: assume that we only get permission for a saliva sample for the barman and the staff who were still on site after one o'clock. For all the others, I look at the black side. With an alibi and no proof that the perpetrator really had intercourse with the victim…"

"We haven't had all the interrogations yet."

"Is there anyone there who hadn't already left the club after the victim was last seen?"

Avila shook his head in frustration.

"Well, let's start small first. Let's see what I can get with the prosecutor." Lobo put his hands on the back of the chair and pushed himself up.

Funchal, Police Headquarters, 14.08.2013–10:04

Avila looked very closely at his opposite. Today, William Stuart Jr. made a more tidy impression than on the evening at the golf club. There, although they had been sitting at the same table, he and Avila had hardly exchanged more than three sentences.

Before the conversation, he had spoken with Vasconcellos, who knew the Stuart family well through his relationship with Kate.

"William is actually quite a nice guy. It's just that he's under a lot of pressure as the company's progenitor. His old man is desperate to ensure that Stuart Winery remains one of the leading ones in Madeira. Kate and Colin, the younger brother, are not interested in the business at all. I'm just surprised that William is now starting to take an interest in politics. That was actually always Colin's area, the younger one. He runs a politics blog and has been messing with the government for years. I don't want to know how many libel cases he has and has had. His disputes have gone all the way to the European Court of Justice. Two years ago, William took up politics from one day to the next. He can really get people excited, I'll give him that. His chances in September are pretty good, or so they say. Better than Palmeiro's for sure."

With this information in mind, Avila tried to re-examine the first impression of Stuart that had already settled on him. On closer inspection, he saw the resemblance between William and his sister. The same green eyes that had seemed so dark to him at the club, the narrow oval face and the smile lines at the corners of his eyes. It was only hair that Kate clearly had more of. Stuart had cut the few hairs that formed an implied wreath around his head razor short so that only a dark shadow was visible. He was good-looking, one had to give him that. Avila could imagine that he was successful with women. For a politician, it was definitely an advantage if he could win over his female voters.

William Stuart Jr. had been sitting quietly in his chair the whole time, following the Comissário's scrutiny with an implied smile. Now he cleared his throat and asked in a dark voice:

"I don't want to be rude, but I'm afraid I'm in a bit of a hurry because I have to be at party headquarters at noon. We have some things to prepare for our election meeting tomorrow. Could we perhaps start?"

Quite different from that arrogant Vitor Marsh. Stuart made a friendly impression.

Avila nodded and started with the usual.

"O senhor Stuart, we would like to record the conversation so that we can keep an accurate record of it later. Is that all right with you?"

"Yeah, it's fine."

"Then I'll start now: 14th of August 2013, 10:13 am. Conversation with William Stuart Jr., resident in Funchal. Born on the 28th March 1961, also in Funchal. Is that correct so far?"

169

"Yes, that's right."

"I would like to ask you first about the evening of the 9th of August at the golf club. When exactly did you arrive there?"

"My sister Kate Stuart and I were quite late because my father wasn't feeling well. Kate wanted to stay at home at first, but I managed to persuade her to accompany me. We should have got there about a little before eight." Avila nodded, this was in line with his information.

"Did you have a conversation with the victim, Teresa Ferro, that night?" Would Stuart admit that he had talked to her on the putting range?

"Yes, I did. You should know that too, Comissário. After all, you and Diretor André saw us both outside. It must have been a little after eight." Avila was annoyed, he had hoped he hadn't been noticed.

"Can you tell me what you were talking about with Teresa Ferro?"

"Teresa was a bit nervous about the evening and the exhibition the next day. I wanted to calm her down."

"It sounds like you're still on good terms?"

"Yes, we were. However, we never had a real relationship either, it was more fun between friends. And at some point, we dropped that one part and were just friends."

"Did she mention to you if she was afraid of anyone, maybe felt threatened?"

"She was scared about the exhibition. You probably already know that the gallery is not doing so well. The share the gallery was to get for the sale of the Churchill painting was very important to her. So, when everything went wrong that night and even the guest of honour cancelled, Teresa was pretty upset." Avila remembered the nervous impression Teresa Ferro had made when she had stood next to Ignacio Coelho.

170

"There was nothing else that worried Teresa Ferro?"

"There was another problem with one of their bigger clients in the gallery."

"Why, what was going on there?"

"She wouldn't give me any details. I'm sorry." Briefly, Avila wondered if he should follow up. Did Stuart suspect something? He would put Vasconcellos on the subject. Had there been trouble with Vitor Marsh and he had strangled his former lover in a rage? Unfortunately, the time of death and his alibi didn't fit the ...

"Comissário?" Stuart startled him out of his thoughts. *Time of death.*

"What time exactly did you leave the golf club that night?"

"It must have been around midnight. Kate and I were worried about our father and couldn't take it anymore." Stuart's features tightened. Avila could clearly see the concern for his father.

"Your father is already very old?"

"Yes, that's why I didn't want the questioning to take place at our quinta. He mustn't get upset if possible. Especially over the last few days, he has lost a lot of energy.

"Of course we take that into consideration if possible. I hope your father gets better soon." Avila had to agree with Vasconcellos, Stuart really did make a nice impression and the concern for his father seemed genuine. He noticed his mind starting to wander again as he thought of Leticia and his current worries. He really had to pull himself together.

"Can anyone testify that you did not leave again that evening?" he returned to the conversation.

"I sat down with my father because he couldn't sleep, as he often can't. He always talks about the past and just needs someone to listen. Kate must have heard us, if she didn't fall asleep right away."

"We will also question Kate about this in the next few days. But it may be necessary for us to question your father as well." William Stuart straightened up in his chair and looked at Avila menacingly.

"Is that really necessary? I told you he isn't well! You should have consideration for his health!" *There are his cracks*, Avila thought. *He wants to protect his father. I wonder if my child will be like that with me one day.*

"At the moment, a conversation with your father is not necessary. Unfortunately, I cannot promise that it will stay that way. But we will inform you in good time beforehand. From my side that will be it, do you have anything else to say? Did you notice anything else about the evening?"

"No, but if I think of anything else I'll be happy to get back to you." The cracks had disappeared and William Stuart was once again as friendly as at the beginning of the conversation.

Funchal, Jardim do Sao Francisco, 15.08.2013–11:00

*C*aras *amigas, caros amigos.* We are all here today because we want to change something. For Funchal, for Madeira. For too long we have let one party rule our lives. Let's make a statement. This regional election will herald the end of the politics. We will all be free from corruption and nepotism again." Applause and cheers interrupted William Stuart Jr. as he addressed his supporters.

The small square in the Jardim do Sao Francisco was full. People were standing everywhere, waving the blue-green flags of his newly founded party "*Partido Liberal Verde*", PLV for short. Vasconcellos and Baroso had mingled–as inconspicuously as possible–with the crowd. Vasconcellos, however, had not been particularly enthusiastic about Avila's idea, as he hardly thought it possible to be present at such an event without being recognised. This fear was confirmed at that moment when someone tapped him on the shoulder from behind.

"Ernesto, *amigo*, what are you doing here? Are you investigating in secret? Or have you discovered your green heart in your old age?"

Vasconcellos turned around and looked into the grinning face of Romario Palmeiro.

"I could ask you the same thing, what are you doing at a PLV event? Your party has slightly different goals, if I remember correctly?"

"You should always know what the competition is doing. That's how I do it in business and also in politics. So, what have I missed? Has William already given his usual litany against the tourism industry and the destruction of our environment?"

Vasconcellos just shrugged and turned back towards Stuart and the small stage that was set up in the square.

"The tourism lobby and the real estate industry are responsible for these architectural eyesores that are costing us Madeirans dearly. Do you remember February 2010? How many of you lost children, parents or friends in the floods? We have to stop the madness. No more building of ever larger hotel complexes and sealing of green spaces. No concreting of river banks and river beds. No filling up sandy beaches and destroying the image of our volcanic island. All this is the work of the government and we must now seize the opportunity to break its power. Are you with me?" Loud cheering from the throats of those present was the answer.

Palmeiro just shook his head and whispered in Vasconcellos' ear:

"He can make speeches, dear William. But he and this mini-group don't stand a chance against the established parties."

Then he called out loudly to the front:

"Bravo, William. Why don't you tell your followers how exactly you're going to break the power like that with so few people? Are you going to lie down in front of the *municipio* and block the doors? That's all it's going to take!" Loud

174

whistles, but also a few cheers rang out. Palmeiro also had a few of his supporters with him.

William Stuart looked down and made out the troublemaker.

"Well, well, we have visitors. My friends, let's welcome Romario Palmeiro, the new face of our ruling party. Shall we not take the opportunity to question him a little?"

Palmeiro didn't have to be asked twice and jumped onto the stage with two strides. Again, loud booing and clapping.

Baroso looked at Vasconcellos worriedly.

"Do you think we need help? Some of them look pretty sinister."

"If it calms you down, you can tell our colleagues from the Segurança Pública. But there are two of them back there, and I think they are smart enough to assess the situation properly." He pointed to two policemen in uniform who were watching the action from a little distance. Palmeiro had now stepped up to the microphone.

"While I am up here, I would like to ask a question right away. How is it that someone from a family that has profited from politics all these years now thinks he can act as a saviour here? Or weren't your father and grandfather among the close friends of our Presidente?"

Stuart was silent for a moment, then replied:

"We Stuarts have always thought about our workers and the environment. Our factory has the highest safety standards and one of the largest environmental zones in Madeira is financed by my family. What do you have to show for it, Romario? All I ever hear is how disastrous the conditions are on your winery. The cheap price of your products can only be maintained because you pay pittance to your workers! We don't need people like you here in Madeira!" The crowd went wild.

Palmeiro's grin gave way to a baring of teeth. Stuart had clearly hit him on a sore spot.

Stuart followed up:

"And while we're on the subject of money, my friend. Where does your capital for this winery actually come from? How is it that the son of a worker, and that's you, is suddenly playing with the big boys?" Everything was silent.

"Shall I tell you, my friends, how this man here gets his money? He cashes in when someone from honourable society wants to launder his money."

Baroso and Vasconcellos looked at each other in amazement.

"And he used his girlfriend's gallery for that. That's right. His girlfriend who was found murdered a week ago. Do you want someone like that in charge of our Madeira? Who can't even protect his girlfriend and drags her into his dirty business?" A commotion broke out. Supporters from both camps started throwing objects at the stage. The two protection policemen came running up and tried to shield Stuart and Palmeiro from the angry crowd.

Vasconcellos muttered through clenched teeth:

"What a bummer. If there is any truth to the story, we have a problem. We have to go back to the presidium immediately and take another look at the gallery's cash flows."

"I don't understand, how can you launder money through a gallery?"

"There are several possibilities, I'll explain when we get back. Let's go."

Funchal, Police Headquarters
15.08.2013–12:13

*M*erda! Why didn't that Stuart guy tell us about this when we questioned him?" Avila was running circles in his office again. Vasconcellos and Baroso had just told him about the accusations against Palmeiro.

"He probably wanted to have something up his sleeve for his election campaign. Since the press was also there, I'm sure it will be all over the news tomorrow."

"*Porra*!" Avila couldn't stop himself from swearing.

"We have to prevent our colleagues from the press from spreading this around tonight. Vasconcellos, did you see who was there?"

"Yes, I did. An independent newspaper and our party paper. I'm only worried about the non-government paper. I imagine the others will be more silent about this incident because then they won't make the Presidente look good either."

"Vasconcellos, you establish contact with the press people. Offer them exclusive information if they hold it back for another day. And after that, you and Baroso take another look at the gallery's finances. I want to know what Stuart meant by that." Another round of the office followed.

"There is one good thing about today's performance. Finally, we can put more pressure on them. The prosecutor's office has been notified, we'll get an insight into the gallery's financial data. Baroso, go right now and get the records from Duarte. He already knows. If he gives you any trouble, let me know. In the meantime, I'll talk to the wolf and explain that we need to subpoena Palmeiro again. He won't be thrilled."

Barely an hour later, Baroso and Vasconcellos were sitting over the gallery's financial documents, which Hugo Duarte had made available to them without grumbling.

As Vasconcellos had expected, the pro-government party paper was not interested in "this tall tale", as they put it. The representative of the other newspaper, on the other hand, had needed some persuasion before finally agreeing to withhold the story for twenty-four hours. Vasconcellos had had to make further concessions, however, because the newspaper now also wanted first-hand information about Teresa Ferro's murder. An agreement had been reached for an exclusive story on the murder after the investigation.

"You were going to explain to me how to launder money in a gallery."

"It starts with the fact that sellers and buyers in the art trade can remain anonymous. I know that people have been discussing changing the legislation here for years, but so far it only happens on a voluntary basis when galleries and auction houses register the parties involved in a transaction."

"That doesn't sound good, but I don't understand yet..."

"Let me tell you more. Art deals are likely to be done with cash. Let's say I have a lot of cash of dubious origin that I want to clean up. I give a middleman this money in cash. At an auction or in the day-to-day business of a gallery, an art object of mine with a low value is then offered for sale. My middleman buys this object from me without me appearing as

178

the seller. He pays the gallery in cash the price previously agreed upon with me. The gallery books the transaction on its books as proceeds of sale and I get the money booked to an account of my choice. To disguise it even further, I can even add other accounts in between, but in the end my money returns to me laundered that way."

"Phew, sounds complicated."

"It's actually quite simple. And for sales of up to 15,000 Euros, the bank won't ask too many questions. Only after that do things have to be declared in more detail."

"Do you think Palmeiro acted as a buyer then?"

"I think he's too clever for that. I suspect that he only made the gallery available. But that would hardly have worked without Teresa Ferro's knowledge. It is probably the case that he and Teresa got percentages on every deal and so always cashed in nicely."

"Do you think they will be able to prove it?"

"It will be very difficult. And neither of us are experts. We need to get help from our money laundering team. Let's go over to their office." Vasconcellos packed up the documents and went with Baroso over to the colleagues at the *Unidade de Informação Financeira*.

"Do we have anything to confront Palmeiro with?" asked Avila when the two came back to his office two hours later. Baroso's face was red from exertion and Vasconcellos also looked tense.

"We have spent two hours going through the financial transactions of the last six months with our colleagues. We could see that there were conspicuously many smaller transactions up to 15,000 Euros. The art objects that were sold seem to have been chosen very arbitrarily. Various artists are listed, but they are not listed in the catalogues of the big auction houses. Our colleagues suspect that the works were all sold well above value. Which could speak to our suspicion of money laundering."

"Can we connect Palmeiro to this?"

"No, unfortunately not. Teresa Ferro instructed all the transactions. It may well be that Hugo Duarte had no idea about the existence of these transactions. How we are going to prove that Palmeiro was involved is beyond me. Baroso and our colleagues still want to check whether a connection can perhaps be established through the artists."

"Let us assume that William Stuart's statement is true. What do we think? That Teresa Ferro wanted out and someone objected?"

"Do you want to hear my opinion? A possible scenario: Teresa Ferro wants to get out, she argues with Palmeiro, complains about him to her former boyfriend William Stuart. Palmeiro observes this, is afraid that Teresa Ferro will betray him, and kills her that very night. He then fakes a robbery to divert attention from himself."

"How did he get back into the club unnoticed? We also have the statement of his housekeeper that she did not hear him drive away again."

"What if it wasn't Palmeiro who committed the murder, but one of his so-called business associates? The one who might have mingled with the staff?"

"That would be possible. We have to check the staff again. Speaking of, is there a result from the DNA samples yet?"

"Expected tomorrow at the latest."

"This is all taking far too long for me! I feel like we're just not getting anywhere. Always new loose threads." Avila fretted. How did this money laundering story fit in? If it had been a contract killing, it had to have been planned long ago. This would argue against Vasconcellos' thesis that Palmeiro had seen Teresa Ferro with William Stuart that night and then someone from organised crime had taken over the murder. No. The club site was very risky, with all its camera surveillance. The volcano must have erupted that night, regardless of the fact that there were better places for a murder. But what event had triggered the eruption?

When Vasconcellos and Baroso had left the room, Avila started travelling through his office again. He could think best while walking. Maybe he should swap the confines of the office for a walk through the old town and a snack in that place next to the market halls? After barely getting a bite down yesterday out of concern for Leticia, his stomach was now audibly making itself known.

He decided to make another quick phone call to see if she was really in bed and if Ana had already stopped by as promised. He dialled her number.

"*Tou*? Fernando, is that you? Are you going to check that I'm a good girl in bed?" Leticia laughed. Avila was glad to hear her laugh. It had been quite a scare for both of them.

"Before you ask, Ana has just been to see me. She even made me an *açorda*. Yes, and there is still enough left for you to have a large portion tonight. Ana even thought of your beloved *bacalhau*." Again, Leticia laughed. She knew her husband's weakness for Ana's bread soup. "Wait, there's someone at the patio door. Urso, go see who it is…" Leticia put the phone down.

A short time later, she got in touch again.

"Don't worry, I didn't get up. It's Carlos who wants to look after things. Did you make him my nanny too?"

Avila grinned, he could rely on his friend. He had met him last night while walking with Urso and told him about the excitement. Carlos had agreed to spontaneously drop in on Leticia every day. Avila noticed how he became calmer. The balloon lost some air and could float more leisurely again. Now he could really go out to eat.

"Talk to Carlos for all I care, I just wanted to hear if everything was alright. I'll see you tonight, *meu amor*." He hung up and looked at his watch. He still had about an hour before Palmeiro would be back here at the presidium. That should be enough for a late lunch.

Funchal, Police Headquarters
15.08.2013–16:02

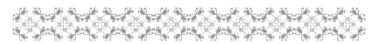

I see I'm getting special treatment now. The boss himself!" Palmeiro flattened himself casually on the chair in the interrogation room.

Avila sat down.

"You are still familiar with the procedure from the interrogation two days ago, I assume? I will record our conversation."

"Before you continue, my dear Comissário, I would like to know briefly what this is all about. You have already received a witness statement from me and I am frankly a little surprised to be summoned by a uniformed official with an official letter. My patience and helpfulness can run out quite quickly in such circumstances." Palmeiro changed his relaxed posture only marginally, but his voice took on a slightly threatening undertone.

"You are here because there are some new aspects to the case that we would like to discuss with you."

"New aspects? You don't mean William's abstruse accusations? I might have guessed that Ernesto would run straight to you with them."

"Subcomissário Vasconcellos has, of course, immediately informed me of Senhor Stuart's remarks. But I am sure that together we can shed light on this matter. May I now officially begin our conversation?" Avila pointed to the recording device.

"Do what you can't help doing."

After the usual formalities, Avila got straight to the point.

"This morning the suspicion was expressed by Senhor Stuart that Teresa Ferro's gallery was being used by you for money laundering. Do you have anything to say about this?"

"Nothing except that's completely absurd."

"Senhor Palmeiro, we know that you had worthless art objects sold through the gallery for a pre-arranged price in order to launder money."

"What nonsense. I earn my money legally through my winery. Go to the supermarket here, you'll see the Madeira from 'Palmer's Winery' everywhere. My investment in Teresa's little gallery was just to diversify my assets. Tadeu Parry recommended the gallery to me. That's how Teresa and I met. Why don't you ask old Parry about it?"

"It is quite possible that at first you really just wanted to diversify, as you so nicely put it. But you certainly came across the opportunities offered by the art trade very quickly. Perhaps you were also made aware of it by a few business friends."

Avila presented Palmeiro with a printout that Vasconcellos had pressed into his hand shortly before.

"What is it?"

"This article pretty much describes how to launder money through galleries and auction houses. Nowadays almost the only way left, as there is much more control through laws and regulations than in the past."

Palmeiro raised an eyebrow.

"Just for curiosity's sake and since I'm not an expert. How exactly is such business supposed to work?"

Avila let himself in on the game.

"Buyer and seller agree on a certain and overpriced purchase price for a cheap art object. The buyer receives the agreed price in cash from the seller. He buys the art object with the money. The gallery handles the transaction without naming the buyer and seller. This way, the dirty money can be neatly booked through the gallery's accounts." Palmeiro frowned, but remained silent.

Avila decided to bluff.

"We can prove that you collected money for all these transactions."

"Oh yes, how exactly are you going to prove that? I'm curious about that." Still no cracks appeared in Palmeiro's façade.

"Teresa Ferro left records, probably to cover herself. In it are the transaction numbers and the payments made to you."

"She didn't. She wouldn't be that stupid…!" Palmeiro had jumped up. The volcano's eruption was brief. He sat down again, folded his hands and looked at Avila.

"I will not say another word. If you want to accuse me, please get my lawyer. Otherwise, I will end our conversation now and leave. What do you want, Comissário?"

"We will end the conversation now, Senhor Palmeiro. However, I would like to ask you not to leave the island for the time being. You are free to consult a lawyer. In due course we will then take further steps." Avila himself knew how hollow this threat sounded, but unfortunately that was all he could do with the current evidence. After all, Palmeiro's reaction had shown him that there was definitely something to the accusations. It would be worthwhile to drill down further there. He would ask the director to allow Palmeiro to be monitored to see if he tried to meet with his business partners.

Funchal,
08.01.1950

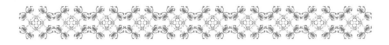

W here have you been all day? Diana and I were already worried."

"What's going to happen to me here on the island, Cat? I can hardly take a step without someone recognising me."

"Knowing you, you hardly took a step either, but let yourself be driven around in the Rolls Royce all day. And don't think I don't know about the bar in the boot! As if you would paint. James and your secretary, that Bill Deakin, they're just covering for you!" Her eyes sparkled and he could see behind them the strong-willed young woman he had married over forty years ago.

"Cat, we didn't even use the Rolls Royce today. Jorge took us to a beautifully secluded bay in the west."

"Who, pray tell, is Jorge?"

"The brother of Fred, the barman. We arranged last night for him to show me around the island. Would you like to come with me in the next few days? I really want to go back there again. The colours of the rocks in the rising sun were just indescribable."

"Rising sun? That sounds very early..." Cat looked at him suspiciously.

"We have to be there around six in the morning." He looked at her innocently, he knew what was coming.

"Are you crazy? Six o'clock? No, do it nicely without me. As punishment for leaving me alone for so long today, you will dance at least two dances with me at the ball tonight, my little pig."

He groaned. He hated dancing. And he didn't like his new nickname, "pig", either. At the beginning of their marriage, she had called him "pug". That had been a lot more affectionate. Although he had to admit, with a look at his handsome belly, that he had clearly outgrown the little pug.

"Did you and Diana buy anything nice?" he asked as he tried to change the subject.

"We have found four wonderful little wicker chairs for our salon in London. They are being shipped tomorrow. With a bit of luck, they'll be there when we get back. I thought of you too, by the way. But I don't even know if you deserve this." She playfully threatened him with her finger. "On the way back, we passed a sugar cane factory and I brought you a bottle of aguardente." She went over to the bedroom of her small suite and returned with a bottle of the sugar cane liquor.

He took it in his hand and examined it.

"Aguardente de Cana Açuca reserva, Burke LTD.", he read. "Sounds good. Shall we try a sip right now?" Without waiting for her answer, he loosened the cork and filled two small glasses from the bar cabinet with the golden liquid.

"Can you drink it like that? I thought it was just mixed?"

"If it's well made, and it looks like it is, it's like a good rum. It's nothing but sugar cane liquor." He toasted Cat and finished half the glass in one gulp. Cat wasn't quite as quick as he was, but she too drank a big gulp.

"You're right, it tastes good. Much smoother than I expected." She set the glass down. "After such a refreshment, it should be no problem for you to dance with me later. I'm sure you'll float across the dance floor. And if you say now that you've forgotten the steps because it's been so long: I've taken care of that too. We'll have a dance lesson on the terrace right after high tea at five. It's all planned." She winked at him. Bloody hell, he'd really hoped he could get out of this one.

A few hours later, he was standing at Fred's bar having his second martini. He had completed the dance lesson with as much dignity as he could under the circumstances. Of course, many spectators had turned out as he had pushed his round self across the terrace with Cat.

Now he had got ready for the big event tonight and was waiting for his two women, who took a little longer than he did to get ready.

Two young men stood next to him at the bar and ordered an Aguardente Reserva from Fred.

"But one of us, please, Fred!" the more bullish of the two let himself be heard. When Fred placed the same bottle that he had almost half emptied with Cat earlier in front of the two men, he eyed the beefy type more closely.

He looked familiar to him somehow. Was that perhaps...? The next words of the second young man confirmed his suspicions.

"What does Milly actually say about you wanting to be at sea with your yacht for the next few weeks? I bet you spent the whole day on your great love today too!"

"What are you implying, Cecil? Are you jealous?" The brawny one grinned broadly at his friend. The old man began to wonder if the two boys were really talking about the yacht.

"I don't have to, my friend. I also have my way of making my free time enjoyable." Both friends laughed.

He hoped that Cat and Diana would take a little more time with their wardrobe, this was quite entertaining after all.

At that moment, a beautiful young woman joined them. She was wearing an off-the-shoulder black cocktail dress with a wide skirt. Her hair framed her delicate face in dark waves. *What a beautiful woman, almost like an elf,* he thought. But he would not allow Diana to wear one of those new-fangled dresses, it really left little to the imagination.

The young lady snuggled up to the brawny man who encircled her waist with one muscular arm. *This is definitely not the woman from the yacht.*

"I might have guessed I'd find you two here. Fred, can you make me a poncha? I can't get the aguardente down that neat!"

"Milly, I was just saying to your husband that I'm sure it's not going to be easy for you when he says goodbye in two days for the sailing trip."

Milly turned to the bull and looked at him reprovingly.

"Oh, you've heard it too? I've only just found out. Yes, I've already scolded him for leaving me alone with my old father. Two weeks he wants to stay away. Impudence." She laughed, which took some of the edge off her words.

"Don't you think you should have prepared the whole thing a little better? It's a bit unreasonable to plan such a tour in a few days", Cecil said again.

"Now don't scare Milly, or my wife will end up forbidding me to go sailing to the Canary Islands. I know what I'm doing. After all, I'm out on the Atlantic almost every evening. I know the waters well. We're leaving the day after tomorrow."

"If you don't come back, may I comfort your wonderful wife, old friend?" Cecil now also wrapped an arm around Milly and pressed a kiss to her cheek. The young woman was clearly enjoying the attention of the two men and let out her laugh again.

"I thought you were already doing that?" The brawny one playfully bumped his friend's shoulder with his fist.

"Sir, Lady Churchill sent me. She and Miss Diana will now be ready and waiting for you at your table." Grumpily, he took his half-full glass of martini and followed his secretary.

Funchal, Gallery,
15.08.2013–17:22

E xcuse me, may I ask you something?" The old man in
his worn suit stood in front of Hugo Duarte and looked
at him shyly.

Hugo Duarte raised an eyebrow and looked the old man up
and down. What was someone like that doing in his gallery?
What if someone had seen him? Such types were not allowed
in his gallery, it could damage his reputation.

Impatiently, he snapped at the other.

"What do you want? Do you think you are in the right
place? There are works on display in this gallery that I'm sure
you can't afford."

The old man's eyes widened in horror. He clearly could not
handle such an outburst. He lowered his head and nervously
tugged at his sleeve.

Hopefully he will disappear soon, Hugo thought.

But the old man had apparently composed himself, raised
his head and continued speaking in a low voice:

"I really don't want to disturb you for long. My wife and I
just have a question about the picture of the yacht hanging
there in the front." He pointed towards the head of the gallery.

Hugo looked irritated in that direction. The old man was indeed referring to the most important exhibit in the exhibition, "Sunbathing in Madalena do Mar". To the right of the painting, Hugo saw an elderly woman looking tensely over at them. Judging by her clothes and age, she certainly belonged to the strange old man.

"The painting? Good man, the painting is really, without any doubt, not within your financial scope."

The old man looked over to his wife for help, who encouraged him with a brief nod of her head to continue asking.

"We don't want to buy the painting either, we're just wondering where the sketch and the photo are."

"What sketch, what photo?" Hugo Duarte didn't understand. What did the crazy old man want from him?

"Senhora Ferro got a sketch and a photo from us, which she really wanted to hang up next to this picture. But now there is nothing hanging there." The old man pointed to the empty space next to the painting, which Leticia Avila had already pointed out to Hugo.

Duarte thought about it. That sounded really strange. He decided to invest a little more time and ask.

"What exactly is this supposed to be about?"

"A sketch Sir Churchill made of the yacht and the print from an old photograph his secretary took of him and me. He sent both to me months later with a little dedication. It's very important to us, you see."

Hugo Duarte began to sweat. A sketch by Churchill? Disappeared in the gallery? What a disaster. He wondered if the insurance covered it. Damn, what had Teresa done there? He really needed to check all the handwritten notes preparing for the exhibition. She always had a thick black notebook for such occasions, in which she meticulously noted down the pictures, with little background stories, photos and sketches. Until now, he had not bothered about it, as she had prepared the everything wonderfully before her death. The police had not asked about it either, only about the finances. So it was still in its usual place, on the table in their little kitchen at the back of the gallery.

At least he had thought until now that she had everything under control. *Caramba*. He had to fix this.

With a broad smile, he turned to the old man.

"My dear friend, I am sure there is a misunderstanding here. Due to the death of my partner, we are still a little behind on the exhibition. I will get back to you in the next few days, I promise. May I ask what your name is?"

"Jorge, Jorge Rocha."

16.08.2013–08:17

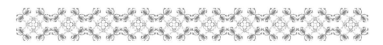

I thought we should talk in private. Man to man like that. Just the two of us."

"What makes you think I want to talk to you?"

"Teresa, whom we all cherish, has left me some information."

"Did she?" He tried to make his voice sound as uninvolved as possible.

"Yes, she did. One or two of the things could be extremely interesting for you."

"I doubt it."

"The information concerns the gallery."

"Why should I care?"

"Because dear Teresa was a control freak and took meticulous notes on everything."

"And you come to me of all people with this?"

"I put two and two together and I am very sure that you are the right person for me."

"What's with these vague hints? Don't monkey around with me!"

"How about we meet and I show you something. Then we can decide together what it's worth to you."

"Will you be quiet if I meet with you?"

"As I said before, it's for your own good."

"While I'm sure it's complete nonsense, please... My suggestion would be to meet at the gallery tomorrow morning. I'll be around anyway."

"Hmmh, not today?"

"I'm sorry, but it's not possible today. Either tomorrow or not at all."

"All right, I'll see you at the gallery tomorrow at ten." A click at the other end of the line ended the conversation.

Now he had almost twenty-four hours to fix the problem. That should be possible.

Funchal, Police Headquarters, 16.08.2013–10:03

W e got a hit, chefe!" Vasconcellos had stormed into Avila's office without knocking and threw a folder on his desk.

Avila, who was reading one of Leticia's birth preparation books and was wondering if he really wanted to be present for such a bloody affair, looked at him absent-mindedly.

"What is it?"

"The results of the DNA analysis are back, and we now know who Teresa Ferro had intercourse with on the evening shortly before her murder!"

Avila dropped the book and pulled the folder towards him. He browsed through it, but couldn't make out anything at first glance. This could also be due to the fact that he had quickly thrown his reading glasses to the side with the rushing in from his Subcomissário. He just felt old with the things on and didn't want to hear Ernesto say anything about it.

"Don't keep me in suspense, who is it?"

"Otavio Jesus. Without a doubt."

Avila looked at Vasconcellos and pondered. The barman? The wolf would like that. Not one of high society and a newcomer to boot. Madeira would be clean. But why? Why leave his stamp first and murder her the same night? He had to know the police would find out, didn't he?

He sighed. Maybe the young man just wasn't very smart.

"Go get him."

"I sent Baroso out with two colleagues a quarter of an hour ago, they should be here soon. And before you ask, I've already applied to the public prosecutor's office for a search warrant."

Vasconcellos could be relied upon as always.

"Good. Then it should go quickly. With a bit of luck, we'll have the first results during the interrogation. Speaking of which, would you like to do the interrogation? I would then be the silent observer."

"If you want. By the way, I haven't told Diretor André yet. I thought we should hear what Jesus tells us first."

"Very good. We should avoid presenting him as the culprit early on. If the *Diretor* asks why Jesus is here again, we'll say there are still a few follow-up questions about the evening."

"He'll soon realise that's a lie, though."

"I'll take that on my head."

Half an hour later, Avila stood behind the glass and watched Otavio Jesus. If he had only made an uncertain impression the last time, he was now in a state of great agitation. Again, he paced up and down the room, stroking his curly short hair again and again. By now it was sticking up wildly from his head.

"He's completely off his rocker. If he's not dirty, I don't know what he is, boss." Vasconcellos had joined Avila at the window. They had agreed to leave Jesus to stew for a while before Vasconcellos began the interrogation.

"What do you think, is he ready?"

"Yes, go in and see him. I almost feel sorry for the boy."

When Vasconcellos entered the room, the barman practically stormed him.

"Why am I here? I've already told you everything!"

"Please sit down so that we can talk in peace. Before we begin, I must point out to you that anything you tell me can be used against you later."

Jesus turned pale and sank down on the chair.

"I, I didn't mean..." His voice died away.

"I will start the recording now." The Subcomissário pressed the button.

"Do I need a lawyer?"

Vasconcellos sighed. The question was now on tape.

"Would you like to exercise the right that you have and prefer that we continue the conversation in the presence of a lawyer?"

"I don't know." The young man propped his arms on the table and buried his face in his hands.

Avila watched what was happening through the window. The boy was desperate. *If Vasconcellos puts some pressure on him, he will talk, even without a lawyer. But we shouldn't risk not being able to use this in the end.*

He pressed the button on the intercom, which connected him directly to a small receiver in Vasconcellos' ear.

"Stop the interrogation. We'll continue as soon as the lawyer gets here. It has no value."

Vasconcellos looked towards the mirror and nodded briefly in confirmation.

"Senhor Jesus. To answer your question, of course you can get a lawyer now. Do you already have legal counsel or should we get you one?"

Jesus raised his head and looked at Vasconcellos. His eyes were moist.

"Please, get me one. I don't know that many people here in Madeira."

"Good, then we'll interrupt this now."

An hour later, a slender man in his late thirties wearing jeans and a brown leather jacket with a scuffed leather briefcase under his arm entered the police station. Vasconcellos was already waiting impatiently next to the entrance door.

"Gee, Chico, how long are you taking?" he greeted him and gave him a pat on the back.

"You're lucky I got here so quickly at all. If the hearing in court this morning hadn't fallen through, you would have had to wait a few more hours. No matter how much you cry my ears off about time being of the essence. Now where's that poor boy you've got on your hands?"

"I'll take you to him in a minute. Before that, I'd like you to meet my boss, Comissário Avila. I don't think you know each other yet." Avila had joined them in the meantime and the lawyer approached him with his hand outstretched.

"I am happy to meet the famous Comissário. Belmiro is always raving about his boss."

"Belmiro?" Avila looked from one to the other, uncomprehending.

Vasconcellos laughed.

"It's such a stupid nickname that Chico came up with when we were younger."

"Yes, because all the girls used to adore you all the time, my beautiful. And we all know, not much has changed there either." The lawyer laughed again.

"Okay, let's get serious. This joker here is Francisco Guerra, the lawyer I got for Otavio Jesus."

Avila shook his hand.

"Pleased to meet you. Ernesto already told you what it's about?"

"There hasn't been time for that yet. Belmiro, I suggest you briefly explain what you have on my client and then give me time alone with him. Please make sure that all microphones in the room are turned off. Have you lectured him on his rights?" Guerra's cheerfulness had now given way to a calm professionalism that suited Avila well.

A good hour passed before Vasconcellos, this time in the presence of Guerra, was able to continue the interrogation.

After the formalities, he got straight to the heart of the matter.

"Senhor Jesus, has your *advogado de defesa*, Senhor Guerra, informed you of the results of our investigation yet?"

Otavio Jesus nodded his head slowly. Guerra answered for him.

"I have informed my client, Otavio Jesus, that his DNA matches the DNA found on Teresa Ferro."

"What is his explanation?"

"My client admits to having had intercourse with Teresa Ferro that evening at the golf club shortly before midnight. They went to the club's wine cellar for it."

Avila was beginning to wonder what kind of golf club this was, with members like Teresa Ferro making out all over the place. And his Leticia was a member there? He didn't like that at all.

"This makes him the last person to have had demonstrable contact with her. Does he realise what that looks like?" continued Vasconcellos.

"I didn't kill Teresa!" Jesus burst out. Guerra put a reassuring hand on his shoulder.

"At this moment we are searching your flat, Senhor Jesus. Are you sure you want to stick to your testimony?" Guerra raised his eyebrows, but remained calm.

He must have thought that under these circumstances we would get a search warrant immediately, Avila interpreted the lawyer's behaviour.

Jesus looked over at Guerra for help.

"I would like to speak to my client again." Avila looked at the clock. By now it was just after one o'clock. His stomach was beginning to tell him. He really hoped they were through here quickly. At that moment, Baroso came in the door, once again with a red face.

"We found something, boss." He waved two bags, in which Avila could make out a large ring decorated with a blue stone and a credit card.

"The credit card belonged to Teresa Ferro and the jewellery also matches the description we have. She was wearing it that night at the golf club."

"I guess that's it then." Avila felt a slight regret. Secretly, he had hoped that the young man was not responsible for Teresa Ferro's murder. But the evidence was clear.

"I'll tell Vasconcellos and Advogado Guerra."

Funchal, Police Headquarters, 16.08.2013–13:51

I t wasn't me, she was already dead when I found her!" Otavio Jesus had been muttering these sentences without interruption for half an hour.

"My client admits that he appropriated Teresa Ferro's property when he found her at the lake."

"It didn't occur to him to inform the police?"

"My client has had a few experiences in the past which have unfortunately strengthened his distrust of the police. However, he will now do everything he can to support the police. Please Senhor Jesus, describe to Subcomissário Vasconcellos exactly what happened." Guerra nodded encouragingly to Jesus.

The latter sat up in the chair in which he had been slumped and took a deep breath.

With a slightly trembling voice, he began to tell the story.

"I finished cleaning up around two and wanted to smoke a cigarette in peace before going home. Since that's not allowed in the clubrooms, I went outside. I looked at the course from the putting green. That's when I thought I saw movement by the lake. Doutor Ignacio had been complaining lately that unauthorised people were on the course. I wanted to make sure it was really one of the guests who was out there. So I put out my cigarette and walked towards the lake. When I arrived, I saw Teresa lying dead in the water. I panicked. The contents of her bag were scattered on the ground. I only pocketed the cash and credit card and took the ring."

"Why the ring?"

"Teresa told me it was worth a lot. I thought I could turn it into money and get out of here."

"I am very sorry, Senhor Jesus. You are accused of murdering Teresa Ferro on the night of 9-10th of August 2013. We are going to arrest you now." The two officers who had been in the interrogation room for the last half hour stepped forward and handcuffed Otavio Jesus.

The latter looked briefly at his lawyer.

Guerra cleared his throat.

"Senhor Jesus, I will arrange everything necessary. Please do not speak to anyone when I am not present."

Jesus allowed himself to be led away without resistance.

Vasconcellos looked at his friend.

"I'll let you have everything we have on Jesus."

"Good. If there are any further questions, I'll be in touch." They said goodbye.

When Vasconcellos, Baroso and Avila had lunch half an hour later in Rua Maria, they were all silent. To an outsider, they did not look like three policemen who had just convicted a murderer, but rather like participants in a funeral. Even Avila poked listlessly at his *carne vinho e alhos*, although he normally loved the pickled pork.

He nevertheless raised his glass of Madeira and toasted his staff.

"To the conclusion of our case. You both did a good job. Diretor André will be very pleased. And even though sometimes a case doesn't turn out the way you want it to, we have Teresa Ferro's killer behind bars. The evidence is overwhelming." He knew how lame that sounded, but he didn't have anything better for them right now.

Garajau,
16.08.2013–20:23

W hat is it, old friend? You don't look too happy. I thought you found the volcano? You arrested the young barman, didn't you?"

"How do you know that again?"

"Oh, the nice thing is, most people tend to overlook me. Not everyone puts up with a street sweeper like you do. And so I can watch and listen in peace to what is being said. Not to mention that even at the bakery here in Garajau it's the topic of the day. Apparently your Aspirante wasn't very discreet either when he picked Jesus up this morning. Ernesto would probably have managed it more discreetly."

Avila looked at Carlos. They were both sitting on one of the benches along the path to Christo Rei, watching the sun slowly bathe the Atlantic in fire. Carlos had his broom between his legs and was now propping his arms on it, while Avila had leaned far back on the bench and was looking up at the sky. He had released Urso from his leash and he seemed to have discovered something very interesting at the base of the statue. At least he had been sniffing there for at least ten minutes now with his tail up in tension.

"You're right, we arrested Otavio Jesus. So, we found a volcano, but I can't imagine that its eruption really resulted in Teresa Ferro's death. He's too weak. On the other hand, there's all that evidence. The case is closed though, I have to come to terms with it."

"Take it this way, now you have your head free to take care of Leticia. Today at noon she seemed quite happy when I came by. But I can well imagine that the horror is still in your limbs. Remember, your balloon must not burst, it must rise to the sky." Carlos looked up as if he saw Avila and Leticia's balloon flying into the reddish evening sky.

"Shall we take Urso and have another poncha in the bar upstairs?"

"Good idea. I wasn't very hungry at lunch today either, maybe I'll have a few more *lapas*."

"I share your preference for rum with lemon juice, my dear friend. But our snails, I don't know. Have you ever noticed that they have little faces when you take them out of their shells and look at them closely?"

"You're supposed to eat those things, not look at them! Come on. I have now gathered enough strength that I can complete the climb reasonably quickly. Now I just have to collect my dog. Where is he? He was just over there."

"I think he discovered Senhora Schmidt's pigeon food. I've wanted to tell her a few times that she also attracts the rats with the food. But feeding the birds in the morning is her only joy."

Avila tightened the leash on Uso's collar and pulled the reluctant retriever away from the grains.

"You really do eat everything, you glutton!"

When Avila returned home two hours later, a visibly impatient Leticia was waiting for him in bed.

"The walk took quite a while! Don't tell me, you probably went for a poncha with Carlos, didn't you?"

Avila lowered his head guiltily.

"Yes, but only one. I checked my phone in between to make sure you hadn't called either."

"It's all right. It's just that in bed it's so terribly boring! Inês brought me some magazines, but I find them boring too. And there's nothing on TV but soaps and talk shows."

Avila sat down with her on the edge of the bed.

"What can I do to make you less bored?"

"Tell me about the case and how you solved it", it came like a shot from a pistol.

Avila groaned inwardly, he should have guessed that Leticia was curious.

"I'll get a Madeira from the kitchen quickly, then I'll tell you a bit. Shall I bring you a juice?"

"While you're in the kitchen, can you make us a plate of bread soup, how's that?"

Avila went into the kitchen with a lively step. The evening had turned out quite nicely after all.

Garajau, 17.08.2013–5:31

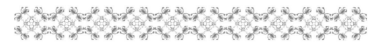

The phone rang. Avila fumbled half asleep on his bedside table to find it. As he did so, he knocked over the alarm clock.

Leticia turned to him.

"Answer the phone already, Fernando!"

Cursing, he turned on the light and picked up the phone:

"Tou?"

"Boss, it's me. Not good news. Hugo Duarte has been found in his gallery. He's dead."

"What? How?" After last night, during which a whole bottle of Verdejo had been killed, Avila was not yet in the mood for complete sentences.

"He was stabbed. The cleaning lady discovered him half an hour ago."

"Where are you?"

"I'm still at home, but I'll be on my way to the gallery in the next ten minutes. Shall I pick you up?" Vasconcellos lived a little further north-east of Garajau in Camacha. Which was very convenient for Avila, because Vasconcellos more or less had to drive by him on his way to the presidium.

"Yes, come and get me. I'll be ready in a minute too." Avila ended the conversation, gave Leticia a kiss on the cheek and got out of bed.

What the fuck was that? Duarte, stabbed? That would probably mean they'd arrested the wrong guy. *As if you didn't know that,* his inner voice told him. And that didn't make it any better.

When they arrived at the gallery half an hour later, forensics and Doutora Souza were already there. Some joker had changed the sign outside the entrance to "*Fechado*". Now that the last owner had passed away, the gallery would probably remain closed permanently. Avila shook his head and went through the door. After he and Vasconcellos had put on white protective clothing under the strict gaze of the Doutora, they were allowed to go to the actual crime scene in the kitchen.

In the furthest room of the gallery, which served as a kitchen, Hugo Duarte was lying with his upper body on the table. A knife was stuck in his back. Blood had seeped through his light-coloured suit and formed a bizarre pattern. *Like that Rorschach test,* Avila thought. *The image is almost symmetrical. Looks like a red butterfly or a leaf.* He stepped closer to the dead man.

"Please don't touch anything, Comissário! It was already very nice of us to let you in this room." Doutora Souza looked at him grimly.

"Don't worry, we're good", Vasconcellos intervened, winking at his godmother.

"Doutora, can you tell me anything yet?" Avila let himself be heard.

"Well, the cause of death at least. He has a knife in his back." She laughed her deep, dry laugh.

Avila scowled at her.

"Don't look so angry, my dear Comissário. Or can't you take a joke this early on a Saturday morning? Well, seriously. Death was caused by a pericardial effusion. That is, the perpetrator hit the heart directly and there was a tamponade, an effusion in the pericardium. The fluid obstructed the ventricular filling."

"Meaning?" Avila had to pull himself together so as not to get impatient. At some point he had to get a medical non-fiction book so he could do something with all this technical jargon from Souza.

"It will most likely have led to cardiogenic shock and the deceased died of cardiovascular failure. But I can only tell you more details after a post-mortem examination."

"Why didn't he fight back?"

"If the stitch is well executed, and it looks like it is, fainting occurs in a very short time."

"Must the perpetrator have had medical knowledge?"

"Nowadays you can read all about it on the internet. You can even find pictures where the exact puncture sites are marked."

"And the death occurred tonight?"

"Hmm, I don't think so. Do you see the death marks?" She carefully turned the corpse over. Then she pressed on one of the marks.

"They are no longer reversible. That means more than twelve hours must have passed since Duarte died. Rigor mortis is also fully developed. I'm going to take the core temperature now. Let's see what else Duarte tells us."

A short time later, she removed the thermometer.

"That's what I thought, 21.3 degrees. Look at the air conditioning over there, Ernesto. How many degrees is it set to?"

Ernesto went to the controller for the system, which was located right next to the door, and looked at the display.

"Exactly 21 degrees."

"So, the body is already at ambient temperature. I'll do a few more tests at the institute: Check stomach contents and maybe we'll get lucky and the pupils will still respond to stimuli." Avila didn't even want to know how Doutora Souza did it. In his mind's eye he saw her wiring up the dead man and making him twitch with electric shocks. He shook himself.

Doutora Souza looked at him with raised eyebrows. Had she said anything else? Seeking help, he looked over at Vasconcellos.

"Doutora Souza said just now that at this point she can say that the death was at least twelve hours ago, three days at the most."

"We need to find out when Duarte was last seen alive. And we need to check when he last used his mobile phone."

"Unfortunately, we haven't found a phone yet. It is possible that the perpetrator took it with him."

"Then we need the connection records from the telephone company. Also, I want us to take another look at the gallery. I want Baroso to look not only at the financials, but everything else. Has anything been stolen? I want him to make sure that all the paintings from that Churchill exhibit are still there. They must be worth a fortune. And how did the murderer get into the gallery unnoticed and stab Duarte in the back?"

"I'll ask the cleaning lady who found Duarte to accompany us to the presidium so we can take her statement. I'm sure she'll be glad to get out of here."

Vasconcellos pointed to a woman in the salesroom whom Avila had not noticed so far. She squeezed herself sheepishly into a corner and looked anxiously over at them. Avila felt sorry for the young woman in her tight shorts that stretched dangerously across her thighs and stomach. She had certainly imagined the day going differently.

"Good, then let's go to the presidium and do our work. Doutora Souza, we'll hear from you as soon as you have more for us. *Bom Dia*."

Doutora Souza was already engrossed in her dead body again and only absently waved her right hand at them briefly.

Funchal, Police Headquarters, 17.08.2013–9:23

Avila tried to compensate for the night's lack of sleep with a third *bica*. Unfortunately, the expresso did not have the desired effect. He still had to pull himself together so that he didn't fall asleep. As a precautionary measure, he had already exchanged his armchair for the desk chair, but the desktop as a possible headrest also seemed to be becoming more tempting to him by the minute.

Vasconcellos stuck his head through the door.

"Shall I briefly report what the cleaning lady told us?"

"Yes, come in. I was just about to make myself a galão, would you like one?"

Vasconcellos nodded, sat down in the armchair and watched as Avila foamed the milk for the galão.

When the steaming drink was in front of him, he began to report.

"Senhora Ventura, the cleaning lady, told us that she entered the gallery shortly after five. She used her key to do it."

"Isn't there an alarm system there?"

"Yes, there is. According to Senhora Ventura, it was also armed. She has about ten seconds after opening the door to enter the numerical code into the control box right next to the door. If she doesn't, the security company will be there within fifteen minutes. Apparently, this happened to her a few times in the beginning. Therefore, she could report that there is a deafening alarm when the system goes off. So, we can assume that the system was definitely not triggered."

"That would mean that either it was not armed when the perpetrator entered the gallery or he has a key and knows the code."

"I suspect the second. Because you need the code to arm the system again. And if our perpetrator can't conjure himself out of closed rooms, he must have left the gallery through the entrance door."

"That means we assume the perpetrator had the key and knew the code. Were the keys of Teresa Ferro found at Otavio Jesus' place?"

"No, not so far."

"We have to wait and see when Duarte was last seen and what else Doutora Souza gives us. In terms of time, Otavio Jesus could still be our man if he killed Duarte before we arrested him. But my gut tells me otherwise. Teresa Ferro's killer is still out there, and he has Duarte on his conscience now too."

"I agree with that. I'm trying to reach your Ana about that right now."

"What does Ana have to do with this?"

"She also keeps Duarte's flat clean. I hope she can tell me when she last saw him. Maybe she also knows what time he usually leaves his house, so we can narrow down the time of the crime further."

"Good. Is Baroso in the gallery yet?"

"On the way there. Forensics just finished recording and released the crime scene. It's not much that they found. Right now, they're also searching Duarte's house, so I hope we'll find more there."

Three hours later, they knew that the perpetrator had done a good job. Neither in the gallery nor in Duarte's house was a laptop or a mobile phone to be found. The tracking of the phone, which Vasconcellos had immediately initiated, had also come up negative. It was switched off.

"Caramba! You've got to be kidding!" Avila was travelling around his office again, Vasconcellos and Baroso watching him.

There was a knock at the door. An Aspirante from the Segurança Pública came in.

"Ernesto, a Senhora Ana Pinho is on the phone for you." Vasconcellos jumped up and disappeared.

Ten minutes later he came back in with an impenetrable expression.

"And?" asked Avila, pausing for a moment.

"Ana was able to tell me that she last saw Hugo Duarte yesterday morning at just before half past nine. He left at that time to go to the gallery. The gallery usually opens at ten o'clock."

"A little after nine? How long does it take Duarte to get to the gallery?"

"He lives in Monte. I guess about twenty minutes, maybe even longer."

"Let's assume he was in the gallery shortly before ten. Was it possible for Otavio Jesus to ambush him there, stab him in the back and then be found by Baroso at home in Câmara de Lobos shortly after ten o'clock?"

216

"No, that's too close in time. Even if he drove home from the gallery like a maniac, he couldn't have made it before Baroso."

Baroso nodded his agreement.

"I found Senhor Jesus at home at 10:07 am. He was still in his pyjamas and gave me the impression that I had woken him up. That's what my report says."

"If we are not dealing with two perpetrators, Otavio Jesus is innocent. My gut tells me Teresa Ferro and Hugo Duarte fell victim to the same perpetrator. I just wonder how he got the code. It's no use, we have to start all over again. We're missing something. The perpetrator must have come onto the golf course without the cameras picking him up. What can you come up with?"

Vasconcellos shrugged his shoulders.

"I am still thinking about delivery vehicles for food and drinks. Like if the perpetrator used them to get onto the premises during the day and hid until the evening. But how did he get back down from the site? The next day would have been far too risky, after the discovery of the body the place was swarming with police."

"I have no other idea either. It has to be one of our suspects who was on the premises that evening. Please look at the alibis of Marsh, Stuart and Palmeiro again. Especially Palmeiro's alibi, he had the most to lose based on what we know now. What if he had taken a taxi back to the club? Then his housekeeper wouldn't have been able to hear anything either. Or did we miss someone else? Who else was there? Go over everything again, please. If only we could prove one of them was at the club later that night after all. Maybe the security guard was bribed? Stopped the camera recording briefly so someone could sneak in?"

"I'll go to Palmeiro and see if I can find out anything else."
Vasconcellos stood up.

"If it is all right, I would then like to look at the statements
of Senhor Marsh and Senhor Stuart again", Baroso let himself
be heard in a low voice.

Avila agreed with him.

"Alright, that's how we'll do it. I'll go by Doutora Souza's
place again in a few hours. I suggest we meet on Monday
morning, say at half past seven? We all need some sleep and a
day of rest. But one thing is clear, if something unforeseen
happens, a quiet Saturday night and Sunday won't be
happening, agreed?" Everyone nodded.

Funchal,
17.08.2013–13:03

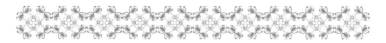

Vasconcellos was sitting in a wicker chair on the terrace of Palmeiro's townhouse in Funchal, waiting for the master of the house. The somewhat shy elderly housekeeper had let him in about fifteen minutes ago and led him to the covered veranda clad in dark teak. Palmeiro had not yet shown himself.

Vasconcellos looked around. The view over the well-tended garden down to the Atlantic was spectacular, but he doubted that Palmeiro stayed here often. He had another property in Madalena do Mar with a tennis court and a small putting range, where Vasconcellos had also been once for a celebration of the mountain sports club. Compared to the huge house there, this city villa was tiny. Palmeiro probably only used it during the week when he had business in Funchal. It was all the more surprising that he was here today, on a Saturday.

Vasconcellos listened, he could hear voices. One was clearly a female voice, but it did not sound as creaky as the old housekeeper's.

He decided to see who Palmeiro's lady visitor was. Quietly, he got up and walked through the open patio door towards the entrance hall. He could make out Palmeiro in a pair of running shorts and a tight running shirt, talking to a young blonde woman. Wasn't that ...?

Vasconcellos cleared his throat and the two turned to look at him. He looked into the chubby face of Aurelia Gomes, the assistant to Tadeu Parry, the bank manager. Interesting. She wasn't wearing business clothes this time, but had on a short, colourful summer dress. Now you could clearly see how young she actually was. Vasconcellos wondered what she was doing at Palmeiro's on a Saturday afternoon.

The latter looked at him with his typical grin.

"My dear Ernesto. I'm sorry to have kept you waiting. But Senhora Gomes was kind enough to bring me some documents from Tadeu Parry just now. A service that only special clients enjoy." He turned to the young woman.

"Thank you very much, Senhora Gomes, and give my regards to Doutor Tadeu." Vasconcellos looked around the hallway. Whatever Aurelia had brought over was nowhere to be seen. The mahogany sideboard was completely empty, except for a pot with a lush white orchid, and no documents could be hidden in Palmeiro's clothes either. So, what was going on here?

Aurelia Gomes spoke up in her squeaky voice.

"Doutor Romario, I will pass on your greetings to Doutor Tadeu, I wish you a wonderful weekend." She bent down to pick up the large handbag she had set down on the floor. The small leather latch holding the bag opening together was not properly fastened and Ernesto caught a glimpse inside. A hairbrush and some red lace. It didn't look like the usual handbag stuffing to him. He raised his eyebrows and looked at Palmeiro.

The latter had seen the look in Ernesto's eyes and was now grinning from ear to ear.

"I think I'll escort Senhora Gomes out for a moment and then you and I can talk about what brings you here today." He pushed Aurelia towards the door.

Five minutes later, he was sitting on the terrace with Vasconcellos and they both had a chilled, non-alcoholic Coral in front of them.

"Before you ask, Ernesto. Yes, Aurelia was here overnight. You'll find out anyway, after all Madeira is a village." Palmeiro allowed himself a big gulp of the cold beer.

"Then your grief for Teresa Ferro must be really great if you have to be comforted by Senhora Gomes", Vasconcellos commented dryly and also took a deep sip. It was quite hot again today and the cold drink was good. After the last interrogation with Palmeiro, Ernesto had decided not to let Palmeiro's confidential tone bother him this time, but to go with it. Maybe he could get a little more out of him that way.

"Oh, Teresa and I didn't look at it so closely before either. She still had one or two others she was having fun with, and she knew about Aurelia."

"And Aurelia Gomes also had no problem with Teresa Ferro being the official wife at your side?"

Palmeiro thoughtfully turned the beer can in his hand.

"Now that you mention it. Aurelia may not have been quite as easy-going as Teresa. But she accepted it. The alternative would have been for me to end the affair with her."

"Senhora Gomes was also the one responsible for organising the opening dinner at the golf club, right? A task that, according to my information, she did not fulfil to everyone's satisfaction. Teresa Ferro was certainly not very well disposed towards her that evening. And surely one could expect better organisational skills from the personal assistant of a bank director? Her tasks in this private bank are not that much different. How could she forget to organise the guest of honour's trip?"

"What do you mean? That Aurelia acted so stupidly on purpose, to spite Teresa?" Lost in thought, Palmeiro wiped the drops that had formed on the cold can with his fingertips. "Hmmh, come to think of it. It's possible. She's a sneaky one, that one. But are you also suggesting that Aurelia killed Teresa? That's bullshit. The little bitch isn't capable of that. When she's in trouble, she acts like a little girl. That's how she manipulates most of the men around her. Whether it's old Ignacio or Tadeu Parry. When Aurelia presses the tear button, she gets what she wants from them. And no, Ernesto, that trick won't work on me. Aurelia knows that too. With me, she pulls herself together and drops the act. But one thing is also clear: she couldn't be dangerous to a woman like Teresa." He put the empty beer can on the table and leaned back in the wicker chair.

Vasconcellos remembered the appearance of the young woman in the bank and Leticia's descriptions. He had to agree with Palmeiro. How could this little person overpower and drown Ferro?

Aloud he said:

"I'm also here for another reason. As Teresa Ferro's partner, do you have access to her gallery?"

"You mean a key and the door code for the alarm system?" Palmeiro got straight to the point. "I don't have a key. When Teresa asked me to get something from her gallery, she gave me hers."

"But you knew the code for the alarm system?"

"Of course I know the code: 04111977."

"You have a good memory for numbers."

"It's not much of an art. And I bet every one of Teresa's exes knows it. It's her date of birth."

Funchal, Forensic Medicine, 17.08.2013–19:11

T here you are at last, Comissário!" Doutora Souza greeted him as he entered the forensic department.

"Come with me to my office, I'm afraid I don't have much time."

Avila trotted dutifully behind her, glad not to have to enter the section room.

When he closed the office door and turned to look at her, he noticed to his astonishment that she was wearing a dark blue evening gown under her white coat. She also seemed to have put on make-up. This was something he had never seen on her face once in the last three years.

Apparently, she had noticed his astonishment.

"Don't look so astonished, my dear Avila. There are also occasions when I dress up. Tonight is one of those evenings. That's when someone like me gets all dolled up." She laughed throatily.

"May I ask what the occasion is?"

"You may. It is the ninetieth birthday of William Stuart the Elder. I suspect the name is familiar to you after the investigations of the last few days. At least, I heard you interrogated his son." Avila didn't even want to know how the Doutora knew that. Nothing went unnoticed in Madeira.

"But first let's devote ourselves to the dead. Surely you want to know if Hugo Duarte has told me a few more secrets?"

Avila nodded.

"My suspicion that he died of pericardial tamponade was confirmed. The bleeding in the heart led to unconsciousness after a few seconds. That's why we couldn't find any defensive marks on his hands or arms. The stabbing must have come completely unexpectedly for him."

"And the time of death?"

"I checked to see to what extent the pupils still reacted to external stimuli. But could not elicit any pupillary response after injection of mydriatics."

"And what does that mean exactly?"

"The victim must have been dead for at least 16 hours before I could tamper with him. I administered the drugs at six o'clock."

Avila calculated quickly.

"That means he must have been killed by noon at the latest. So, we have a window of time from ten in the morning until then, when he was killed."

Souza confirmed his calculation.

"Yes, that also fits the body temperature. Unfortunately, I can't be much more specific."

"That's already a good restriction. Do you have many..." Avila's phone rang.

He looked at the display for a moment.

"This is Vasconcellos, I'm afraid I have to take this. Excuse me, please. *Tou*?"

Silently he listened. Meanwhile, Doutora Souza was already taking off her smock and going to the small washbasin placed in the left corner of her office. She began brushing through her short hair with quick strokes.

"I don't like this, Ernesto. If the code for the alarm system is really such an open secret, then it's actually easy to gain access to the gallery with the key from Ferro despite the alarm system being switched on ... Yes, I also think that Palmeiro has a strong motive with this possible money laundering. We must try to prove it. Have you talked to your friend, the lawyer? ... Good. I assume we're only going to charge Jesus with theft. Our murderer is still on the loose." Avila sighed. "But let's call it a day, it's time for the weekend to begin. I'll see you Monday morning." Avila made a move to end the conversation with Vasconcellos. He had heard enough.

"Comissário, please ask Ernesto if I can see him later. I'm sure Kate would be overjoyed."

Somewhat reluctantly, Avila passed on the doctor's question. Vasconcellos' answer was short but clear.

Avila turned to Souza.

"I guess it looks like Ernesto is indisposed tonight."

"Give me the phone, please." Doutora Souza held out her hand energetically.

"Ernesto. What's this I hear about you trying to back out again? It's about time you started standing up for your relationship with Kate… What? Family gatherings aren't for you? Don't tell me. Family gatherings at the Vasconcellos house have never happened without you. And you were always one of the last!"

Avila had to grin. He wondered how Vasconcellos was going to get out of the act.

"I can't imagine Kate being okay with you not coming… Open relationship? Don't make me laugh! But I don't have the time or the inclination to argue with you any further right now.

Young man, you and I are still going to do some talking. The subject is not yet settled." She ended the conversation.

"Why do young men these days just not want to commit? I don't understand it. Kate really is a nice girl and Ernesto's mother is more than pleased with the relationship." She shook her head.

Avila remained silent. He would not interfere in this matter.

The Doutora, however, was not through with it, and continued to speak.

"It would be satisfying for old William if something good finally happened in the family again. There have been so many scandals and misfortunes over the years. I was surprised that he actually wants to celebrate his ninetieth in a big way. But maybe he is doing it for the sake of his son. As support for the upcoming elections. William junior would really make a good president. If only his mother could have lived to see it."

"Did you know her?"

"Yes, but it was a long time ago. She died when Kate was born. It was amazing how late she had children. No one thought it was possible anymore, then all of a sudden little William announced himself. I remember it like it is today. I was still at school, but my mother was friends with the Stuarts and I was the first babysitter of the two little boys. There's also Colin. He was born two years after William. That must have been 1963."

"Then Kate really was a latecomer. She can't be more than in her mid-thirties."

"Yes, her mother was in her late forties when Kate came. Too much for her. She died shortly after giving birth. William was completely broken. Which, to be honest, did surprise me. Because he was always known for leaving no stone unturned. He and Cecil Franco even shared a mistress or two. Even though they were both married at the time. But that's all water under the bridge. I shouldn't tell so many of the old stories."

Avila's interest was aroused.

"Cecil Franco and William Stuart senior were friends?"

"Yes, they used to be very close friends. Then something happened. The story with the missing Irish woman was the beginning. After that they fell out. Not an open fight, that's not what I mean. More of a gradual process over a few years."

"A missing Irish woman?"

"Yes, a young woman, daughter of Irish immigrants. She disappeared one day. William and Cecil were questioned about it at the time, but it was never clear what happened."

"When exactly was that?"

"At the beginning of the fifties, unfortunately I don't remember more precisely. I was only just born then, so I only know the story from my mother's stories." She looked at the plain white wall clock hanging just above her office door. "Twenty to eight already. I would love to chat with you some more, dear Comissário, but I have to be at the Stuarts' quinta at eight. I will finish my detailed report on Hugo Duarte on Monday and send it to your office. You should also go home to your wife now. I heard she went into premature labour. A new life is really more important than the dead, Fernando. Believe me." She opened her office door. The sign for Avila to leave.

Funchal,
18.08.2013–08:34

I really don't know why I'm going along with this." Kate pulled the blanket off the bed and wrapped it around her waist.

"Because I'm so irresistible." Vasconcellos remained lying down and eyed the cloaked Kate, who was walking towards the bathroom.

"You do realise I've seen you naked before, right?"

"I just don't like it when someone looks at my bare bottom."

"And you have such a beautiful backside."

"Stop it. Don't think you can make up for letting me down like that last night with a few compliments."

"Kate, we've talked about this before. I'm not a good boyfriend to show off. You knew that before we got together, though." The teasing undertone had disappeared from Vasconcellos' voice.

Kate turned to look at him and frowned.

"I know we have talked about it. But we've been together for almost four months now. I just expected you to change your mind."

"*Meu amor*, you are a wonderful woman, but please let's not discuss this now."

Kate came back to the bed and sat on the edge of it.

"My brothers warned me about you." She raked her hand through Vasconcellos' hair.

"They were probably right about that too. Tell me, how was it last night?" he asked conciliatory.

He and Kate hadn't had time to talk yet because he had only arrived from his get-together with his friend Chico at four in the morning. Actually, he had only wanted to drop by Chico's to tell him that his client was most likely no longer considered a murder suspect. But as so often with the two of them, the friends had gotten talking. Chico had put a bottle of aguardente on the table and before he knew it the time had flown by. They had discussed everything and anything and, of course, women. At the end of the evening, Chico had persuaded him to stop by Kate's place to reconcile them.

"She's good for you, Belmiro. Maybe it's time to commit slowly after all. You should still go there and spend the day with her tomorrow. It's better than being alone, don't you think?"

So, he had stopped by the family's quinta, where Kate lived in a side wing with a separate entrance, to which he had also had a key for some time. She had already been asleep and had only snuggled up to him, grumbling softly, when he had crawled into bed with her.

"It was a very nice evening. There must have been fifty guests and my father lasted until shortly after one o'clock in the morning. A lot of people asked me why you weren't there." Kate looked at him out of flashing eyes.

We are not quite reconciled again, Vasconcellos thought to himself. *I have to think carefully about what I say now. The best thing to do is to change the subject.*

"Your old man is still quite spry for his age. Didn't you tell me that he spent the whole night talking to your brother after the evening at the golf club?"

"Yes, I heard him talking to William until shortly after four in the morning. The two of them had been sitting in the grand salon and the windows were open. Then you can hear almost every word in here."

Vasconcellos looked over at the large, almost floor-to-ceiling windows. What worked one way would most likely work the other. Fortunately, the windows were firmly closed. He didn't want the old man to hear Kate and him having breakfast in the lounge. If he was already up and about after such a long evening.

Kate hadn't noticed Vasconcellos' look, she kept talking.

"Poor William. He must have been dead tired, but he couldn't persuade our senior to sleep. So, in the end he just listened in silence while father talked for hours again. Of course, I couldn't understand a word, but the steady hum of his voice kept me awake. It didn't bother me, I felt like I used to when my father sat by my bed and told me bedtime stories. Besides, I was so happy that he was feeling better again. It was a nice feeling that evening, but sometime in the early morning I fell asleep over the murmuring. William looked completely exhausted when we had breakfast together the next day. He said that the evening with the old man had been very long. Unlike him, our father was completely fit." She smiled.

"Your father must be quite happy with you already." Vasconcellos knew how much Kate cared for the old man. But William also spent a lot of time with him.

"By the way, I also talked to your godmother for a very long time last night", Kate interrupted his thoughts.

"I can well imagine that. And the subject was probably all my transgressions of the last few years. I can only be glad that your father didn't invite my parents too. My mother would have been only too happy to join in the conversation." Vasconcellos laughed.

"You're not taking any of this seriously. I should have sent you home."

"But you didn't, *meu amor*." Vasconcellos slowly stroked her right bare shoulder with his fingertips.

"Oh, my problem is really just that I can't stay angry with you for long. Do you actually have to work today? If so, that's no problem."

"What would you do if I wasn't here today?"

"Colin suggested we go for a sail in the nice weather. Would you like to come along?"

Vasconcellos did not share the Stuart family's enthusiasm for sailing. His father had already regularly taken part in regattas and won. His children were not inferior to him in this. Kate and Colin in particular were excellent sailors and Kate's living room was full of trophies.

Kate correctly understood Vasconcellos' hesitation.

"I can see you don't feel much like it. Colin and I don't want to leave until noon either. You and I could kill some time until then." She bent over and let the blanket slide off her shoulders.

Funchal, Police Headquarters, 19.08.2013–08:17

We have to look at everything completely anew. There's something we're missing." Avila looked at Vasconcellos and Baroso. "Let's take Palmeiro first. He's the one with the strongest motive and his alibi for Teresa Ferro's murder is weak."

"But we have not been able to verify Stuart's accusations of money laundering so far", Vasconcellos interjected.

"We'll stay on it. I don't like this Vitor Marsh either. Is there anything else in his past that could have been used by Teresa Ferro to blackmail him and then later maybe again by Hugo Duarte? Did forensics find anything else in the gallery?"

"They have not been able to discover anything useful. No laptop, no notes. Which, if you ask me, is suspicious once again."

Baroso came forward shyly.

"I know Senhor Duarte had a laptop. When I went to him last week to get the documents on the finances, he sent everything to the printer via the laptop."

Vasconcellos added:

"Forensics didn't find a computer at Duarte's house either. So, the murderer must have taken it with him."

Avila ran his usual circles around the room again. To Baroso's relief, however, he was a little calmer this time and the furnishings were not maltreated by beatings.

"There must be something. Baroso, you go back to the gallery. Check if there might be a hidden safe or other documents that we might have overlooked. Maybe Duarte has a confidant he could give documents to for safekeeping. Talk to the housekeeper again."

Baroso stood up immediately.

"I'll be off in a minute then!" He was obviously happy to be entrusted with such an important task. *Or maybe he's trying to avoid another outburst from me. I really need to learn to pull myself together more. I should be calmer by the time the child arrives at the latest.*

Avila turned to Vasconcellos.

"Let's talk about Teresa Ferro's murder again. We missed something in the alibis. I can't imagine our killer not being among our original suspects."

"Shall we go to the meeting room where the board with our suspects is hanging?"

Avila groaned.

"Ok, but let's have a quick galão before we go into the ice chamber."

A short time later, they were both sitting in front of the blackboard.

"The time of Ferro's death on the 10th of August was fixed by Doutora Souza between one o'clock in the morning, more likely two o'clock, and four o'clock." Vasconcellos tapped the photo of Teresa Ferro under which Baroso had written the time in his careful handwriting. "By then the event at the golf club had broken up and the invited guests had left the premises. As evidenced by the camera at the entrance."

"Let's ignore that part for now." Vasconcellos looked at Avila in amazement.

"That has been our problem from the beginning. We rely on the camera to show us the facts. The access to the site. That's where we made a mistake. Coelho's statement about the 'impassable' wall–pieces of glass, motion detectors–and the only access being through the gate. That limits our view. Let's look at the people first. What do we have?"

"You mean the alibis for the time of the crime?" Avila nodded.

"Vitor Marsh told us he went home with his wife shortly after midnight. Which the cameras", he glanced apologetically at Avila, "confirmed."

"His wife gives him an alibi for the night, right? Do we know if the two of them are sharing the marital bedroom again?"

"Well, that's exactly the point. Senhora Marsh certainly claimed this when we spoke to her. But the maids say otherwise. Namely, that she usually denies Senhor Marsh access and that he has therefore converted one of the many guest rooms in the house into his personal bedroom."

"What would be his motive? He has shares in the gallery, it would be good for him if the exhibition had gone well. With two dead owners and the botched exhibition and auction, it will probably be a losing proposition for him."

"True. And the relationship with Teresa Ferro is water under the bridge. So it shouldn't bother him or the wife that much."

"Let's move on to my favourite, Palmeiro. He had a fight with Teresa that night and left her alone at the club. If she no longer wanted to play along with the money laundering, that would be a very strong motive. Just because his housekeeper didn't hear him leave in the car doesn't mean he couldn't have snuck out."

"Romario has a racing bike. If he used that, he would have been back at the club from his house in no time and the housekeeper wouldn't have noticed anything."

"Please see if there is CCTV in the streets around his house, we might catch Senhor Palmeiro in the night. What about William Stuart junior?"

"Kate testified that she went home with him and then he spent half the night talking to his old man. She even told me on Sunday that she heard the conversation until she fell asleep. The father must have spent hours telling old stories again."

"Let's also check here for the sake of completeness if there are any possibilities that we can view the surroundings of the quinta via CCTV. But what would be Stuart's motive? The relationship with Ferro was long over and just like Vitor Marsh, a living gallery owner gets him more than a dead one with his shares in the gallery."

"I'll get right on it and find usable CCTV footage. I'll also get statements from Marsh, Stuart and Palmeiro as to where they were at the possible time of Duarte's murder. I wouldn't want to subpoena them for that though, just send an Aspirante over. There will be enough dust if we go back to the three of them. The wolf will certainly not be happy about it."

"He won't. But he's even less happy about the fact that a murderer is on the loose in the middle of the holiday season. Thank God the election has just given the newspapers other stuff for the front pages."

"Diretor André wants to hold a press conference this afternoon around three, has he notified you yet?"

Avila sighed, this was bound to happen.

"Do you think we need to be there?"

Vasconcellos knew how much his boss hated such press conferences.

"I have already clarified this with him. He'll be running the conference, we just need to brief him carefully in advance. His concern seems to be that you might strike the wrong note on the possibility that someone from Madeira's high society is involved in the murders. That's why he doesn't want you in front of the press cameras. I don't know where he gets that idea from." At Vasconcellos' broad grin, Avila could very well imagine who had put the idea into the wolf's head.

"You did that really well. Thank you. Now let's gather as much information as possible so that the Diretor can also offer something to the press pack. I'm going to take a look at the golf club wall, which is so insurmountable. Baroso has printed me a map and I will walk it from the outside. Afterwards, I will pay a visit to Ignacio Coelho. If Baroso contacts you– which I assume he will–tell him to meet me back here at the presidium at 11 o'clock. Then we'll have enough time to feed the wolf with news."

Funchal, Gallery, 19.08.2013–09:33

C arefully, Baroso removed the barrier tape and the seal on the door to the gallery. He was so concentrated on leaving everything as intact as possible so that he could simply close it again later that he almost tripped over the large cardboard box that stood directly in front of the entrance door.

When he entered the gallery, he took the package and put it on the table in the small kitchen. He looked at the sender. It was a local printing house.

"It won't hurt anyone if I see what's in the package", he said to himself and took his Swiss Army knife, which he always carried, out of his trouser pocket.

A short time later, a catalogue of the Churchill exhibition, still smelling of fresh paper and printing ink, lay in front of him.

"Let's hope for the printer's sake that the order has already been paid for. I can hardly imagine anyone else needing it", he muttered.

He picked up one of the colourful booklets with the famous photo of Churchill painting in Câmara de Lobos printed on the cover and scrolled through it briefly. Right at the beginning of the catalogue, the only painting up for auction was advertised. "Sunbathing in Madalena do Mar" took up a double page. *A really beautiful picture*, Baroso thought to himself. He turned the page.

What was that? He whistled through his teeth. This could be interesting. He flicked to the front again, yes, it was the same yacht. A beautiful sketch. Someone had also photographed a handwritten note for the catalogue. It said: "For my dear friend Jorge. In remembrance of the 'Last morning' on beautiful Madeira. Winston Churchill, London, June 1950."

"I don't remember that picture at all." Baroso put the catalogue aside and went into the gallery. He calmly looked at each of the paintings. The sketch was nowhere to be seen. He stopped in front of "Sunbathing" and pondered the arrangement of the picture.

"I wonder if that's the way it should be?" He reached for the phone to call Vasconcellos.

The latter answered shortly afterwards.

"Baroso, is there something important?" Silently he listened as the Aspirante told him about the missing picture.

"Hmm, I still don't understand what this could have to do with our murders. But you're right, we need to look at every angle. Did you find any other records? Something we can use to nail Palmeiro on the money laundering?"

"Unfortunately, no. But how am I supposed to deal with the picture now? I have no idea who this Jorge could be."

"Think about it. Do you have any other clues?"

"It looks like Winston Churchill knew Jorge personally and gave him the sketch. He was here in Madeira in 1950."

"That means that if this Jorge is still alive, we are looking for a man who would have to be at least eighty years old, right?"

239

"Right. I should check the civil registers." *Merda, that would take forever.*

"Or you ask someone who knows all the old stories. What about your grandmother? Maybe she can help you? Now, if you'll excuse me, I don't have that much time to filter anything useful out of the CCTV footage. You can manage on your own now, can't you? See you at eleven!" Vasconcellos hung up.

Baroso called his mother, in whose house his grandmother lived. After some back and forth, he finally had the old lady on the phone.

"*Monstrinho*, what do you want from me?"

Once again, Baroso wondered when he would be able to break his grandmother's habit of calling him "little monster". But there were more important things to focus on now.

"*Avó*, I need your help. I'm looking for a man with the first name Jorge, who should be around eighty years old. And he had dealings with Winston Churchill when he was here in Madeira."

"With that Englishman? I can still remember what a fuss there was when he was here in Madeira. He was always driving around in a big car and having himself one drink after another. He had a huge bar in the boot. Those English..."

"Do you remember who he was in contact with?" Baroso interrupted his grandmother.

"No, I was still a child then. I don't remember it so well. If Cecil Franco was still alive, I would have told you to call him. He knew so many people here in Madeira. And he was older then ... You know what, call Dona Luana. I'm sure she can help you."

"Dona Luana? Oh no." Baroso dreaded calling Luana Alves. The old lady had scared him since he was a child when she used to come to his grandmother's house.

"Dona Luana can help you, I'm sure. Don't make such a fuss. She's still pretty spry for her age. I'll give you her phone number, wait, she must be here somewhere."

After his grandmother had given him the number and ended the conversation, not without asking him if he was eating enough, Baroso took heart and called Dona Luana.

The old lady answered after only one ring with a creaky voice.

"Tou?"

"*A dona* Luana? I'm sorry to disturb you so early, this is Filipe, Saila Baroso's grandson."

"Oh, little Filipe? I hear you're with the *Seguranca Pública* now?"

"Actually, I am with the *brigada de homicídios*", Baroso corrected her, not without pride in his voice.

"In homicide? I remember when you were a little boy. You fell into my garden pond then because you wanted to have a closer look at the fish. It's like it was yesterday."

"Dona Luana, that's exactly the point. I know what a good memory you have and maybe you can help me."

"I'm listening?" Fortunately, Dona Luana was not one of those garrulous old ladies. She always got straight to the point. She was very direct and nothing escaped her notice. Which was also the reason why many people had a lot of respect for her.

"It's about a name. A man who should be over eighty now, if he's still alive. His first name is Jorge."

"Jorge? You don't have anything else for me?"

"He has something to do with Winston Churchill."

"That's easy. You mean Jorge Rocha, the brother of Fred the barman." Baroso was flabbergasted. Was it supposed to be this simple?

"Dona Luana, are you sure?"

"Oh yes. Jorge spent half his life talking about nothing else. Always the story of how he drove the English Prime Minister across the island. He didn't achieve much else in life. But he was proud of that."

"Do you know where I can find him?"

"He lives with his wife in Câmara de Lobos. Quite close to the harbour. But that's all I know. Does that help you?"

"It does! Thank you very much Dona Luana!"

"I am always happy to help Saila's grandson."

Funchal, Golf Club,
19.08.2013–10:14

"A m I glad this golf club doesn't have eighteen holes." Avila wiped the sweat from his brow. He had spent the last hour walking around the golf club, which was in the middle of a residential area below Monte. Leticia had chosen the golf club mainly for its beautiful location and not for the opportunity to go the full eighteen-hole distance. For her, the nine holes were enough to get some exercise and, above all, to catch up with friends. At least that's what she had told Avila and that's what he remembered now. Not that he was particularly interested in golf. He wouldn't think of ever taking up the sport. Besides, now he had one more excuse after the murder on the course. Secretly, he hoped a little that Leticia, too, would distance herself from the whole golf thing when she was fitter again after the birth. He didn't like the sport, or the people who hung around this club.

The wall surrounding the club was very high indeed. Coelho had not exaggerated here. So far, Avila had also not seen any way to easily overcome the obstacle. There were no overhanging branches of trees, nor was this bulwark dilapidated at any point. At four metres, it towered well above his head. Smooth grey stone that offered no means of climbing up it without tools. He wondered what the residents thought of this sight. It really could not be called beautiful. He was not surprised that the golf club had been given permission to build this structure. Old-boy networks in the ruling party and money were certainly the key. It was about time they had a new government. The wall beside him made a sharp right turn and he followed it along the small side road. That's when he saw it. A transformer house was built right up against it. The roof was slightly slanted and overgrown with flaming red bougainvillea. The two grey-green double doors that took up almost the entire front of the little house were made of slightly slanted slats. A splash of colour next to the grey monstrosity.

Avila stepped closer. The marks of a multitude of shoes were clearly visible on the slats. He reached for the phone. The forensics team should take a look at this. After a short phone call with the head of the team, who promised to send someone right away, he hung up.

Vasconcellos would probably try to climb up there now. What had Leticia told him a few days ago, that he was getting stiffer and more immobile? That was when he had found it so difficult to clear the gutter of leaves at her cottage. He almost fell off the ladder trying. He had to admit, he had been a bit stupid. Leticia's laughter still sounded clearly in his ears as he had climbed the ladder with effort and groans. "My old man", she had called him. Again, he looked up. He could easily reach the roof of the cottage with his hands, that much was certain. If he tried the side where there were no traces, the forensics would still have enough material. To be on the safe side, he took a few photos with the camera of his mobile phone, then he started to climb up.

He tried to find a foothold with his right foot at a height of about one metre and then push himself upwards to reach the

244

roof of the little house. It worked. *Old and immobile, my ass. Leticia has no idea.* He was now holding onto the edge of the roof with both hands and slowly manoeuvring himself up with his feet. This was another one of those times when he wished he had a slightly more favourable mass-to-force ratio. He should really start doing sports and lose a bit of weight.

Now just don't give up. Finally, he managed to push his upper body over the roof and he landed somewhat inelegantly face-first in the bougainvillea. He brought up his legs and looked around. It did look pretty high from up here. Perhaps he should have left this climb to Vasconcellos. Carefully he crawled towards the wall. What if the roof collapsed under his weight? He noticed how he had begun to sweat from exertion and stress. The sweat ran into his eyes and burned slightly. *I'm really not in good shape, Leticia is right. What an idiot I am to try to prove myself here.* His hands touched something under the red flowers. What was that? He pulled out a folded large piece of sail and a thick rope about two metres long. He looked up at the wall, on which one could now clearly see the shards of glass described by the club president. Was this the way? He really had to stop now. He looked down at the transformer house onto the road. The grey asphalt looked terribly hard. The ground on the other side of the wall was covered with soft grass, he was sure. Was he supposed to sit on the little house and wait for forensics? No, that was too humiliating. He would pay for his mistake later, but not like this. Carefully, with pointed fingers, he pushed the rope to the side. Again he took a few photos with his camera. Then he folded the canvas twice and threw it over the broken glass. Gingerly he felt around with his hand. Sure enough, the thick sailcloth withstood the shards. That had to be the solution. Slowly he pulled himself up onto the wall of the golf club, always expecting glass shards to cut through the fabric or for him to set off the alarm. Nothing happened. He heaved one leg over the wall, then the other. Now he could catch his breath and take in the surroundings.

The golf course stretched out in front of him. About a hundred metres away as the crow flies, he could see the lake where they had found Ferro. Right next to the piece of wall he was sitting on was a tree with a large branch sticking out in his direction. With a spirited leap, an intruder could get there and lower himself down. *Why the hell didn't we see the branch? Because we didn't walk the terrain carefully, but relied on that darn wall. Merda! I have never made so many mistakes as I have in this case.* Now this climbing game crowns it all. *The head of forensics is going to rip my head off. Maybe there are at least usable fingerprints on the rope, at least I didn't touch that.* It was too late now, he would go through with it. The jump was manageable and if not, there was thick grass under the tree. He took photos of his surroundings again. A little hesitantly, he bent towards the tree, jumped and tried with both hands to get a hold on the branch fork. A short time later, he found himself in a hanging position on the branch, which creaked ominously under his weight. He looked down. The ground was still quite far away, but what other solution was there? He let himself fall. Actually, he had wanted to roll off elegantly, as he had once seen those parkour runners do on television. But there was no question of elegance. He landed on both feet and then fell lengthways, face forward, into the grass.

"*Porra!*" He got to his feet and looked around. Had anyone seen him? Indeed they had. Two ladies in pastel quilted waistcoats, polo shirts and matching trouser skirts were standing in front of him, staring at him with wide eyes.

"Don't worry, ladies. I'm from the police and this is an investigation." He tried to cover his embarrassment, pretending that it was the most natural thing in the world for a Comissário to plop lengthwise out of a tree onto the ground.

"Comissário Avila?" One of the pastel-coloured ladies came closer. What a bummer, she knew him. He bet Leticia would know where he was hanging out and hear this story in no time.

"I'm Celia, Celia Mendes. A friend of Leticia's. We met last year at the flower festival here at the golf club. We had talked about Lisbon for a long time then. I was born there."

Avila remembered darkly. It had been another one of those awful evenings when he had found no excuse not to accompany Leticia to the golf club. But the conversation about Lisbon with this Celia ... True, she had lived in the same part of town as him.

"Dona Celia, how nice to meet you again." He indicated a bow, which visibly pleased the two pastel-coloured ladies. "If you will excuse me, please. I need to speak to Senhor Ignacio urgently." He walked towards the clubhouse, glad to have escaped the embarrassing situation with as much dignity as possible.

As he passed the lake and walked across the putting range through the open glass doors into the great hall, he ran straight into the arms of the club president, who was talking to a member of staff.

"Fernando? Where did you come from?" Astonished but also slightly piqued by the policeman's sudden appearance, the club president eyed him up and down. Avila was all too aware that the light-coloured trousers he had put on in the heat this morning showed clear traces of the grass patch whose acquaintance he had just made. But that didn't matter now. He could not imagine that Ignacio Coelho knew nothing about the back entrance to his golf club.

"Senhor Ignacio, I need to speak to you urgently. Can we talk in private without being disturbed?"

Coelho said a brief goodbye to the young man and then walked ahead towards his office.

Looking at the dark mahogany desk, the other use of which the owner surely had no idea, Avila sat down. Coelho took a seat behind the desk and looked at him, waiting.

Avila got straight to the point.

"As you must have noticed, I did not enter the compound through the main entrance." Coelho's eyebrows shot up, but he remained silent playing a game of wait-and-see. "I took the back entrance, you might say, and I'm sure I'm not the only one who knows how to get into the golf club by other means. So, tell me, how many times has it happened that you've had unexpected visitors here?"

Coelho cleared his throat.

"I must say, Comissário, you surprise me. Until now, I was not aware that you could enter our club in any other way."

"Oh really? If I ask around a bit among the guests and staff here, they'll all confirm that for me?"

The club president drew in his breath audibly.

"I thought you promised me you would be discreet about the whole thing."

"Discreet? We have two people dead. And if you hadn't led us to believe that your wall was an impregnable bulwark, we wouldn't have focused on the wrong man. That might have prevented the murder of Senhor Duarte." Avila was fed up with this stupid talk about discretion.

The piqued façade collapsed.

"I'm sorry. I should have told you." Coelho hung his head. "There have been complaints a few times in the past about golfing on the premises at night. You'll have to take my word for it, though, that I don't know where that access point might

248

be. I promise you that I will correct this. If only this doesn't become public."

This guy was terrible. The correction, as Coelho put it, came too late for Teresa Ferro. It was clear that her killer knew this way in, and about the transformer house. Now all they had to do was catch Palmeiro via the CCTV. Avila rose from the armchair and left the room with a brief goodbye.

Funchal, Police Headquarters
19.08.2013–11:05

Y es, that won't happen again. I'll come by later and you can take the prints of my shoes for the tread comparison." Avila hung up. Baroso looked at his boss uncomprehendingly, Vasconcellos smirked. He had taken the call when the head of forensics, audibly enraged, wanted to talk to this "irresponsible Comissário who had destroyed important evidence with his climbing."

For the third time that day, Avila tried to cover his embarrassment. He was annoyed. What kind of devil had gotten into his head? But really, it was Leticia's fault. If she hadn't always teased him about being so unathletic, then he would have waited for the forensics team. Hopefully, at least the piece of rope would yield some fingerprints and his photos would help with the forensics.

On the other hand, his surprise visit to the club president had not been so bad. He had run after him and, while escorting the Comissário from the premises, had told him that members of the club had also been caught by the security staff during night-time golf games. But since they had been highly respected ladies and gentlemen, as club president he had left it at a discreet reprimand. That "discreet" attitude again. Avila's insides were boiling up again when he thought of Coelho's face contorted into an embarrassed smile. Fortunately, he was not so discreet in the end that he did not tell Avila the names of the gentlemen. And lo and behold, all their suspects were there. Even three ladies had been in on it: Teresa Ferro, Aurelia Gomes and Kate Stuart.

"So, we now know that Marsh, Stuart and Palmeiro must know about the entrance via the transformer shed. The footprints that the forensic team were able to take are unfortunately very numerous and varied. Impossible to determine the perpetrator from them because we can't place them in time either." This circumstance had relieved Avila somewhat. But it still could not be ruled out that the head of forensics would complain about him to the wolf. But that didn't matter now, the main thing was that they were finally getting closer to the culprit.

"Did the CCTV evaluation yield anything?"

"Yes, Palmeiro really did leave his property on his bike shortly after one o'clock in the morning. I'm still trying to reconstruct his route from there via various cameras. But I can already say that so far his route leads along the promenade in Funchal and then across the market halls. The only question now is whether it will continue towards the golf club. The direction is definitely right!"

"That's good. How much longer do you need?"

"I have given the sighting of the footage to one of the Aspirantes. He should be in touch any moment."

As if on cue, there was a knock at that moment and a young man poked his head through the door of Avila's office.

"I have now been able to trace the path of Senhor Palmeiro. Unfortunately, there are no cameras in the outskirts of Funchal. But the last shot shows him on Rua Conde Carvahal, not far from the Jardim do Miradouro Vila Guida."

"From there it's only a few hundred metres to the transformer house! That must be enough for an urgent suspicion. Let's tell Diretor André. Maybe he'll be able to report an arrest by the time of the press conference."

Baroso cleared his throat in embarrassment.

"Do you still want to hear about my findings from the investigations in the gallery and the phone call with Dona Luana? There are still a few interesting aspects."

Avila looked from Baroso to Vasconcellos. The latter noticed that Avila actually had little desire to leave the trail he had now taken to Palmeiro.

"Perhaps you could give us a very brief summary, Baroso. It will certainly help to round off the picture about Teresa Ferro and the background of the gallery. Then please write a detailed report as well."

Avila looked at his Subcomissário. Ernesto had used exactly the right words not to discourage the young man. He himself had been on the verge of saying, "Not now. That won't help us." It was good that Vasconcellos had spoken up quickly. He was also quite right, they still had the time now.

"I'll make us all another bica, you tell us about the gallery and this mysterious missing painting. And when the expresso is finished, I'll go and notify the wolf." Baroso beamed happily at his boss and started talking about the exhibition catalogue and his phone call with old Dona Luana.

Garajau,
19.08.2013–12:27

Have you heard that Hugo Duarte was found stabbed to death in his gallery?"

"No, how terrible! Poor Hugo! How could this have happened? I thought they had arrested Otavio Jesus for Teresa's murder. Unbelievable! Fernando just won't tell me anything. When is that supposed to have happened?"

"As early as Friday. But they didn't discover him until Saturday morning."

"That was certainly the reason why Ernesto called so early. I had tried to get something out of him when he came in on Saturday night. I'm beginning to understand. That's probably why the daily paper isn't here this morning. Fernando will have taken it with him. I think he's imagining this whole murder thing is bad for me now that I'm pregnant."

"Leticia, you gave us all a big scare. So, it's only understandable that Fernando is worried. But I think a little gossip can't hurt. Otherwise you'll be bored to death. Oops, I probably shouldn't say it like that."

Inês was right about the boredom. Leticia had even started reading some of Fernando's old science fiction novels. There was just nothing decent on TV and she didn't feel like reading women's magazines at the moment. There were only super-slim models and looking at them made her feel even more out of shape.

"So, it wasn't Otavio then? In a way, I'm glad. He was always so nice and polite."

"But he definitely managed to steal from the dead Teresa, we must not forget that."

"You're right. What exactly did André tell you?"

"Not as much as I would like to hear. He always dodges my questions and says he doesn't know more. I'm not sure if that's really because your husband hasn't given him all the information yet or he just doesn't want to tell me."

Leticia had to grin. She could well imagine that the wolf was sparing with internal information around his wife, since it was common knowledge that Inês liked to pass on gossip. But she was not allowed to complain. As a result, there was never a dull moment with Inês. Fernando usually held back from telling her stories about his current cases. So, she was always grateful when Inês let her share her knowledge. Especially now, when it was so dull for her in bed, this story was a welcome change. No, that wasn't nice of her. Poor Hugo was dead. She didn't feel quite as sorry for Teresa, she had to admit. But she had got on well with Hugo.

"Do you know how it happened?"

"Ask your Ana. I heard that Ernesto spoke to her on the phone. She also cleans at Hugo's."

"Right, you're right. I forgot all about that. Ana is even upstairs doing our bedroom right now."

"Aren't you lying in your bed? If Fernando finds out, you'll be in trouble."

"Ana and I went downstairs together very carefully this morning and she set up a camp for me here in the living room

254

on the sofa. In the bedroom under the roof it's totally stuffy and if I leave the air conditioner running all the time, I catch a cold because of the dry air. Here I can look out into my garden, the patio door is open and I can hear the activity from the street outside."

"You'll know what's good for you. Why don't you ask Ana what the men wanted from her? I'll stay on the line."

Leticia called upstairs:

"Ana, can you come here quickly?"

She heard Ana running down the stairs.

"Dona Leticia, are you all right? We should have listened to Senhor Fernando and not taken you downstairs! Shall I take you back to the bedroom?" Ana bent down to move Leticia's blanket aside and help her up.

"No, Ana, it's all good. I just wanted to talk to you for a minute. Do you want to make us a galão? Dona Inês is on the phone and we thought we women could have a quick chat."

Ana frowned in surprise, but then wiped her hands on her smock apron, which she wore while working, and disappeared into the kitchen.

"Can you turn up the volume even more and put the phone closer to you? I can't hear you very well", Inês' voice sounded from the phone.

Leticia obliged her and a short time later Ana appeared with two glasses of milky coffee. She sat down somewhat stiffly opposite Leticia on one of the armchairs and looked expectantly at her employer.

"Dona Inês and I are talking a little about the events of the last few days. What happened with Senhor Hugo is really bad", Leticia got straight to the point.

"Yes, terrible. Poor Senhor Hugo. Ernesto, Dona Marea's son, called me this morning, he wanted to know when I saw Senhor Hugo last. I told him what I knew."

It was typical of Ana that she also knew Vasconcellos' mother. If anyone here in Madeira was well informed, it was Ana. Leticia knew that Inês was thinking the same thing on the other end of the phone.

Leticia leaned forward and looked at Ana expectantly.

"Alright, I'll tell you. Senhor Hugo left the house shortly after half past nine on Friday morning, as usual, to open the gallery. But believe me, Dona Leticia, he hasn't been himself for the last few days. The death of Dona Teresa has taken its toll on him. Besides, he was very worried about the gallery. I know business wasn't that good. He was constantly sitting at his laptop looking at figures. That's why he had also asked me to clean his house only once a week. He wanted to save money."

Leticia had also heard about the finances. She knew how important the exhibition with the auction of the Churchill painting had been for the gallery.

"Did he say anything else or was anything unusual?"

"He asked me a few days ago about an old Madeiran, about Jorge Rocha. I had wondered about that a bit."

"Who is this Jorge Rocha?"

"Oh, I always forget that you're not from here. Almost everyone on Madeira knows Jorge. The old guy has scraped by all his life with odd jobs here on the island. Kind and nice, but if he hadn't had his older brother Fred, he and his wife would be completely impoverished today."

"And what did Hugo Duarte want from him?" Leticia continued. Was this Rocha the old man she had seen with his wife in front of the gallery?

"I'm afraid I don't know. But that's definitely the most unusual thing I've noticed about him in the last few days. And that's what you wanted to know, isn't it, Dona Leticia?" Ana looked slightly reproachful and stood up. "I'd like to go upstairs now and close the windows I opened for air. If you don't need me anymore, I'll leave to take care of my husband and children then. I promised to take them swimming today."

"Thank you, Ana, for taking such good care of everything. I'll see you on Wednesday then." Leticia felt guilty for having squeezed Ana like that. Hopefully she wouldn't hold it against her, or worse, tell Fernando about it.

"I'm happy to help you and Senhor Fernando", Ana said conciliatory and left the living room.

Leticia reached for the receiver.

"Have you been able to understand everything?"

"Yes, but unfortunately it wasn't much."

"Do you know Jorge Rocha? Or his brother, this Fred?"

"No, unfortunately not. Never heard of them."

"Too bad. But I have an idea of who I could ask. I'll get back to you later, I have to make a phone call now."

Funchal, Police Headquarters, 19.08.2013–13:15

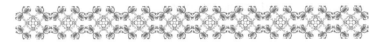

"A re you sure? You've got to be kidding!" Avila was beside himself.

"It is unfortunately the case. Aurelia Gomes has confirmed Palmeiro's statement. He went to see her the night Teresa Ferro was murdered and stayed until the early morning." Vasconcellos looked up from his notes.

"And this Gomes really lives near the golf club?" Avila was still suspicious.

"Yes. According to her, that was also the reason why she joined the club in the first place. She can walk there and doesn't have to drive in the evening after work if she wants to play golf."

"*Porra*! It fitted so well. But that Palmeiro. He goes to the event with the one woman. Then leaves her there alone, only to meet up later with the one who spoiled the whole evening for Ferro. I don't like that man anymore."

"You are right. Unfortunately, it's not enough to arrest him. But the issue of money laundering is not over for him yet. After Baroso and I spent our time with colleagues from the *Unidade de Informação Financeira* checking the gallery's finances, they have tasted blood. They want to get Palmeiro too. I've already given them all the data we have on it so far."

"At least that's something. But back to our murders. Palmeiro is indeed eliminated now." Avila's phone rang.

"Damn, who's calling now?" He reached for the receiver. "Tou? Dona Luana is on the phone? ... For Baroso? ... She says it's important?" He looked in amazement at his Aspirante, who shrugged awkwardly. "Well, put her through, please."

"Dona Luana? This is Comissário Avila. We met some time ago at the golf club ... Yes, I am Leticia's husband. I was told you have something important to tell us? Yes? May I put you on speaker? Subcomissário Vasconcellos and Aspirante Baroso are in my office."

The loudspeaker emphasised the natural creak in the old lady's voice.

"I remembered something else after talking to Filipe, I mean Aspirante Baroso, on the phone. I think it could be important."

"We are listening, Dona Luana."

"The night at the golf club when Teresa Ferro was murdered, I had a long conversation with her. We also talked about Jorge Rocha. Teresa showed me a photo of a sketch she was going to present at the exhibition the next day." Baroso looked at the other two triumphantly.

"That sketch seems to have disappeared, Dona Luana", Vasconcellos hastened to say.

"Do you know what it's all about exactly?" her voice creaked.

"No, not exactly."

"I'm afraid I have to backtrack a bit. Jorge Rocha showed Winston Churchill some hidden corners on the island back then. His brother Fred, who was a barman at Reid's, had arranged it. Jorge has been scraping by with odd jobs all his life. Luckily, he has Fred to support him all the time. Otherwise, he and his wife would surely have starved. Tourism was just starting up again in the 1950s after the war and Reid's was the place where Madeira's rich people and well-heeled tourists met. We went to Reid's for a sundowner or even teatime. And what beautiful balls there were back then." She sighed at the memory. "Where was I? Jorge. Fred put Jorge up at Reid's as a temporary waiter. But of course that wasn't enough to feed the family. So, Jorge played chauffeur for Churchill for a few days. As a thank you, Churchill gave him this sketch. Jorge guarded this gift like the apple of his eye. He could have made good money out of it all these years. But he didn't want to. I think he felt that this painting made him special. And he was a little bit right. Everyone in Madeira knew the story of Jorge and the Prime Minister at that time. I never saw the picture. Until the weekend before last. Teresa showed me a photo of it."

"We did not find a photo", Vasconcellos interjected.

"It shows a sailing yacht", the old lady crooned. "The yacht belonged to poor late Cecil. Teresa already knew that, she had done her research. Actually, she had wanted to talk to Cecil about the history of the yacht, to include the historical background in the exhibition. But there had been nothing more than a brief telephone conversation about the sketch between the two of them. Shortly afterwards, he had an accident."

Avila noticed how the hair on his arms stood up. Was the key this picture? And even worse, could it mean that their murderer had not only struck twice? Baroso and Vasconcellos also seemed to have this train of thought, and they listened spellbound to Dona Luana's words.

"I told Teresa that she should contact the original owner of the yacht. The one who sold Cecil the piece sometime in the mid-fifties. At the time the picture was painted, the yacht still belonged to him. Teresa was very excited. She thought that now she could also rewrite the history of the actual centrepiece of the exhibition, the painting 'Sunbathing in Madalena do Mar'. It would be a sensation, she told me, and her gallery would be saved. Actually, I had wanted to go to the exhibition to take a closer look at this painting. But unfortunately, I haven't had the chance yet. Now I don't think it will be possible either." You could clearly hear the regret in her voice.

"Who was the original owner of the yacht?" asked Avila, although he already suspected the answer.

"William Stuart senior."

Funchal, Police Headquarters, 19.08.2013–13:41

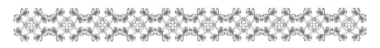

W hat does it all mean? We have to find out what Ferro meant by it being a sensation! Was there anything else in the catalogue about this sketch?"

"Only that it should have the title 'The Last Morning'." Baroso had taken a copy of the catalogue with him and was now leafing through it.

"Last morning? What do you mean?"

"I have an idea. What if Churchill was referring to his last morning in Madeira? Or the last morning he spent with Jorge?"

"Good idea, Baroso. I seem to remember Duarte reading a text at the opening about Churchill's trip to Madeira. Can you find it in the catalogue?"

"It says here: 'Churchill was in Madeira from the first of January to the twelfth. His wife Clementine and daughter Diana stayed four days longer'."

"So according to your theory, the sketch would probably point to the twelfth of January. What's so important about the killer not wanting us to find this picture? Baroso, try to find out what happened here in Madeira during that time. Have you tried to reach this Jorge yet? Vasconcellos, we'll pay your almost father-in-law a visit. Maybe he can tell us what's so interesting about this yacht."

"Shall we take my car? Or do you want to drive up in a police car right away?"

"No, let's take your car. It's only a questioning and we don't want to upset the old man unnecessarily."

A short time later, the two drove west in Vasconcellos' small station wagon.

"There was something else", Avila reflected aloud.

"What do you think, boss?"

"I was talking to someone about the old days. What was it?"

"It will come back to you. Let's wait and see what Baroso finds out about the yacht first. Do you think the same thing I do, that Cecil Franco could have been murdered too?"

"That's it, Ernesto. Cecil Franco! Doutora Souza told me something about an old scandal. A mistress, an Irishwoman, who has disappeared. I'll call Baroso right away. Maybe there's something to it." He reached for his phone.

"Baroso, there was something else. Doutora Souza told me about an Irish woman who disappeared. It must have had something to do with Cecil Franco and old Stuart. Maybe you can find newspaper articles on the case. It's supposed to have been a major scandal... Have you reached this Jorge yet? ... No? ... Occupied? Keep trying, but stay on top of this Irishwoman thing. If you have to, check with Doutora Souza again. Get back to me as soon as you know anything. But please call me on Vasconcellos' phone, my battery is about to die."

When he hung up, he turned to Vasconcellos.

"I'm a fool for forgetting to charge my mobile phone again. Baroso will get back to you when he's found something. He hasn't been able to reach that Jorge guy yet. The line has been busy the whole time."

"It's probably like my *avó*, once she starts chatting with an old friend, she can't find an end to it."

"I know that about Leticia too."

"Speaking of Leticia. Who's in charge today?"

Avila looked at the clock, it was exactly two o'clock.

"Ana should have been there until just now. I hope Leticia is taking a nap now. At some point this afternoon, I'm sure Carlos will check on her. I just don't like that she can't reach me by mobile in case something is wrong."

"Then she will call the police station and they will put her through to my phone. Don't worry, Fernando. Does she know about Duarte?"

"I tried to keep it a secret from her so as not to upset her. Don't laugh, but I even took the daily paper with me this morning so she wouldn't read the headlines."

"And you don't think Inês hasn't told her yet? Surely the wolf's wife wouldn't miss a story like that?" Vasconcellos laughed and shook his head.

Avila nodded. Yes, he would not be able to keep Duarte's murder a secret from Leticia for long.

Vasconcellos' phone rang, Baroso. The boy was really fast.

"What do you have for us? I'll pass you on to the boss. He'll put you on loud."

Baroso's excited voice sounded throughout the car.

"I found the Irish woman. Her name was Órla, unfortunately I don't know her last name yet. She disappeared at the beginning of 1950, in January. She was supposed to be a beautiful woman. The men were all over her. When she disappeared, they investigated in all directions. The inspector in charge suspected a jealousy drama. But no body was ever found. The main suspect at the time was William Stuart,

264

because an argument had been observed between him and the Irish woman. But since there was never a body and he wasn't even in Madeira at the time she disappeared, it all went on file."

"Good work, Baroso! We're going to give old Stuart a bit of a run for his money now."

Vasconcellos was silent, thinking.

"What colour hair might an Irish woman typically have?"

"Red", Avila and Baroso answered simultaneously.

"And what colour was the hair of the woman in the painting of Churchill?" Vasconcellos averted his eyes from the road and looked at his boss triumphantly.

Garajau,
19.08.2013–14:08

Satisfied, Leticia hung up. It had been a good idea to call Doutora Souza. The doctor had a memory like an elephant. She had actually been able to tell Leticia quite a bit about Jorge Rocha and the reason for his fame in Madeira. Fortunately, the doctor was busy writing the autopsy report for Duarte that she had promised Avila. So, she did not ask Leticia any further questions about why she wanted to know all this, but hung up right after the brief informational conversation.

At last the story began to make sense. So there was another Madeira painting by Churchill and it was definitely not in the exhibition ... Leticia was now sure that the old man outside the gallery had been Jorge Rocha. These were certainly all important pieces of the puzzle for Fernando's investigation. Let's see what else she could find out.

With difficulty, Leticia got up from the sofa, slipped on her slippers and slowly made her way into the hall. It was lucky that Ana had helped her down the stairs this morning. If she were upstairs in the bedroom now, her little research adventure would be over. Carefully, she propped herself up against the wall and slowly made her way towards the hallway. There on the small telephone table next to the entrance was what she needed now: the telephone book of the Funchal region. She scrolled through it. Doutora Souza had told her that Rocha lived in Câmara de Lobos. Indeed, there was a Jorge Rocha there. On her way to the living room, she typed in the number and then dropped onto the sofa, breathing heavily.

After only two rings, Leticia had the old man on the phone.

"*Boa tarde*, Senhor Rocha. This is Leticia Avila. Please don't be surprised that I am calling you out of the blue. It's about your picture of Winston Churchill."

Leticia had feared that the old man would react dismissively because he did not know her. But that worry turned out to be a mistake.

"You have heard about it? It's such a misfortune. My wife and I let Senhora Ferro persuade us to lend her the sketch for the exhibition. Now poor Senhora Ferro is dead and no one knows where our painting is. Senhor Duarte wanted to take care of it, but we can't reach him."

Leticia briefly wondered whether she should tell Rocha that Duarte was dead too. But the old man seemed excited enough already.

"Senhor Rocha, my husband is Comissário Avila and I will tell him about our conversation. Maybe he can help you."

"*Graças a Deus*! That would be wonderful. We are so grateful to you. Every day my wife and I look at the wall where the painting hung. We should never have given it away!"

"Could you tell me anything about the painting and what Senhora Ferro intended to do with it?"

"You must know Sir Winston Churchill? Such a fine gentleman. I was allowed to show him a few hidden spots on our island in 1950. As a thank you, he then sent me the painting. It's not a finished painting, but a beautiful sketch. Even with a personal dedication! Even when things were going so badly for us all those years, we still never thought of selling it. No, it was our lucky charm. And now it has disappeared. *Está terrivel, absolutamente terrivel!*"

"What exactly does the picture show?"

"What does it show? The yacht. Excuse me, I'm so excited. You couldn't possibly know all that. On his last day of leave, very early in the morning, I showed Sir Churchill another place. And there it was again, the yacht, the same one we had seen together before. He was thrilled that we had found it again. But this time the boat was deserted. Without the woman he had painted before. Did you see the painting in the exhibition? It was hanging there when my wife and I were there last week. Only our sketch has disappeared."

"You mean the 'Sunbathing in Madalena do Mar'? With the red-haired woman?"

"Yes, that's exactly what I mean! I was there when he painted it. The woman was even more beautiful in real life than in the picture. She must have known we were standing there watching her. My wife always tells me that if Sir Churchill had given me a sketch with that woman, she would have destroyed it. '*Que piranha*', those were always her words."

"Did you know the woman in the painting?"

"Oh yes. That was Órla, the Irish girl. Everyone knew her at the time. A few days after Sir Churchill painted the picture, she disappeared. To this day, no one knows what happened. But I remember well that she was not alone on the yacht. A man was also there, but you couldn't see him at a distance. I only knew it was Órla because of her hair. No woman in Madeira had hair like that."

"Surely Senhora Ferro found the story very interesting?"

"Oh yes. I was able to tell her exactly when Sir Churchill painted the Irish woman on the yacht and when he did the sketch without the woman. She wanted to write this in the catalogue. Unfortunately I didn't get a catalogue, and she wanted to send us one as soon as it was printed. As a souvenir for us."

"When exactly were these two pictures taken?"

"The painting was on the 8th of January 1950 and the sketch four days later", the information came like a shot from a pistol.

"But you didn't see Órla on the yacht that day?"

"In retrospect, I think she had already disappeared. But at first nobody really thought about it. We all thought she would turn up again. But she didn't. The police even investigated. But nobody knew anything."

"Was anyone suspected?"

"Unfortunately, I don't know. I could only tell Senhora Ferro that I saw the yacht again a few years later. At some point she was anchored in Câmara de Lobos."

"Did you see anyone on board then?"

"Yes, Doutor Cecil Franco, God rest his soul. That's what I told Senhora Ferro."

"Was that before or after Senhor Cecil's accident?" An evil foreboding crept up in Leticia.

"Just before that ... Do you think something happened to him because of that? That is, I could be to blame for his death? Oh, *meu Deus*!" The old man's voice began to tremble. Leticia feared he would start crying at any moment.

"I'm sure it's just a stupid coincidence. Please don't get upset, dear Senhor Rocha. We'd better stop talking on the phone. I'll tell my husband everything and I'm sure you'll find your picture again."

Immediately after hanging up, she tried to reach Fernando to tell him about the pictures. And he would also have to hear about her suspicion that Cecil Franco's fall might not have been an accident.

Only the announcement from his voicemail. Had he forgotten to charge the mobile phone again? Should she call Ernesto now? No, that was too much. Besides, it wasn't her fault that Fernando didn't know how to use a mobile phone. Anyway, it would be better if she told Fernando about it calmly tonight, when he had a full stomach and a glass of Verdejo in his hand. Then hopefully there would be no trouble about the fact that she had done research on her own.

Could she find out more by then? She preferred not to call Doutora Souza and disturb her again to ask about Cecil Franco's yacht. Who else did she know who sailed?

She reached for the phone to dial Kate Stuart's number. A short time later, a male voice answered.

"Tou?"

Quinta Pôr do Sol,
19.08.2013–14:33

"Have you ever been to Quinta Pôr do Sol?" asked Vasconcellos.

"No, is that the name of the Stuart family quinta?"

"To be precise, it's actually the Burke family quinta. Old William married into it in the forties. That's what Kate told me. The family had been in Madeira for a long time and had a sugar cane factory at the beginning of the twentieth century. The Aguardente de Cana Açuca reserva from Burke LTD. was legendary. Kate let me try some of this treasure once. Tasted really good."

"So, William Stuart senior married a Burke?"

"Yes, and the only daughter and heiress, Millicent. He was said to have come from a poor background in England, if I remember correctly. But he must have been a gifted engineer who modernised the factory."

"And in return he got the daughter?"

"I guess you could say that."

"Souza told me that Stuart and Franco seem to have been getting it on pretty thick. Hence the mistress."

"I can hardly imagine that. Are you sure? The old gentleman I know, all he talks about is sailing and hare coursing. And that means real rabbits, if you want to ask."

"What do you know about his wife?"

"He doesn't talk about it himself, but Kate told me that he had completely withdrawn after her death. From one day to the next he was pretty much just at home."

"No friends?"

"Kate never mentioned any. I only know about his friendship with Cecil Franco through you. According to Kate's description, her father is more of a recluse, just work and his children, with whom he went sailing from time to time. Or to hunt rabbits. Only recently has he become more active again. He is insanely proud that his eldest wants to go into politics and he tries to help him wherever he can. Hence the big celebration for his ninetieth I suppose."

"If he really had something to do with the disappearance of this Órla, it could certainly disrupt his son's political career", Avila mused.

"Let's just ask him", Vasconcellos said, turning onto the quinta's driveway covered in light-coloured gravel.

Avila held his breath. He had already visited some of the quintas in Madeira with Leticia, but this one was really impressive. The driveway took a right turn up a small hill on which the quinta was perched. The roof tiles of the quinta shone in the August sun in the same bright orange-pink as the roofs of most houses on Madeira. But that was the only similarity between this mansion and the small houses of the island villages. The main building was brightly painted and two storeys high. The floor-to-ceiling windows were framed by dark green, open shutters. Adjacent to the main house were single-storey outbuildings to the right and left. Everything was framed by various colourful, climbing bougainvillea and hibiscus. These did not grow as wildly as in Avila's garden, but were neatly trimmed. Like coloured eye shadow on a woman's eyes, they adorned the quinta and made it shine.

They stopped in front of a flight of natural stone steps leading up to the entrance.

"Is the building perhaps also used as a hotel?" Avila could hardly imagine that only one family lived here. Moreover, he knew from Leticia that none of the children of old Stuart had any descendants yet.

"No, old Stuart lives in the main building and Kate and William each in one of the two outbuildings. Plus, of course, a few servants. You can imagine that it takes a lot of manpower to keep this place in good shape."

"I am impressed."

"Wait until you see the inside. It's even more impressive." Vasconcellos let the old-fashioned doorknocker smack against the heavy entrance door. Surprisingly, the expected dull thump of metal on wood did not sound, but instead there was a bright ringing. A short time later, the door was opened for them by a man in a dark suit.

"Senhor Vasconcellos. Senhora Kate is not here, unfortunately. She went into town an hour ago to do some shopping."

"That's fine. We would like to speak to Senhor Stuart senior."

"I'm not sure Senhora Kate would like that." The clerk looked over his shoulder uncertainly, as if Kate were standing behind him and looking at him reproachfully.

"I'm afraid it has to be. Could you please tell Senhor Stuart that Comissário Avila and I would like to speak to him?"

Reluctantly, the clerk disappeared inside the house, revealing the entrance hall. They entered.

Avila whistled through his teeth. Vasconcellos had not exaggerated. This was even more impressive. The floor was lined with a geometric pattern of light and dark woods. The pale heavy armchairs spread across the hall were the same colour as the columns decorated with vines that divided the large room into smaller sections. To the right and left, two curved staircases led up to the first floor onto a kind of balustrade. Here the clerk now appeared and beckoned them up.

"However, I would like to ask you not to upset Senhor Stuart too much. He has not been well the last few days. I will now take you to his salon."

Silently they followed him down the long corridor.

Quinta Pôr do Sol,
19.08.2013–14:39

The heavy oak door opened and Avila looked into old Stuart's room. Immediately, a gush of stale, musty air rushed out. It was dark, the shutters half-closed, barely letting in any light. Avila could see nothing in the room, his eyes still adjusted to the bright surroundings outside. Only very slowly did they get used to the semi-darkness and he was able to take a closer look at the salon.

Hadn't Vasconcellos told them that the old man was feeling better? This was not the room of a healthy and contented person. Someone had made an effort to bring some life into the room with large bouquets of fragrant flowers. But these could not mask the sour smell coming from the person sitting in front of them in the semi-darkness in a large armchair, similar to the armchairs downstairs in the hall.

The clerk cleared his throat briefly.

"Senhor Engenheiro, these are the gentlemen from the police. Comissário Avila and Subcomissário Vasconcellos." He paused for a moment, then added: "Ernesto Vasconcellos, your daughter's friend." Then he turned and quietly closed the door behind him.

They were alone with the old man. Avila was struggling with a rising nausea, the first thing he would have liked to do was to throw the windows wide open to get some air into the room.

He was still wondering how best to start the conversation when a weak, trembling voice sounded.

"I was expecting you, gentlemen." Avila stumbled. "You are surely here to question me about my past", the voice from the darkness continued. "My past, which has now caught up with my children too. I should have said something much sooner. But I wanted only the best for my three after Millicent's death. She would have so wanted her eldest to guide the destiny of Madeira. She would have really liked that." The rough voice became quieter and quieter and Avila thought they could hear that the old man was fighting tears.

Avila tried to make out Vasconcellos' expression in the darkness. Was he thinking the same thing as he was? That there might be something to the theory they had developed in the car?

Stuart took a rattling breath, then continued.

"It would certainly never have come out if it hadn't been for", his voice took on a harsh undertone, "that little bitch sticking her nose into our business. She was clever. But not clever enough. First she pestered poor Cecil with questions about the yacht and the painting of Órla. This painting, I had no idea it existed all these years. Why did Churchill paint this of all things?" Talking more to himself, he continued, "But why should he have been any different from me. Everyone who saw Órla could not take their eyes off her. She was so beautiful. My golden princess." He fell silent.

Avila and Vasconcellos remained silent and gave the old man time to collect himself. Quietly, they sat down on two smaller armchairs that stood in the room.

The old man regained his composure.

"She tried to blackmail Cecil first, you know." Now he had to be back to talking about the "little bitch". Avila guessed he was talking about Teresa Ferro. "Cecil then came to me. He wanted me to tell the police everything and put an end to it. I wish I had listened to my old friend." He shook his head.

"Cecil talked to me that day. He didn't know in all these years. It was only when Ferro came to him and showed him the pictures that he understood. We argued, he yelled at me to do it for my children. There it was again, that roaring in my ears, I pushed him and he was gone. Just gone. Like Órla." The whispering died away.

For what felt like an eternity, with the old man seemingly suspended in his memories, Avila heard only the slight rattling of breath from the armchair. Then Stuart returned from his thoughts.

"No, Cecil was not gone. Not like Órla. They found him, after all. How I had hoped that would be the end of it. But that Ferro didn't stop asking. That night at the club, Luana made her realise that I, not Cecil, owned the yacht at the time. She went straight to my William with it. He didn't understand what she was telling him. As soon as he and Kate came back from the golf club, he came to me and wanted to know what Ferro had been talking about. Should I have kept quiet then? Would that have stopped everything?" The old man sighed.

"Do you always know what is right and what is wrong, Comissário? I lied to my children for decades. It was no longer possible. I had to tell him. If he had heard it from strangers, it would have been even worse. So, I told him. Would you like to hear the story now?"

Avila and Vasconcellos nodded silently.

In a quiet but now firm voice, William Stuart began to narrate.

Madalena do Mar,
08.01.1950

W hat do you want to talk to me about? What could be
the reason for you to cut off your beautiful hair?"

"Can't you guess? As a mother, I have to be a role model
and fit into society for my child. Don't look so surprised. Yes,
you got it right. We are having a child." Triumphantly, she
threw her head back.

He felt cold, then hot again. What did Órla say?

"A child, impossible. Milly and I have been trying for
years and now you're claiming that after two months you'll be
having a child with me? I don't believe it!" He banged his fist
on the small wobbly table she used as a dining table and also
for kitchen work.

"Watch it, you'll break everything", she hissed at him as the
table made a distinct crackling sound of bursting wood.

"I'm ruining everything? That's you! We still have to talk
about that!" He stormed out of the hut, the rage rushing in his
ears so that he barely understood the words she shouted after
him.

"We'll talk about that too! Don't think that I'll put up with it
if you don't take care of us properly. I no longer want to live

by fattening pigs and selling them at the weekly market in Funchal. Those days are over now. I'm sure the fine Burke family won't like it if you have a bastard!" She slammed the door behind him.

The pigs in the fence were not bothered by all this, but continued to eat the kitchen scraps that Órla had thrown into their trough. Their smacking accompanied him as he ran up the winding path to the road. The climb was steep and he felt his anger slowly fade through exhaustion. His head cleared and he began to feel calmer. He could not lose his nerve now, but had to find a way to end it all. It couldn't be that Órla would destroy everything he had worked hard for over the last few years. He reached into his trouser pocket and pulled out his pocket watch. The only thing he had from his family. This pocket watch. His father had guarded it like the apple of his eye and solemnly presented it to him when he left for Madeira. His father. Did he want to live like him again? In poverty? Without any prospects? Perhaps even return to Wales? No, he would not trade the life old Burke had given him. Not for anything in the world. He looked at his watch. In two hours he would be at the ball at Reid's. By then he would have to know what to do.

As he made his way to Funchal, he passed Ribeira Brava. In the harbour basin, a few fishing boats bobbed up and down on the waves. In a few hours they would be off again in search of the scabbardfish that rose up in the dark.

His yacht, anchored here, stood out against the shimmering pink evening sky. This boat meant freedom for him. How many times had he talked to Milly about sailing to the Canaries, but she had always dissuaded him because he would be away for so long. The Canaries. An idea ripened in his head. This could be the salvation.

Three days later, he was at Órla's door late in the evening with a large bouquet of strelitzias.

When she opened the door for him with a searching look, he said:

"The colour of the flower reminded me of the gold of your hair. I hope our child will have hair like gold too." She smiled at him and took a step aside to let him in.

"Didn't you write me that you were on a sailing trip to the Canary Islands and wanted to plan the future with me afterwards in peace? What are you doing here again?"

"I have something to do." He fetched the large knife he had hidden in the bouquet and stabbed. The stab was precise, right in the heart.

Órla gasped briefly, then sank down, her eyes fixed on him in amazement. When it was over, he opened the door. Examining it, he looked around. But there was no one in the small secluded valley except him. And the pigs. He went back into the house and fetched the colourful blanket from her bed, the one that Órla spread over it during the day to make it look more homely. When he stepped back into the living room-kitchen, some blood had already flowed from the puncture mark, even though he had left the knife in it. He would still have to clean. Gently, he spread the blanket on the floor and laid Órla on it. How peaceful she looked. Why had she had to break everything? He forced himself not to think about the unborn child in her womb and wrapped her in the blanket. Then he carried her outside. Now came the worst part. Fortunately, Órla sometimes did the butchery of the pigs herself and behind the house in an offside of the small barn he found everything he needed.

He put on her heavy apron, took the knife and heaved the body into the large metal tub. He would dispose of the blanket at some point on the way to the Canaries, there had been a distinct bloodstain. For the next five hours he worked completely mechanically, barely noticing the ferrous smell of her blood. When he was finally ready and the pigs began to finish his work, a feeling of happiness almost welled up inside him. He would be able to go on living, with Milly. This life here would soon be gone, disappeared in the stomachs of these pink, bellowing masses.

As he walked down to the water where his yacht was bobbing on the waves in the sheltered bay, he knew he would make it. A faint pink streak appeared on the horizon. The sun slowly wiped the grey of the night from the sky with golden-red long fingers. The few clouds were bathed in a dark pink-golden light. A soft red glow like Órla's hair. It would be a beautiful crossing to the Canaries. And at home, Milly was waiting for him.

Garajau,
19.08.2013–15:11

He quietly opened the garden gate. No squeaking, the landlord seemed to keep things in good shape. No wonder, given his profession, he certainly had to be pretty meticulous.

Hesitantly, he looked towards the small house with the veranda. He wondered if she had already seen him. On the way here he had thought about what to do. The other two murders had been so simple, almost frighteningly easy. Had he had it in him all along? Like father like son?

His father had told him the whole story that evening. About Órla, the beautiful Irish woman who had bewitched him and finally threatened to destroy his life.

"It was the most natural thing in the world to kill her. I devised the plan in less than an hour before I went to Reid's for the ball that night with your Uncle Cecil and your mother. You, your brother and sister, you wouldn't exist if I hadn't acted then."

Strangely, he did not feel any disgust for his father's deed. It all seemed logical and consistent to him, too. In the same way, he had then decided that Teresa had to die. When he called her that night and asked her to meet him on the golf course–"in our place, you know, where we always met at night"–he had been completely calm.

He was sorry that he had to be here now. He had hoped that the killing would now come to an end. But after her call, he had had no choice. She was on to him, even though she might not know it yet. This was the only chance to save it yet. She was still home alone, he had to act now. No time to make a plan and come to rest before then. Like a madman, he had raced here from the quinta. He paced quietly through the small garden. The patio door was open.

"Fernando? Is that you? I wasn't expecting you back so soon. I think I've found something out. Why don't you go quickly to the kitchen and make us a galão? Then I'll tell you everything."

Quinta Pôr do Sol, 19.08.2013–15:18

E xhausted, the old man leaned back in his chair. Avila and Vasconcellos remained silent. They had to process what they had heard.

Avila was the first to find his language again.

"Senhor Stuart, then what exactly happened in the weeks after the crime? Did no one suspect you?"

"Oh yes, they did. I was the first one this inspector showed up for. What was his name then? Pinho? Or Pinheiro? I don't remember. He was like a little terrier. Got stuck on the idea that I had something to do with the murder. I didn't deny that Órla and I were having an affair. Half the island probably knew that." He stroked his eyes with a trembling hand. "Milly knew it too. And kept quiet. I'm sure you can't understand it, but my affair with Órla had brought Milly and me closer again. The Irish woman didn't understand, I would never have left my Milly for her."

"And when the police accused you of having something to do with the death?"

"Then all my friends and family testified that I had left for the Canary Islands two days before. The inspector could not refute that. I hid my sailing yacht well in plain sight for those two days. Until I had to go back to Órla to finish it."

"And in the process you were seen and the yacht was painted."

"If I had guessed that that damned picture of old Jorge's would show my yacht, surely I would have acted decades ago. Maybe Cecil would still be alive then."

"You killed Cecil Franco. What about Teresa Ferro and Hugo Duarte?"

"I'm not saying anything about that."

"Senhor Stuart, I beg you! We all know that you are not able to scale the high walls of the golf club. So, who was it? Which of your children did you use for the other murders?"

"I didn't mean to." The old man's voice was barely audible.

"Senhor Stuart? Where is Kate? Is she really shopping?"

"No, not Kate. Kate would never…" Ernesto's voice died away and he shook his head violently. Avila looked at him. Would he have been better off coming here with Baroso? Wasn't Ernesto too involved?

"It's not Kate. She's completely innocent." The voice had become louder again.

"Then talk! Or shall I rather just tell you which of your children has the greatest interest in ensuring that there is no scandal? Where is William?"

"He's not here."

"Where is he?"

"You can't imagine what it's like to have children. They are my everything. Milly and I had not even dared to hope that we would have children. How could you understand what it's like?"

"Whether you want to believe me or not, Senhor Stuart, I know what it is like to want children. I am also about to become a father and we were no longer expecting it either.

But that does not mean under any circumstances that I would murder for my child or let my child murder for me."

"You're going to be a father? Your wife is pregnant?" The old man's voice was again little more than a whisper. "This is not good. It's going to happen again. Why didn't William say so? He must know, surely?"

"What is not good? What is he repeating?" A slight vibration, as if a crack opened up and slowly the glowing lava rose.

"I shouldn't have let William…" Now the voice died away. Was the old man crying?

"Senhor Stuart. What is all this about your son? Where can we find him?"

"Your wife shouldn't have interfered…" That's all Avila needed to hear, he stormed out of the room, closely followed by Vasconcellos. The volcano erupted.

12.01.1950,
early in the morning

There it was again, the yacht he had seen a few days ago. What luck that they had found it here in this little bay. Apparently its owner had decided not to sail to the Canary Islands after all. He wondered if this whole sailing trip was just an alibi to have some undisturbed fun with his mistress in this hidden bay. It was still quite dark and the sun would surely need a good hour before it bathed the rocks in red. He was too far away to see anything.

This morning he was out with Jorge and his secretary even earlier than a few days ago. Yesterday at noon he had had a long discussion with Cat about it.

"Do you have to go back to painting on our last day together?"

"You won't even notice that I've been away. I'll get up while you're still asleep and be back for breakfast, I promise. Then we still have half a day before I have to go back to London."

"Shouldn't we accompany you home after all? How does it look when the future prime minister comes back from holiday alone?"

"It looks like he has an emancipated wife. Besides, we don't know yet whether I'll win the election next year. Let's wait and see if the British turn back to my party." He stroked her arm tenderly.

"I know it. Who else would they want as prime minister for this time? It's not good that you're doing so much again. A little more rest would have done you good. Especially after last year."

"I'm doing splendidly! Didn't you think I led you around the dance floor like a young god a few days ago?"

"Young god with lead on his feet maybe. My toes are still green and blue."

"Maybe you should dance with Bill Deakin next time then. He's certainly a more gifted dancer than I am."

"Any man is more gifted than you, pig." She laughed.

"We will have a lot of time together, I promise you. And I'm sure we'll come back to this island again. There are still a lot of things I would like to paint."

Cat laughed.

"I already understand. Then, for God's sake, go paint in the morning. But you better be there for breakfast."

"I promise. Since you're worried that I'm not getting enough rest: How about a restful nap before we get back into the fun? What do I actually have to learn tonight? Archery? Basket weaving? Or have you hired a tango instructor for me?"

Cat acknowledged him with laughter again.

"No, tonight is just going to be a leisurely dinner and then we'll see what else the evening brings."

"Wonderful. But a little sleep can't hurt now anyway. If you please, my lady?" He jokingly held out his arm to lead her into the bedroom.

Last night, himself, Cat andDiana his secretary had ended the evening quite comfortably with a game of bridge in the salon. But if he was honest, being out here now and slowly watching the day approach while looking across the Atlantic was more his world. It was too bad he couldn't experience this with Cat.

He pulled out his pocket watch. He had almost four hours left before they had to leave for breakfast at Reid's.

"Jorge, do you think we can get a little closer? I'd like to do another sketch of the yacht. Maybe I'll have time to make a painting of it in London."

"I can try to go down that dirt road over there a bit more. But it is very narrow and slopes very steeply to the left. I'm afraid we'll only be able to drive a little further and then have to continue on foot so you can get a better view, sir."

"Then we will do that."

Carefully, Jorge steered the car down the dirt road. The old man had to laugh inwardly when he saw the tense face of his secretary, who was trying hard not to look down into the abyss on the left. About fifty metres further on, the car came to a halt in a small bulge.

"This is as far as we can go. I suggest I carefully turn the car around once you two have gotten out. Then I'll show you the spot I have in mind for you, sir."

Another ten minutes later, they were only about thirty metres away from the yacht. The rising sun sent delicate harbingers; the horizon slowly turned pink.

"The place is perfect, Jorge. From here I might even be able to recognise the name of the yacht later. They all seem to still be sleeping on board. Too bad, I would have liked to see our red-haired beauty up close." He sat down and began to sketch the yacht. He already had a suitable name for the picture in mind, it was to be called "The Last Morning".

Santo Antônio,
19.08.2013–15:34

Answer the fucking phone!" Avila shouted into the receiver as if by doing so he could get Leticia to pick up the phone. But only the steady toot sounded. No Leticia, nothing.

"Fernando, we will make it. Baroso is also on his way with the Segurança Pública. Everything will be fine. Leticia probably just won't answer the phone because she's upstairs in the bedroom."

"I don't think so. Something happened. I know it."

"Is there anyone even closer than Baroso you can call?" Vasconcellos' voice came through faintly. There was a rush in Avila's ears, a heavy stone in his stomach.

"Carlos has no phone and our neighbours are out of town. I've already tried everything."

Vasconcellos sped along the VR1 motorway towards Garajau. The screeching sounds of the siren stabbed like knives into Avila's temples. Everything blurred before his eyes, he could only think of Leticia and what William Stuart might do to her.

They were not moving fast enough. At this time of day, rush hour traffic was starting to arrive and many tourists had decided to spend the afternoon in Funchal. The road was full. Vasconcellos did his best and drove using one risky overtaking manoeuvre after another. But in the almost one-kilometre-long Marmeleiros tunnel, the time had come: they were at a standstill. No way to push past the tinny avalanche in front of them. Vasconcellos sounded the siren.

"*Porra*! Why can't those idiots in front of us form an alley! You've got to be kidding!" Avila put his hand on the door handle.

"What are you going to do?"

"If need be, I'll push that one off the road!"

"It's no use, Fernando! Stay in the car!"

Vasconcellos sounded the horn. Finally, the metallic mass in front of them started to move and an alley formed. As fast as he could, the Subcomissário drove between the cars. They could see the cause of the traffic jam at the end of the tunnel: the roadway was being renewed and the left lane was completely closed before the next tunnel, which passed underneath Quinta da Palmeira. Without further ado, Vasconcellos drove all the way to the right. In doing so, he had to balance with his right wheel on the slightly raised, narrow footbridge, which acted as another obstacle to the balustrade in front of the abyss of the valley.

"Watch out, there's a lamppost up ahead, it won't be enough of a gap!" Avila narrowed his eyes in anticipation of the collision.

Vasconcellos managed to manoeuvre the car alongside the lamppost, but in the process he touched the grazed it, which was acknowledged this with a piercing squeal. The sound seemed to have an even more violent effect on the cars in front of them than the wailing of the siren. They all now made an effort to drive as close as possible to the closed lane to let them pass. Shortly after, the road became two lanes again and they could continue their wild ride towards Garajau.

About ten minutes later, Vasconcellos took the exit to Garajau with squealing tyres. In front of them, right on the bridge, a Segurança Pública car appeared, also with a siren on its roof.

"Damn, that must be Baroso. We have to turn off the sirens so Stuart doesn't hear us coming!"

Fortunately, the car in front of them seemed to have had the same idea: as if due to an invisible sign, both sirens fell silent. They drove into the centre of the village and Vasconcellos turned sharply behind the patrol car into the gate to Avila's residential street. A few metres further on, both cars stopped and the occupants of the patrol car jumped out. As expected, it was Baroso accompanied by three policemen. They were wearing protective clothing and were armed. Baroso was also wearing a bulletproof vest. Avila and Vasconcellos wasted no time in putting on body armour and ran to the small group. Baroso looked at them tensely.

"Chefe, I'm sorry, I couldn't go any faster. What happens now?"

Again Avila felt the blood rushing in his ears. A plan, a fucking plan had to be made now. He tried to think, but the fear of what was happening to Leticia in there paralysed his brain.

Vasconcellos stepped forward.

"I have an idea. Fernando and I will go first, we'll use the entrance via the terrace. Isn't that the way you usually go?"

Avila nodded silently.

"Good. We should be very quiet, but try to look completely relaxed, not like we're on a mission. No guns drawn. If we're seen from the house, make it look like you've taken your

Subcomissário out for a beer after work. If we're lucky, William won't be there yet and we won't scare Leticia unnecessarily. You, Baroso, and fellas: you gain entry through the front door when I give you the signal or if we're not out of the house in the next five minutes. Fernando, please give them your key." Wordlessly, Avila took his key out of his pocket and gave it to Baroso.

The latter looked at Vasconcellos, completely unsettled.

"Is it right for you to go in there like that without protective waistcoats? At the police academy we were told…"

"Filipe, no discussions, please! We can't take any notice of that now! Fernando and I act at our own risk. You behave according to the rules, all right?"

The three patrolmen nodded silently and disappeared with a reluctant Baroso towards the small alley that led to the front entrance of the house. Quietly, Avila opened the garden gate. Where was Urso? Normally the retriever would have greeted him with a joyful yelp. Now it was clear that something was wrong in the house.

"No dog", Avila whispered and drew his Beretta; Vasconcellos, without hesitation, did the same. They ducked behind the large hibiscus that the previous owner had planted many years ago and that screened half the terrace from the rest of the garden. How often had Avila scolded the hibiscus and wanted to cut it down because it blocked the view into the garden. Now he was grateful for the shrub, which was over a man's height and offered shelter with its dense foliage and many red flowers. Straining, he and Vasconcellos tried to make out something inside the house.

"I think I can see Leticia sitting on the sofa. Someone is sitting next to her." Ernesto's eyes were clearly sharper. Avila could see nothing through the reflection of the living room windows.

"Do you see Stuart?"

"There's someone else in the chair opposite. That could be Stuart."

"We're going in. Take aim at the person on the armchair." Avila knew Vasconcellos was a much better shot than he was. He would try to take out the person next to Leticia, whose back was turned to them, if need be. They began to move in.

"Police, nobody move! Hands up!" Avila heard Urso yelp, no sound came from the people in the living room.

Garajau,
19.08.2013–15:55

With weapons drawn, Avila and Vasconcellos stood in the living room and looked into three frightened faces that turned towards them.

Avila resisted the impulse to take Leticia in his arms and take her away. With clenched teeth, he eyed the scene and tried to perceive every detail.

Vasconcellos had seen correctly. Leticia had been sitting on the sofa. The man next to her was Carlos, who looked tense but calm. On the armchair opposite the sofa sat William Stuart, who made no effort to move. Crouched in front of him was Urso, who gave a regular, rumbling growl and did not take his eyes off the intruder. The retriever blocked the man's access to a pistol in the armchair, which lay at Leticia's feet in front of the sofa. On closer inspection, Avila noticed that Stuart was bleeding from a wound on his right hand. Was this the work of Urso's sharp teeth or the large kitchen knife that lay prominently on the street sweeper's lap?

"Fernando, it's all right. You don't need the gun anymore. Nothing happened to us."

Vasconcellos bent down and picked up the pistol with a handkerchief.

"Is that your gun, William?"

Stuart just nodded and buried his face in his hands.

Vasconcellos took a pair of handcuffs out of his back trouser pocket and put them on the politician. In doing so, he refrained from twisting his hands behind his back, but left him sitting in his position on the armchair. It was clear to all present that there was no longer any danger from the broken figure.

"I'll just let Baroso and the others know." Vasconcellos walked down the hall and opened the front door.

A short time later he came back into the living room with Baroso. In the meantime, Avila had put his gun away and pulled up a chair so that he had a good view of William, but also of the surprisingly calm Leticia.

Again, it was Vasconcellos who turned to William Stuart.

"William. I'd like to take a moment to advise you of your rights. Anything that…"

"I already know Ernesto, don't bother", the other interrupted him. "It's over. I was just about to tell Leticia and the senhor here everything."

"William, I think we should wait until we get to the Bureau and you have a lawyer."

"Please, Ernesto, I want to talk." Vasconcellos looked questioningly at his boss. Avila nodded slowly. William Stuart took a deep breath and began to talk.

Funchal, Golf Club,
09.08.2013–19:53

N ow that Cecil Franco is dead, there is only one man who can tell me about this yacht."

"I don't want you to talk to my father, Teresa! He's not doing very well and the death of his old friend Cecil has taken a lot out of him."

"Oh, has it? Don't tell me anything more. They haven't spoken to each other for years. Why should it affect him now?"

"You don't understand. The two of them used to be very close friends. Them and my mother were inseparable in the fifties."

"That's exactly why I want to talk to your father. I'm sure he can tell me who the red-haired woman on Senhor Cecil's yacht was. I need all the background information for the exhibition. You must understand that. If we don't get a good price for the painting, I will have to close the shop. And then your shares would be gone too, William!"

"Let bygones be bygones, Teresa! That's my last word!" He turned and stomped angrily across the putting range back into the hall.

The whole evening he had watched her full of anxiety. But at some point he had become calmer because Teresa was getting more and more drunk and hardly talking to anyone. Apart from her heated argument with Palmeiro, which was going on at the next table.

When Kate became restless shortly after midnight and asked him to go home to check on the old man, he had immediately agreed. Out of the corner of his eye, he had seen Teresa heading towards the wine cellar with the barman, this Otavio. He could imagine what the two of them would do down there. It wasn't the first time Teresa had used the cellar for a little tryst. Two years ago, he had also been too happy to follow her down into the cool vault. But those days were over. What had he seen in her? As soon as the elections were over, he should see to it that he also said goodbye to his shares in the gallery. Then the chapter of Teresa Ferro would finally be closed for him. He helped Kate into her coat and pushed her towards the car. Thank God the evening was over. As soon as possible, however, he had to talk to his father and prepare him for the possibility that Teresa Ferro might contact him. When she was sober again, she would surely try to talk to him about this yacht.

As his car creaked its way up to the entrance of Quinta Pôr do Sol, his mobile phone rang. A quick glance, it was Teresa. Was she not going to give him a break?

"Kate, you go on to father, I'll take the call for a moment."

Fortunately, Kate was too worried about her father to waste any thought on who was calling him so late. She was swallowed up by the large double doors of the quinta.

"Teresa, what more do you want?"

"I spoke with Dona Luana. She told me something very interesting." Her voice was a little washed out by the alcohol, but clearly understandable.

"And that something can't wait until tomorrow?"

"Dona Luana told me that the owner of the yacht was not Cecil Franco at all at the time Churchill painted the picture."

"Oh no?" An uneasiness rose in him. What was she talking about?

"The yacht belonged to your father. Dona Luana was very sure that your father sold the yacht to Senhor Cecil much later. And I also know that the red-haired woman on the yacht was an Irish woman named Órla."

"If you want to tell me that my father cheated on my mother with that redhead, it's nothing new to me. My father confessed it to us years ago. My mother also knew about it."

"Do you also know that the Irish woman has been missing for decades? And Senhor Cecil and your father have both been questioned by the police?"

She interpreted his silence correctly.

"Hah, so you don't know that. Dona Luana also told me that your father quickly moved out of the police's focus because he wasn't in Madeira at the time. He was on his way to the Canary Islands with his yacht."

He darkly remembered that his mother had told him about this solo venture of his father's. That must have been in the fifties.

"But you know what's funny? The sketch where Churchill also shows the name of the yacht has a title."

"I don't know what's funny about that."

"It's 'The Last Morning'."

"So, what's that supposed to tell me?"

"It tells you that your father's yacht was in Madeira on the 12th of January 1950. And not on its way to the Canary Islands, as he had led the whole world to believe." She groaned audibly. The woman really had had too much to drink. What had he felt for her once? Now she only disgusted him.

"What's the big deal?"

"Normally nothing. But if that was his alibi at the time of Órla's disappearance, quite a lot."

William went cold. His father? That couldn't be. Teresa had to be mistaken. Feverishly he thought about what he could do. He had to talk to his father first. If there was any truth to Teresa's story, it was all over. A presidente with a murderer for a father, that would not be possible.

"Teresa. I have to talk to my father about it first to be sure. You understand that, don't you?"

"Do that, but I'll move the exhibition tomorrow morning and announce a sensational unveiling. You'll see, my gallery will be famous all over Portugal, maybe even the world!" She hung up.

William went into the old man's room where he found Kate.

"Kate, you go to bed, I'll sit with father for a bit and keep him company. You've done enough today." He closed the door behind her and sat down.

An hour later he knew everything and had made his plan. He opened the windows of the room leaving them ajar and left his father alone. The old man knew what his son was doing now and would spend half the night talking to an empty chair next to his own armchair. That way Kate, sleeping in the neighbouring wing, would have the impression that the two men had stayed together all night. The best alibi they could have come up with in a hurry.

A reach for the phone.

"Teresa? I've spoken to my father. He wants to clear the air. You and I should talk right away and figure out how to get it out to the press. So that it's as good as possible for your gallery and will also treat my father with dignity."

She seemed a little taken aback by his change of heart. But she did not become suspicious when he suggested that she meet him secretly down by the lake around two o'clock. On the contrary, it seemed more like she was still hoping for an amorous adventure with him in her befuddled state.

Before going outside, he took off his suit and put on dark jeans and a blue hooded jacket. In the protection of the hood, it would be difficult to see his face in the cameras that had been set up everywhere in Madeira by now. On his way out, he grabbed one of his golf clubs from the golf bag next to the front door. Outside the gate to the driveway was, as always, their gardener Nuno's old Mercedes, which he and his siblings had used for nighttime joyrides for as long as he could remember. As always, old Nuno had hidden the key under the doormat on the driver's side. The gardener knew about the Stuart children's use of his car and had tolerated it quietly all these years. In return, the siblings always made sure that the car was filled up with petrol and were generous with donations for upcoming repairs.

Shortly before two, he stood in front of the transformer house that they had so often used as an entrance to the golf course for their nightly golf games. He looked around scrutinisingly: the small street was deserted. With a quick pull-up, he hoisted himself onto the roof of the house. Carefully, he felt under the bougainvillea for the package with the canvas and the rope. He would not need the rope today. He draped the canvas onto the glass shards and swung himself onto the wall. The chill of the stone crept up inside him, displacing the sultriness of the night. His thoughts became clear. Usually, Kate or Teresa went first because they were the lightest. They then threw the rope to the following men, which they would have had tied to a thicker branch fork beforehand. This time he had to make the short jump to the overhanging branch of the old jacaranda tree. Hopefully it would hold his weight under the swing. The branch groaned briefly as he caught it with his two hands in a leap, but it held. Slowly he let himself slide down from it onto the grass, damp from the night. As he walked towards the lake under the cover of darkness, he could already see her: her hair illuminated by the moonlight. Was it a coincidence that her hair was also reddish, just like that of the Irish woman who had started it all? Quietly, he crept up behind her. He didn't want to waste time or talk to her. What had to be done, he had to do quickly, without hesitation. Like his father. Teresa was having difficulty standing up straight, she swayed, but continued to stand with her back turned to him. She was even drunker than a few hours before. It would not be difficult. Just a few more metres and he was there.

A withered branch cracked under his feet, broken from one of the large dragon trees that grew around the lake. Before Teresa could turn around, he knocked her down with a blow from the golf club he had brought with him. She fell lengthwise like a felled tree. As he knelt beside her to finish it, he smelled the salty, smoky scent of rum emanating from Teresa's body. He pushed her to the ground, her head in the pond. Her body twitched a few more times, then it was over.

Again, he looked around. It was quiet and dark. Only the cracking, rustling sound that the hard dragon tree leaves made when they were moved by the wind from the Atlantic could be heard. Next to Teresa's dead body lay her handbag, which had been cracked open by the fall and the contents of which had spilled out onto the stretch of gravel in front of the lake. Illuminated by the pale moonlight, he quickly found what he was looking for: the photo of the sketch with the yacht and her keys. He couldn't lose any time, the work wasn't done yet. Just as quietly as he had come, he disappeared again across the spot on the wall. Now he had to get to the gallery first and foremost and remove the other traces. After that, he would pay another visit to Teresa's flat, although he was convinced there wouldn't be much there. Teresa had always done all her business at the gallery. A "clean separation of private life and business", as she called it, had always been important to her.

He got into the old Mercedes he had parked a few streets away and set off in the direction of the gallery. His hands on the steering wheel, covered with an old leather cover, were sticky with sweat. He was nervous. In a moment it would be decided whether Teresa had died in vain or whether he could remove the traces left in the gallery. He stopped a few side streets away. Here, too, all was quiet, no one was on the street. His hands shook slightly as he slid the key into the lock. With a soft click, the door opened. In the darkness, the red warning light of the alarm system glowed. There was no turning back now, he typed: 04111977. A barely audible metallic clack and the alarm system was deactivated. Teresa had not disappointed him, the code was still her date of birth. The rest was now a piece of cake. He walked through the exhibition and let his torch roam over the paintings. There it was. The damn picture with the red-haired slut and next to it the sketch with the yacht. Should he take both pictures? No, better just the little sketch. The painting was, after all, the main attraction of the exhibition and it disappearing would mean too much attention. With any luck, the absence of the small sketch would not be noticed so quickly, let alone be linked to Teresa's murder. He tucked the sketch under his jacket, activated the alarm system again and carefully locked the door behind him.

His drive to Teresa's house up in Monte also went smoothly. Mechanically and emotionlessly, he searched cupboards, drawers and pockets. Even her favourite hiding place in the kitchen on the top shelf of the kitchen cupboard in the old flour tin contained only some cash and jewellery, nothing else. He had not expected it any other way. After all, she had only understood the actual context that evening at the golf club and had not had a chance to record her conclusion. The only clues that could lead to the Stuarts were now in his possession.

Less than an hour later he was sitting with his father again, listening to a story about how Cecil Franco and his old man had hunted hares on the Paul de Serra.

Garajau,
19.08.2013–16:35

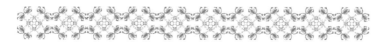

B ut what about Hugo? Why did you kill poor Hugo?"
Leticia, like all the others, had listened spellbound to
William Stuart's story.

"He tried to blackmail me. I had forgotten that Teresa
always kept these notebooks. In them, every exhibition, every
appointment, simply everything to do with the gallery was
carefully planned and described. In them she had mentioned
the little sketch with the yacht that I had stolen from the
gallery. I should simply have searched more thoroughly that
night. But I only thought about the sketch."

"And Hugo found these notebooks?"

"He called me three days ago and only hinted at it. That he
knew everything and we should talk 'man to man'. Luckily I
was able to put him off until the next day, so I could take my
time and figure out how to make it happen." William's voice
sounded completely calm; Leticia found it hard to recognise
the brother of her friend Kate in it, Kate whom she had
always cherished. What would have happened if he had been
so cold towards her too and she and Carlos had not been able
to persuade him to give up?

William continued emotionlessly.

"I got my father's old Beretta from the gun cabinet. But then my worry was that it might be too loud because I didn't have a silencer. So, I looked on the internet to see how I could stab a person. Hugo is not particularly athletic and I knew that I was far superior to him physically. Fortunately, it didn't have to come to that. I hid in the gallery a few hours before our meeting and waited for him. Then, just before half past nine, he appeared. He sat down in the kitchen with a bica and Teresa's notebooks and waited. Hugo couldn't have known that I was already there. I crept up quietly and stabbed him right in the heart from behind. He didn't even groan. He just collapsed. Afterwards I took the notebook in which Teresa had mentioned the second picture. I set the alarm again. I turned the sign on the gallery door to 'Fechado' and locked the door again behind me. I was so relieved when I pulled the door shut behind me. It was over. Until you called, Leticia, and wanted to talk to Kate about Cecil Franco's yacht. That's when I knew you were on to me."

"I knew it!" Avila looked angrily at Leticia. "Why didn't you tell me, and why did you have to interfere? Do you have any idea how scared I was for you?"

"For once in your life, if you charged your phone properly, I would have called you too." Leticia knew it was unfair to blame Fernando like that. But why did he have to bark at her like that in front of everyone now that everything had gone well?

"We'll talk about that later", he growled.

"I just jumped in my car and raced here. Without a plan. The Beretta was still in the glove compartment. When I got here, though, I realised it wasn't going to go the way it did with Teresa and Hugo. Leticia heard me coming through the garden."

"I thought you'd be home early, Fernando. But Urso started growling. That's when I knew something was wrong. Suddenly William was standing in front of me with his gun drawn. First Urso bit his hand, then he stood in front of me growling and barking." She proudly patted the retriever's head, who enthusiastically began licking her hand.

"Your dog was making such a racket that I heard it when I walked past your house", Carlos now interjected. "I took out the spare key you had given me and quietly came through the front door. That's when I saw him", he pointed to William slumped in his armchair, "and I armed myself."

"Suddenly Carlos was standing in the doorway with your favourite knife in his hand. You should have seen that. He almost scared even me." Leticia actually managed a smile.

William hung his head again.

"I just couldn't do it. Shooting everyone, what good would that have done? I would never have gotten that image of Leticia with the child in her belly out of my head. History would have repeated itself. I just couldn't take it anymore. It's good that it's over, Comissário. It should never have come to this."

"William put the gun on the floor and sat down in the armchair. Just as he was about to start telling us everything, you came. The baby and I knew you couldn't be far, Fernando." Tenderly, Leticia looked at him, then slowly stroked her belly.

Avila would have loved to take them both in his arms and not let them go for the next few hours. But duty called.

"Senhor Stuart, we will now take you to the presidency. There, Subcomissário Vasconcellos will take your statement."

"Fernando, I suggest Baroso and I go back with William. You should stay here for a moment and look after Leticia."

Avila was just about to drop into the seat next to Leticia, which the prudent Carlos had cleared for him, when Urso claimed it for himself with a leap and laid his head in Leticia's lap. Briefly, Avila considered chasing his dog away. Then he just patted his head and pulled the armchair, where William Stuart had been sitting a moment before, to the sofa.

"See you in an hour at the presidium, thank you Ernesto."

Garajau,
21.08.2013–19:41

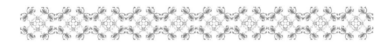

The steady scrubbing of Carlos' broom across the path was only accentuated by the damp slapping of the waves breaking on the cliffs down on the beach.

"Come on over here, old friend, and sit with me."

"Let me sweep up the last of Senhora Schmitz's grains. At noon today I was already watching the fat rats feasting on them. And now the old lady can't see me. She will think her beloved birds have cleaned everything away."

"But tomorrow morning she will feed them again."

"And I will sweep the leftovers away again tomorrow afternoon. That's how it goes now, day after day, a cycle of life." The bin rattled as Carlos opened the lid to throw the grains in. Urso had been watching the whole process with his head tilted and was now whimpering softly.

"You didn't just take away the rats' dessert." Avila searched in his trouser pocket for a dog biscuit. Immediately the retriever's fluffy tail thumped the ground in joyful anticipation. "Come here, Urso. You've more than earned this one." Urso inhaled the small cake with one bite and looked expectantly for another. "That'll have to do for now, glutton. We don't want you to end up with a belly like your mistress."

Finally, Carlos dropped down on the bench next to Avila and looked with him past Christo Rei into the evening sky.

"How is Leticia? Did she take the scare well?"

"She's doing very well. Apart from the fact that she's terribly bored and keeps me on my toes with all kinds of requests."

"Don't think that will change much when there are three of you."

Avila sighed.

"Sometimes I don't know what to wish for. That the wait is finally over or to be able to enjoy the time as a couple for as long as possible."

"You'll see, your balloon will go up into the sky and you'll be a wonderful little family."

"I hope so too."

"Speaking of family. Do you know how Kate and Colin took the whole story? It must have come as a shock to them that their father and brother are murderers."

"I met Colin Stuart yesterday when he accompanied the family's lawyer. He seemed very calm and collected to me. But Kate…"

"What about her?"

"She has completely collapsed. Dona Luana is taking care of her."

"I'm sure the old lady will guard her like Cerberus."

"You can say that again. Ernesto has tried to reach Kate several times, but has always failed because of Dona Luana. She has taken up residence at the Quinta Pôr do Sol to look after Kate."

"But Dona Luana only means well. Did you know she was one of Millicent Stuart's closest friends? I think Kate is in

310

good hands with her. Do you think Kate and Ernesto's relationship will survive the trial and what comes after?"

"It's hard to say. But if you ask me, I'd say 'no'. If their relationship was still intact, Kate would have holed up with Ernesto and not shut him out."

"Anything to do with the police is probably now 'the enemy' for them."

"Yes, that's how I see it too. It's going to be another hard time for the family. Old Stuart is under house arrest at the Quinta and William is on remand here in Funchal until the trial. The Stuarts have appointed several lawyers and I expect this trial to be a spectacle the likes of which Madeira has never seen."

"The newspapers are already full of them. Why do I only see your boss's portrait and not yours on the front pages?"

"Just leave me alone when it comes tothe reporters. I'm glad that the wolf likes being in the public eye so much. Ernesto and I can do our work in peace. But fortunately, this one is also almost over. Apart from our statements in court, the case is closed for us. We even managed to get all of old Jorge's property back. Stuart had hidden the sketch in the quinta. We finally found the photo with the dedication in the notebook from Teresa Ferro that Stuart had also taken to the quinta. I sent Baroso and Vasconcellos to return their treasures to the old people. That way Baroso also got to see the nicer sides of our profession."

"So, how do you see it, what ultimately caused the volcano to erupt?"

"Ambition and vanity. Old Stuart did not want to lose the privileges he had created for himself by marrying into the Burke family. No one would have accepted a pregnant mistress. He would have been chased from Madeira in disgrace. Young Stuart was worried about his political career.

With a murderer for a father, he would never have become Presidente."

"That's one way of looking at it."

"What's your opinion then?"

"Maybe I'm looking at it too humanely, but what if Engenheiro William really loved his Millicent and was afraid of losing her? From what I've heard, the world collapsed for him after her death. His children were his everything after that. To protect them, he also killed his old friend Cecil Franco. And his son wanted to protect his father's legacy and his siblings from the truth that their father was a murderer. Then the volcano would have erupted for the love of family."

"Love of family? I would do almost anything to protect Leticia and our child. But murder? ... Still, there's something to it I guess, in the end it was about family. I'm glad the case is over."

"We should have another poncha to that at the Bar Rodriguez down in Caniço de Baixo, what do you think?"

"I'd rather we drink our poncha here in Garajau. If there is something going on with Leticia, I want to be with her as soon as possible."

"I guess we'll have to get used to that now, old friend." Carlos got up and grabbed the broom and the dustbin. The two of them made the strenuous walk back up to the centre of Garajau.

"Hearing you huff next to me like that, it doesn't fit at all with the image I've been given of you over the last few days." Carlos grinned.

"I don't understand? What do you mean?"

"I'm told you've gone and become one among the climbing artists. That there is still a slight need for improvement in descending trees is, in my opinion, a slight exaggeration."

312

"Say no more. That Celia? You know her too? Then it's only a matter of time before Leticia finds out about my appearance and mishap at the golf club." Avila laughed and noticed how he and Leticia's balloon was headed for the sky.

Portuguese terms, food and drink

Here is a brief overview of the terms, foods and drinks that appear in the book:

Açorda–Portuguese bread soup consisting of bread pieces, garlic, poached egg, savory and olive oil.

Avó–Portuguese for "grandmother".

Bacalhau–stockfish, often prepared as an oven dish with potatoes and cream sauce.

Bica–Portuguese variant of espresso, literally means "spout". But it is also a play on words: Beba Isto Com Açúcar (Drink this with sugar).

Brigada de homicídios–Homicide Squad.

Bual–slightly less sweet version of Madeira Wine, also suitable as a dessert wine.

Caramba–Portuguese for "Damn".

Carne vinho e alhos–pork marinated with garlic, vinegar, savory in white wine, which is fried for dinner and often served with potatoes.

Coral–Portuguese beer.

Cornetto com queijo–Portuguese croissant with cheese.

Desculpem-me–Portuguese for "excuse me".

Engenheiro–Portuguese for the title "engineer". Sometimes used in the form of a polite form of address "Senhor Engenheiro".

Espada preta / Espada com banana–black scabbardfish, often served as fillet with banana.

Espetada de Luoro–Beef in pieces, traditionally grilled on a laurel spit over an open fire.

Fechado–Portuguese for "Closed".

Galão–Portuguese latte, often served in glass cups with handles.

Graças a Deus!–Portuguese for "Thank God".

Jardim Botanico do Monte–Monte Botanical Garden.

Lapas–seasnails fried with olive oil, garlic and lemon juice.

Malmsey/Malwasia–sweet variant of Madeira Wine, the classic dessert wine.

Meu amor–Portuguese for "my love".

Merda–Portuguese for "crap".

Milho frito–fried corn cubes, classic side dish in Madeira.

Oh, meu Deus!–Portuguese for "Oh my God!".

Polícia Judiciária–Portuguese for Judicial Police.

Poncha–Drink made from sugar cane brandy, lemon juice and warm honey.

Porra–Portuguese for "shit".

Que piranha–Portuguese for "Such a bitch".

Segurança Pública–Protection Police.

Sercial–dry variant of Madeira Wine with pronounced acidity, suitable as an aperitif.

Tarte de requeijão–Portuguese small cheesecakes.

Unidade de Informação Financeira–central reporting office for money laundering matters.

Verdejo–semi-dry version of Madeira wine with a delicate bitter aftertaste, suitable as an aperitif.

Recipes

Anas madeiran Açorda

A ctually a soup for winter, but Avila can eat it at any time of the year.

Ingredients:

400 g hard bread
1 bunch savory
Garlic
Olive oil
Salt
Eggs

Preparation:

Break the hard bread into large pieces and place in a soup bowl.

Then sprinkle with the finely chopped garlic, savory and salt.

Poach four eggs and bring about 2 litres of water to the boil.

Pour the boiling water into the soup bowl and stir gently. Then carefully add the poached eggs, leave to infuse for a while with the lid closed and serve.

Variant:

Sometimes Ana takes pity and puts bacalhau in water the day before. The next day, the stockfish is cooked in boiling water for about 5 minutes and added to the soup with the eggs at the end. This is no longer typically Madeiran, but for a mainland Portuguese person like Avila it is a feast.

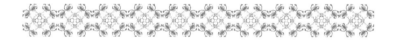

Milho frito

This is the variant of polenta that is cut into cubes and deep-fried as a side dish.

Ingredients:

500 g light maize flour
approx. 1.5 L water
approx. 80 g butter
Herbs (parsley, thyme) and garlic for seasoning according to taste
some cabbage cut into very fine strips

Preparation:

Heat the water with the salt in a large pot. Then slowly stir in the cornflour, preferably in one direction, then there will be fewer lumps. Add the cabbage. It should still be soft. Slowly thicken the porridge over a low heat, stirring constantly. Add the herbs and butter and stir in.

Then place the corn flour on a baking tray lined with baking paper and roll out to about 1.5 to 2 cm. Then chill.

The next day, the mixture can be cut into cubes and deep-fried.

If you don't have a deep fryer at hand, you can also spread the cubed mass on a baking tray, brush it thickly with oil and then put it in the oven at 180–200 degrees. It then takes about 40–50 min, and you should turn the cubes over in between.

Afterword

In writing this book, I was once again inspired by real events.

Winston Churchill actually visited Madeira in 1950 with his wife Clementine and daughter Diana. He had brought his literary secretary Bill Deakin to the island to write his war memoirs with him. Originally, the small party was scheduled to leave together on the 16th of January. However, due to the upcoming British election on the 23rd of January, Churchill decided to leave the island as early as the 12th January. The election in 1950 was the foundation stone for him to become Prime Minister again in 1951. The famous photograph showing Churchill in his coat, hat and parasol painting in Câmara de Lobos inspired my invented anecdote about the mysterious woman on the yacht. The dancing lessons on the terrace of Reid's are historically documented, but unfortunately, I can't say how Churchill fared. At the bar of the legendary Reid's there is said to have been a barman called Fred at that time. However, I do not know whether he had a brother.

In 2013, Madeira held a regional election that marked the start of a political change after many decades in the autonomous republic. I chose this important time of change on the island for the events surrounding the launch of the new crime series about Fernando Avila, his Leticia and Ernesto Vasconcellos, as it fitted so well with the changes now facing Avila and his wife.

The "Rali Vinho da Madeira" has actually been held every summer in Madeira since 1959 and is part of the "European Rally Championship" and since 2005 also of the "Intercontinental Rally Challenge". In 2013, it took place from the 2nd to the 4th of August.

All other events and persons in this book are purely from my imagination. Similarities to living and deceased persons are purely coincidental.

Once again, many people supported me in writing this crime novel. If I have made any mistakes in this crime novel, they are my responsibility.

One or the other bar that Avila visits with his friend Carlos in Garajau and the surrounding area can indeed be found. The same goes for Nelson and his wife's restaurant above Garajau and Caniço. All these places are definitely worth a culinary detour. If, after reading the book, you feel the need to learn more about these places, a recipe or two, or a travel tip, visit my website and blog: http://www.joycesummer.com.

You are also welcome to subscribe to my newsletter to be informed directly about news, new publications and promotions: http://www.joycesummer.de/newsletter-abonnieren/

Acknowledgements

O nce again, many great people have supported me with this book, without whom it would not be possible for you to be holding it in your hands today.

I would like to send a big thank you to my wonderful test readers Ute, Kathrin, Volker and Hatho. I wouldn't want to miss your comments and sharp eye!

I would especially like to thank Dirk for his daily support, encouragement and intensive examination of what I have written. Thank you for walking this path with me.

I would also like to express my gratitude to the staff of 'madeira-reisetipps.com' for providing me with additional information on the Rali Vinho da Madeira and thus making Avila's excursion into the world of fast cars a bit more realistic.

Another thanks goes to Rico, who answered one or two of my questions about police procedures.

And as always, my great thanks goes to you as my readers, whom I hope I can once again take away to one of the most beautiful islands in the world, with this Madeira crime novel.